Expired Hero

LAST CHANCE COUNTY BOOK FOUR

Lisa Phillips

Publisher Lisa Phillips
Cover design Ryan Schwarz
Edited by Jen Wieber

One

There were two people in the diner with the potential to kill him. It was hard to judge skill level outside of a fight, but Stuart Leland's instinct gave enough information to gauge a baseline threat.

He settled onto a stool at the end of the counter. The diner wasn't too busy, even though it was lunchtime. Payday for most people was tomorrow, so it would be packed then. And a Friday. The nine-to-five crowd would be celebrating.

"Coffee?"

Stuart flipped the mug over. "Decaf."

The bleach blonde waitress halted, turned with the carafe, and headed back to the pot. He poured himself water, and she returned with a different carafe and filled his cup nearly to the brim.

"Thanks." Stuart topped it up with cold water from the glass.

Before he set the glass down, a man exited the bathroom. Stuart froze. Dark T-shirt, paint-splattered cargo pants, and work boots. The man had one smashed fingernail that had turned purple and a scar in his stubble on the left side of his cheek.

He passed behind Stuart. Smelled like paint thinner, dirt, and coffee.

Stuart's hand shook. The water sloshed over his hand and spilled onto the counter. The man sat down at his booth with two associates, one of whom also registered on Stuart's threat metrics.

The waitress tossed a rag onto the counter, one thick, dark eyebrow raised. Her blonde hair was bleached to almost white and her nametag said, "Letty."

"Thanks." Stuart tried to sound polite. He didn't smile. When he tried that, people—especially women—tended to look scared and quickly move away from him. So he'd given up attempting to make friends here in Last Chance County.

Besides, it wasn't like he was going to live here forever.

When she took back the rag he'd used to clean the spilled water, Stuart said, "Hot ham and cheese, side of fries."

"Comin' right up." Letty put the order in, then sashayed down to the other side of the counter.

There was another waitress on today, clearing plates from an empty booth in the far corner. He could see through to the kitchen. One guy, white apron. Hollis was back there, her round figure bustling back and forth quickly as though she was busy and agitated. Her stepfather owned the diner and oversaw everything. Although most folks considered it hers now, the entire operation was in his name, and she was paid barely more than minimum wage.

The second waitress lifted a tub of dirty dishes and passed in front of the door just as it opened. She smiled widely. "Kaylee. Good to see you."

The woman who'd entered smiled, tentative but not nervous. "Hi, Becky."

"Looks like your spot's open."

That was a problem, as far as Stuart was concerned. Though, he didn't let it bother him too much as he pulled out his cell phone. Let everyone think he'd fallen into the void of social media. He hardly cared what others' opinions were.

Kaylee had a bigger issue. That being her tendency to eat in the same "spot" every Thursday. The way she grocery shopped on a Monday. Biked the same route to and from work. Went to the gym like it was a scheduled appointment.

Made his life easier, but it was also dangerous.

Stuart swiped to the app on his phone and initiated the scan for Bluetooth-enabled devices nearby. He nearly blinked at the number of phones he could access, in this room alone. People had no idea what hackers were capable of, and they had no idea the ways they left themselves vulnerable to it.

Kaylee's phone was on the list. He knew the serial number, so he tapped hers and ran the program.

Clone in progress.

Some might call it an invasion of privacy, but if she'd done what he thought she had, there was no expectation of being left alone. Not from him, or any of the police officers she worked with.

Could be the whole thing was just to rub their noses in how good she was. Kaylee sat at the police department reception desk Monday through Friday. To keep an ear to the ground so she was the first to hear when things went down? Maybe.

Error.

Letty set his plate down. "Something wrong?"

"Huh?" Stuart looked up, as though she'd surprised him. "No, nothing's wrong. My brokerage account took a hit yesterday when the S&P dipped. Nothing to worry about."

Letty blinked. "Sure. Ketchup?"

"And mayonnaise." He tapped the screen of his phone.

Clone in progress.

"Oh-kay."

As she walked away, he spotted Kaylee, now perched at the end stool. She spoke tentatively, "Fry sauce, right?" Like she wasn't sure if he would reciprocate an attempt at friendliness.

Stuart kept his tone light when he said, "You know it." But he didn't smile due to the aforementioned response he normally got.

Kaylee's round cheeks flushed an endearing pink under the makeup she wore. Her figure had toned up since the spring thaw, what with all the biking she did every day to get to and from work. She had on stretchy black pants and a gray T-shirt, one of those fitness trackers on her wrist with a lavender band. Her dark hair usually had purple streaks. Today they were yellow, and he realized then that, with how often her hair changed colors, they had to be clip-ins.

Meanwhile, he attempted to appear as understated as possible. No one needed to notice him. Stuart's entire life had been about blending in and not ruffling feathers. No one wanted a covert operative working for them who stuck out in a crowd.

Unless they wanted to.

Error.

He frowned at the screen, then tapped through to find the problem. Kaylee had secrets. Stuart needed to find out what they were and what they meant to him. He couldn't wait, and he didn't need technical problems.

Kaylee returned to her book.

Letty decided to chat up two construction workers, while she held the little dish of mayo for him in her hand.

Hollis's movements had become increasingly erratic. She'd gone from agitated to flustered.

Stuart read the technical report for the error. That didn't make sense. It meant… He glanced at Kaylee. She had no idea. What on earth was the woman into?

Another man passed behind Stuart.

He bit down on the inside of his lip to avoid stiffening but, he must have let on somehow. Kaylee glanced at him again.

Stuart ignored her. He ate half his sandwich trying to figure out why this hadn't worked. The error only meant one thing. He'd never be able to get into her phone, or listen in on her calls, or read her messages. Stuart couldn't clone her phone.

Because someone else already had.

Hollis cried out. He was off his stool before the knife she'd been holding clattered to the cutting board.

"Hey!" Letty called out, waving his mayonnaise but making no attempt to stop him. Or come after him.

Stuart pushed through the revolving door to the kitchen, swiped a dish towel from a rack by the door, and strode to Hollis. He took her hand and wrapped her finger while she winced. "That looks bad. What happened?"

"It slipped because the sweet potato was wet."

Stuart could still see the blood, even though he'd covered the cut. He pulled out his phone and pulled up Dean's number from his favorites.

"Cartwright."

"It's me."

"Me?" Dean knew exactly who it was. "It's customary to—"

"Hollis cut her finger. It's deep."

"Diner?"

"Kitchen."

"I'll be there in two minutes." Dean hung up.

"He's close." Stuart offered Hollis a polite, lips-closed smile. "He'll be here ASAP."

She pushed out a breath, face pale.

The chef guy, with the white coat, flipped two burgers. He still hadn't turned.

Stuart said, "Hey!"

Hollis started. Even Kaylee looked up from her book. Her gaze drifted between Stuart and Hollis, both of them standing close to each other. Her brows pulled together and she bit her lip, her focus returning to her book.

Stuart sighed. What did that even mean, and why did the woman take so much of his focus? He was trying to find out what she was hiding, but it was more than that. She had his attention. Her softness. The way she smiled, gentle and tentative. As though she didn't know how she would be received.

"You're squeezing my hand pretty hard."

Stuart jerked back to Hollis. "Sorry."

She grinned, glanced at Kaylee, and said, "Don't mind me." She pinned him with her friendly stare. "She's a kind woman. Sticks to what she knows, lives life quiet. You know?"

He didn't want to nod, but she was right. He did know.

Hollis continued, "Surprised everyone when she gave up the job at the bank and went to the police station to be their receptionist." She leaned closer. "I actually thought she had a thing for Conroy for a while, but…" Hollis shrugged. "Even after the PD was attacked by all those guys, she still stayed."

Stuart had heard about the incident—a local bad guy, dead now, had sent his men to retrieve key evidence. They'd shot up the police station and taken back the cell phone. Kaylee had been there?

Stuart glanced at her, still reading her book.

"It's a shame what happened to her parents."

The steel glint of a blade flashed in his mind; memories. Pain. The smell of blood. He looked down and saw faint scars on the back of his hand. Stuart fought the pull of the past and motioned to the chef with his chin. "What's up with him?"

"Headphones."

"Maybe lay off the knives, yeah?"

She sighed. "I would if my food prep kid actually showed up." She studied him. "How good are you with knives?"

"You think I need a job?"

"Right now, I need all that chopped for a round of cheeseburgers." She indicated the produce with a tip of her head.

Stuart let her hold the towel and went to the handwashing sink. He rolled his sleeves back and cleaned up. One lettuce, four tomatoes. Onions. Stuart chopped and sliced into piles.

When he glanced at her, finished, Hollis lifted her hands together. "Please take the job. *Please.*"

"What makes you think I don't have one?"

"Do you?"

Stuart pressed his lips together, conceding the point.

"Please please please."

Dean strode in. "Where's my patient?"

The chef guy spun, spatula flinging out, allowing a couple of drops of grease to fly. One hit Stuart's cheek, hot oil stinging his skin with a sharp burst of pain. Stuart reacted before his brain caught up with what he was doing. He swiped with one arm, cracking his forearm with the chef's, and then kicked out at the back of the man's knee.

The chef hit the floor with a cry.

Stuart froze.

"Maybe we should—"

Stuart shook his head, not wanting to hear her take back the offer of a job. Even a dumb one like chopping vegetables. "Forget it."

He strode past Dean, not looking at his friend's face because he didn't want to see it. He pushed out the back door and found a rear parking lot. Beyond that, trees and a hill. Stuart broke into a run.

He ducked under a branch and raced up the hill.

The pain from the hot oil lingered. Like every other wound. Every slice and strike. If he removed his shirt, it would be written on him. A map of his darkest moments. Unable to save himself. Unable to make the pain stop.

Sweat beaded on his forehead. He stopped at the top of the hill and spun around to look at the town below.

He saw Kaylee, riding her bike with her backpack on. Headed back to the police department probably. Lunch break over. *Error.* Who had cloned her phone? He was supposed to know by now what she was hiding. Maybe she was nothing but a victim. How did he know?

All he had as a result of his most recent clandestine mission was a job offer.

Which, as with everything else in his life, had likely been taken away.

Leaving him with nothing.

Two

Kaylee swung her leg over her bike and set the kickstand down. On any given day, she'd rather be reading a book than nearly anything else. It wasn't like real life was all that great, anyway. Books had always been a source of comfort and probably would be for the rest of her life.

She could go anywhere. Be anyone but herself, walking around with the memories she kept in her head, even though she prayed every day she would forget them.

Kaylee walked up to the front door of the huge house that was nestled in the trees. Most people probably didn't even know it was here, but she'd done extensive research before she moved to Last Chance. Google Maps Street View had shown her everything—and that included the warehouse behind the main house.

Kaylee had looked up the address on her work computer. The police database indicated the property was owned by Chevalier Holdings LLC, though she knew Dean Cartwright lived here, along with his brother, Ted, who was the police department's tech expert. And also *he* lived in this house.

It was better not to even think his name.

There were reportedly also four others who bunked in the multi-room house along with them, bringing the total to seven. She'd seen the four around town, driving their big, black SUV with the tinted windows. They weren't here much as far as she could tell, but Kaylee steered clear of them anyway.

The way she tried to do with Stuart.

And that was *before* he'd attacked the chef.

Kaylee had called Savannah before she left the diner to tell her what went down, but Stuart had left so fast, no one knew where he'd gone. Not even Dean, and they were supposed to be friends. He'd just attacked that man and then walked away. Like it was nothing.

That "nothing" settled in the pit of her stomach.

She knocked on the front door, then saw the bell. She rang that as well. Ted had told her that Dean was home, so she figured he was the one who would answer the door. Stuart was who knew where. Probably running from the law by now.

It was only after she'd seen Dean at the diner that she'd had the idea to speak with him. Kaylee had been thinking on it all afternoon. How to find out the answers to her questions.

Without actually explaining—to anyone—what was going on.

There was no way she would reveal her secrets.

The door opened. "Oh. Hey." Dean shook his head. "What's up, Kaylee? Is everything okay?"

"What?" Her stomach churned. Why couldn't more of the men who lived in this town be ugly?

She'd been watching her friends fall for them, one by one. Mia. Savannah. Now Ellie had met Dean, and while she wasn't exactly a friend, Kaylee liked her. Then there was Jess, who was Ellie's sister and had a serious thing for Ted, who was Dean's brother. It was serendipity—two brothers and two sisters who fell in love with each other.

Like all good love stories. The kind that ended with a double wedding.

Unfortunately for her, the men were all falling for exciting, adventurous women. Ones who were everything Kaylee was not.

"Kaylee?" He jogged her from her thoughts.

"Um…yes, everything's fine. If, uh, everything's fine here, that is. I mean, is your friend okay? Did the police find him?"

"I can't talk about Stuart." He moved to shut the door.

"I need some help!" She blurted out the words, practically shouting at him.

She didn't want to talk about Stuart, but he was also not the reason she was here. Kaylee didn't need to think about him, either. Not more than she already had, because that would reach creeper territory. Stuart and whatever his deal was didn't have anything to do with her.

And given the way he'd erupted in the diner kitchen, that was for the best.

"I'd invite you in, but I'm the only one here."

He thought she would be inappropriate, or that someone might think something inappropriate might happen?

"That's fine." She grasped her backpack strap with one hand. "I just…"

He waited.

How was she supposed to start?

"It's my brother."

"You have a brother?"

She nodded. "You were in the Navy, right? One of the SEALs?"

"Yes."

"So you know people who do jobs like that."

"Like your brother?"

Kaylee pulled in a slow breath. The truth was far more complicated than that. "He was supposed to have contacted me by now."

"What does he do?"

13

"I don't know. It's black ops, or clandestine, or something."
Or she'd read too many spy thrillers lately. "I'm really worried. I
wondered if you knew anyone that you could call, and then maybe
mention his name. See if someone knows what happened to him,
or where he is? Maybe he's hurt or in trouble." She shivered just
thinking about Brad being in danger. Or injured, unable to escape.
"I know it's a lot to ask, but—"

"It's okay, Kaylee. Give me his name and I'll ask around. I
know a few people with connections in that world. They can find
out if your brother is all right," Dean said. "But one of those people
I know is Stuart."

Dean wanted her to talk to *him*?

"Oh, well… I wouldn't want to bother him. He seems to have
a lot—" She had to clear her throat. "—going on."

The skin around Dean's eyes flexed. She knew he was a
therapist, licensed to help people through their trauma. Hopefully
he assisted Stuart in that way. She didn't want to be judgmental or
anything, but it seemed like he maybe could use professional help.
That, of course, would take plenty of time and meant Dean
wouldn't need to worry about her in the meantime. No one needed
to worry about her.

She was fine.

Dean lifted his chin. "What's your brother's name?"

"Bradley Caldwell."

He opened his mouth but paused a second before he asked,
"Military?"

What was that pause about? Did he know her brother, or
recognize his name?

Kaylee's eyes filled with sudden tears she couldn't blink away.
"Is he dead?"

"What? No." Dean touched her shoulder. "I don't know your
brother."

It took her a minute to compose herself, while she glanced
aside and stared at the trees. "He's not military, but it's some kind
of agency and it's international."

The idea her brother might be CIA had crossed her mind many times before. Usually after reading one of those spy novels. The only problem was that he didn't appear to be affiliated with any one group in particular. He floated around like a transient, living out of the camper that was strapped on the bed of his truck and taking odd jobs when he wasn't off somewhere on a "mission." When he was gone, he was all over the place. He'd come back tanned or suffering from the aftereffects of hypothermia. One time he'd had some tropical skin infection, and he'd had to be quarantined.

Then there were the injuries.

It almost seemed like he was some kind of mercenary. A gun for hire. Maybe a thief, or arms dealer.

Maybe he was a criminal, wanted all over the world, and she would end up exposing him.

She'd considered going to the storage unit where he left his truck and camper, but that would be an invasion of his privacy. The package he'd sent her months ago was enough of a clue that something was going on.

Was he okay?

"I just want to know if he's all right." She blinked away more tears. "He's never been gone this long before, not without contacting me somehow."

Brad knew how she felt about being left with no word of whether he was dead or alive. One time he'd sent a postcard. She'd had voicemails and packages. Even an email. Never the same thing twice and never from the same account or name.

That was how she knew something had to have happened to him.

Dean's eyes softened. "I think you should consider talking to Stuart. He may have the time to spare. If you'd like someone to try and look for your brother."

She saw in her mind, the second Stuart had reacted. Through the opening between the diner and the kitchen, she'd seen his arm swing out. Faster than she'd ever seen anyone move. Like a trained fighting machine. A killer.

"I know you're busy." She took a step back and almost stumbled off the front stoop. "Sorry to bother you. Just...don't worry about me. Okay?"

Kaylee didn't wait around for an answer. If Stuart was the person she needed to help find her brother, then maybe Brad didn't need to be found.

Was that the kind of man her brother also was? She didn't like to think about that kind of violence. Not after what she'd seen with her own eyes eight years ago. The memory was blurred now—except when she dreamed it.

Kaylee flicked back the kickstand and set off, letting her helmet dangle from the handlebars while she pedaled back toward town with tears streaming down her face.

Brad, what did you get yourself into?

He'd always been rough. Not unkind, but far more capable of wading into a mess where a bully picked on someone, or where there were two dogs fighting. He'd broken up plenty of altercations when they were kids. Kaylee had been scared of everything, even *before* the night their parents were killed.

And every day since.

She pedaled fast and when she reached the main road, she stopped to put on her helmet. Biking might be safer than driving a car, but that didn't mean she could go without head protection.

Two people honked, and she lifted her hand to wave at both. Small town life suited her just fine. So long as everyone did what they were supposed to. Kaylee didn't need any surprises, she just wanted things to be the same as they always were. Definitely no scary and attractive, dark-haired men with too much scruff on their face erupting and whacking another man.

What was that about anyway?

Were the police looking for him?

Kaylee wondered if she should ask Conroy. Her boss was the chief of police, but she'd never asked him about an actual case before. Could she do it now or would he question the fact she was changing things up? Getting personal. Involved.

The idea she might need to face her fears was all well and good, but it wasn't like they were unfounded. She had every right to be afraid. Then she would read her Bible. Or go to Maggie's weekly Bible study in the common room at Hope Mansion where she lived with a group of other women. After some songs, and being "encouraged by the Word" or however they put it, she had to admit she would feel better.

It started on the back of her neck. The way it always did.

A tiny itch. The urge to turn around and make sure there was no one behind her. Kaylee heard the rumble of a diesel engine, probably a half-ton truck. Some local, clowning around in their gas guzzler just to pick up milk from the store or whatever.

Kaylee pedaled faster. She was almost to the street where she needed to turn, the road that would take her back to Hope Mansion. The perfect, safe, place for her to be. Everyone knew Maggie had a shotgun.

But first, Kaylee had to make it there in one piece.

Someone was following her.

17

Three

"How much of that did you hear?"

Stuart didn't wonder how Dean knew he was there. His friend shut the front door and turned in time to watch Stuart finish the water bottle he'd filled before he started his workout. Now his long-sleeve, sweat-wicking shirt was drenched, his hair plastered to his forehead.

Dean studied him, eyebrows raised.

Stuart shrugged. "My guess? All of it."

"Wanna tell me what your problem is with her?"

"Who says I have a problem?"

Dean shot him a look and moved through the house to their expansive kitchen. He got a juice from the fridge and twisted off the cap. "Had any thoughts about dinner?"

"It's leftover night." Stuart didn't have time to cook. "Zander and the boys are busy building a new breach house and Ted is working late."

Once a week, at least, they tried to all sit down and eat together. To foster some kind of "fellowship," as Dean called it. When the team was out of town, which was most of the time, they checked in if and when they could. The times they were here, they were always working on one thing or another. Like building a new set-up for their breach house, so they could practice kicking doors down.

Stuart tried to be a lot more subtle than applying his boot—or a small amount of explosives—to solve a problem. But he supposed they came in handy at times.

"Good. Then we have a few minutes. We can go talk."

Water overflowed the bottle and onto his hand. Stuart shut off the faucet. "I don't need to talk about what happened earlier. I was jumpy anyway, and now I'm fine." He twisted the lid on his water bottle even though water from his hand continued to drip onto his sneakers.

Dean didn't look convinced.

"Don't you have things to do? A girlfriend to take care of, a therapy facility to build?"

"Among other things." Dean folded his arms. "If it's close to the surface, you might remember something else."

Stuart didn't want to admit his friend was right, but he also had no basis to argue. As he trailed back through the house to the basement stairs, he conceded the point—to himself—that it was close to the surface. He strode past the huge dining room that had been repurposed into a recreation room for the seven of them to hang out. It was where they'd put the used pool table Stuart found at one of those online buy/sell sites. He jogged down the stairs to the lower level where they'd set up a room that was a near replica of Stuart's worst nightmare.

And Dean wondered why he didn't want to come down here.

His back was tight from the punishing workout he'd used to burn off the stress and lingering adrenaline from reacting when that drop of hot oil stung his cheek.

He didn't realize there was still more in him until he strode across the closet-sized room and punched the wood panel on the far wall. His hand didn't even dent it. Stuart hissed. He'd probably broken bones in his hand.

"I'd ask if you feel better now, but…" Dean didn't finish.

Stuart turned, pressed his back to the wall and slid to the floor. Knees to his chest he looked around, then closed his eyes. He didn't want the chair this time. Or the blindfold. A couple of times, Dean had tied him up and even drugged him the same way his kidnappers had. All of it part of emersion therapy to try and help him remember the details of what happened—the pieces of the puzzle his mind had tried to bury.

It was perfectly safe, but the reproduction of this room and the circumstances of his torment were good enough that it didn't take long for his mind to transport him right back there. It even smelled the same.

Brad gasped. "Stu…don't let them kill me. Promise me… Promise me you'll do it before they do."

Stuart pulled in a long breath and blew it out slowly. Maybe he didn't want to remember.

We were betrayed. That's how they caught us. They knew we were coming."

"Betrayed."

Dean said nothing in response. He didn't speak a whole lot, mostly just a comment or question if Stuart's thoughts needed to be led in a certain direction. One they didn't want to go.

"We were betrayed."

Dean's voice was soft. "Who set you up?"

"He knew." When Stuart opened his eyes, he saw Dean's eyebrow rise. Stuart said, "Brad knew who set us up. I remember him mentioning Kaylee. Clearly she's involved somehow."

"So you came here, where she lives, so you can watch her."

Stuart shrugged one shoulder. "She hasn't made a move yet, but that doesn't mean she isn't up to her neck in it. Maybe that's why she came to the house. She's trying to feel out how much I know."

Why was Dean so sure she wasn't involved? Brad would never have mentioned her if she wasn't.

Dean leaned against the wall. Usually he brought a notebook in lieu of a voice recorder. Stuart didn't want any audio recordings of their sessions but didn't mind his friend writing down notes. Dean said, "If she knew Brad had been captured, why come and ask me to look for him? She'd already know he'd been sold out. Taken by those men."

"She knows *something*."

"Why not just go ask her?"

Stuart shook his head. "I have more surveillance to do."

"Like what? You've been creepin' on her life for weeks. Sooner or later she's going to see you snooping around."

Stuart nearly laughed. "As if. You think I can't get in and out of her room at Hope Mansion without anyone knowing?"

Maybe that would give him a clue as to who else was interested in her. Someone had cloned her phone before Stuart could do it.

He stood. "Good idea."

"No way, dude—"

Stuart held up one hand, palm out. "I appreciate all your help."

"You mean like joining Zander's team to rescue you from that compound? Or are you just breaking up with me as your therapist?"

"I have to find out what she knows." Stuart didn't want to talk about the therapy. "I do appreciate it. All of it. Even though I got myself out, and you guys just picked me up on the roadside."

"If we'd gotten there sooner, we probably would've been able to get Brad's body back."

"There were too many of them." And his kidnappers tended to burn the bodies of men who died under their "care." Which meant, considering Stuart knew Brad was dead, there hadn't been cause to risk the other men's lives trying to retrieve a corpse.

Not with the smoke trail rising into the night sky.

"Like I said."

There was so much regret in Dean's eyes that it made Stuart feel bad for keeping so much from him. But it was in his nature, in the man they'd forged from what remained of him when they picked him up out of that prison cell in France. Since then, the people he'd worked for had trained him as a deceptive killing machine with no feelings and a hair trigger.

Captivity had done its damage, that was true, but he'd already been honed through everything that happened prior to it. The places they sent him on missions. The things they'd ordered him to do.

A ghost, spreading the nightmare of his life, so that it touched the people he touched. Forever changing everyone around him.

"I need to walk."

Dean sighed.

"I don't need your approval."

"No, you don't." A muscle in Dean's jaw flexed. "Hollis gets it. She figured you were military, like the rest of us, and I didn't correct her. But she knows all about PTSD, and she said as soon as you're ready, the job offer will still be open."

Stuart glanced back. "And when the chef finds out I'll be working right behind him and his flinging oil?" He swiped a finger across his cheek where the spot hit him.

He didn't like his reaction to a tiny drop of oil painfully stinging his cheek. He'd been shot recently and hadn't dealt well with that either. Probably he'd be overly sensitive to pain for the rest of his life. There wasn't likely anything he could do about that, except continue working with Dean to process everything that had happened.

Only, if he never told Dean the rest of the story, how would that even work. He'd left out the whole end of the tale—the part he'd remembered.

The part where he held the knife.

And pushed it into Brad's chest.

Stuart's whole body shuddered. "I'm going for a walk."

"Talk to her," Dean called out.

Stuart trotted up the stairs to the ground floor, shaking off the lingering tension. He felt like working out all over again. But even if he tried to exhaust himself into unconsciousness, he still doubted he would sleep.

Promise me you'll do it before they do.

Was that what happened? He'd known down to his soul that Brad was dead. Enough they'd left and not started an unwinnable war to get his body back. Stuart hadn't been prepared to get any of them killed, and he hadn't been in any shape to even help.

Nor had he been able to remember exactly what happened.

With the drugs they'd given him, and the ways they'd twisted his mind until he didn't even know who he was, Stuart knew he couldn't confront Kaylee. It could go wrong in so many ways, and if she turned out to be part of him and Brad getting captured, then it would end with her death.

Something Stuart was almost certain he wouldn't be able to bring himself to do.

He walked the woods around town, the mountain paths and through wooded areas no one had trod in decades, until the sun came up. A few weeks ago, a body had been found in a mine up here. Murder from the seventies. People in this town were up to plenty of things the cops didn't want to know about—a lot he saw when he walked around town—like the murder he'd witnessed. A biker killed behind one of the local bars in town.

He was better off sticking to the wilderness that surrounded the town. Maybe he should build a house up here.

But he inevitably circled around to Hope Mansion.

Stuart watched the house from the cover of trees, sitting leaned up against a trunk. Hope Mansion was bigger than the house he lived in with the guys and housed only women. The place had started as a refuge for women and children who needed safety. Even now, residents who wanted to stay, but who weren't actively in danger, were accepted by invitation only.

So which was Kaylee?

Maybe she needed to live under the radar, her quiet, narrow life. Only, it seemed like she was waiting around for something.

Or someone.

He checked his phone and saw it was just about eight in the morning. She came out just after ten past, buttoning her coat. He hadn't realized it was chilly. Probably almost sixty degrees, but when the high reached nearly ninety, it might feel almost cold first thing in the morning to her.

Kaylee swung her leg over her bike and set off to town for work.

Patrick waited another hour, then circled the house to her window. He'd already scoped out the security system and had been impressed with it. Still, Stuart was through the locked window and inside her room in less than two minutes.

Full size bed. Nightstand, dresser and a small closet. A few family photos and a hairbrush that hadn't been put away.

It took another two minutes to find the hidden camera. Three more were disguised at various points around her room.

Stuart's heart sank. Whoever had cloned her phone?

They were also watching her room.

Four

Every day Kaylee biked to work early so she could read at her desk before her shift started. This morning she was starting a new book, after having finished the last one just after midnight the night before.

She was twenty-two pages in when Conroy pushed the front door open. Mia, his fiancé, followed him. The lieutenant had small cotton buds tucked in her ears, in deference to the damage she'd suffered to her hearing. Watching her navigate through the fear of hurting her ears further, causing permanent hearing loss, was painful, but Mia seemed determined to have a positive attitude about it.

Conroy held the door for Mia, a soft look on his face. Kaylee had never seen him look at anyone else like that. Not until their lives collided the day Mia showed back up into town, harassed by a madman who repeatedly tried to hurt her for the justified killing of his brother. They'd suffered more than enough, yet life hadn't let them enjoy the quiet for long. After them, Savannah had gotten together with Tate, their own story equally as terrifying for Kaylee to watch.

She was ready for life to quiet down.

"Kaylee."

She glanced over at Conroy and realized what he needed. "Right. Sorry, I was miles away."

The door release button was under the counter.

The chief wore his customary suit. He came right to her. "Everything okay?"

"Sure." She patted the cover of her book, then tucked it under the counter so it was out of the way.

"No lingering nightmares or anything from those guys?"

Of course, he wanted to talk about the "incident" as they now referred to it. The police department had been in possession of a phone with incriminating evidence on it. A group of rough bikers who'd worked for a local criminal had stormed the PD with guns, demanded the phone, and shot more than one officer.

Kaylee had been scared out of her mind.

Until one of the bikers noticed how scared she was and hid her out of sight of his crazy friend. In the bustle, no one had even seen what he'd done.

She still wondered why he'd done it. It had probably saved her life, or at the very least, kept her from more harm. And now she didn't have to deal with her mind going places she didn't want it to go—to a place of fear that she'd find herself back in the very place where her nightmares started.

Covered in blood.

"I'm...okay."

Conroy squeezed her shoulder.

She didn't like lying, but she had accepted the job here because she'd figured it was the safest place in town to work. It was exactly what she needed. There was just far more going on here than Conroy would ever know.

Mia leaned against him, and Conroy slid his arm around her shoulders. They were *the* cutest couple she'd ever seen.

"Kaylee, could you print me the file for Gina Harrelson."

Conroy groaned. "Mia—"

She shook her head. "I want to look into it."

Kaylee was grateful they were both so distracted that they didn't even notice her reaction. She swallowed. "Gina Harrelson? Isn't she that girl who went missing nine years ago?"

She remembered because it had been the summer Kaylee moved here. She'd been drawn to the town because it always made her think about her parents. They were the ones who'd told her all about Last Chance, as they'd both lived here on and off over the years and loved this town. The week she arrived, Kaylee had been staying at the motel.

Gina Harrelson had gone missing from the room two doors down.

The police had even interviewed Kaylee, but she'd been so freshly traumatized from the murder of her parents that she'd barely managed to get a few sentences out. Just enough to convince the officer—Sergeant Basuto—that she hadn't seen what happened to Gina.

Mia nodded to answer her question. "There was an article in the morning paper recounting Gina's disappearance, and I thought I'd take a look at it. Just in case."

Conroy didn't seem to agree. "There was nothing to find."

"Maybe." The lieutenant shrugged one shoulder. "But fresh eyes can't hurt."

Mia had been an ATF agent in her former life. Now that she was a lieutenant mostly on desk duty, and the chief's fiancé, she could probably coast by and push paper the rest of her career. But no. Mia seemed to work harder and longer than anyone.

Just this past month, she'd closed three cases from behind her desk. *And* she'd let her officers take the credit for the arrests.

Plus, she ruffled Conroy's feathers just enough to keep everyone's lives interesting.

They headed for their desks, and Kaylee pulled up the file on her computer. She hit "print" and read the notations while she waited for the big printer to warm up.

She'd never met Gina, just knew about the sudden disappearance. The memory of those first few days in town had never left her. She related, probably too much, to Gina Harrelson. A single woman, alone. Kaylee traveled with the gun her brother had given her. Though, after he'd taught her to use it, she'd never even touched the thing. It was tucked up in the closet. Maybe it didn't even work now. Did guns go bad from disuse?

Didn't matter, since Kaylee planned on never *ever* needing to use it. That was probably why she was so vehemently against talking to Stuart. She'd seen the violence he was capable of in his eyes before she ever saw him use it. Now that she had? Kaylee shivered.

She needed to find safety so she could keep the package that Brad had sent her safe. That was her highest priority right now. Until she heard otherwise, or he showed up, she would do what he'd asked her.

She would wait until the right person showed up. And then she would give *them* the package.

The right person was not Stuart Leland. Not with those all-too-familiar demons, from a past he'd survived, swirling in his eyes.

Ones she saw when she looked in the mirror.

"Hey, hey." Savannah's voice cut through her thoughts.

Kaylee looked up at the man who had entered and realized immediately it wasn't her he was talking to.

"Hey, babe." Savannah was sitting at her desk behind Kaylee. She was Mia's partner, and currently the department's only detective.

The man who'd come in was Tate. Another person whose eyes and face reflected the pain and weariness of life's hard times. Still, all that disappeared when he smiled. "Good morning, Miss Kaylee."

"Tate."

"Such warmth. I'm charmed." He leaned across the counter and mock whispered, "Run away with me. Savannah will never know."

Kaylee snatched up her wireless mouse and pretended to throw it at him.

Tate reacted like she'd hit him with a knife to the heart. "Let me in. Please?"

"Maybe I won't after that stunt."

Savannah moved to stand beside Kaylee, where she was perched on her stool.

Kaylee asked her, "What do you think?"

Savannah frowned. "I don't know if he deserves it."

Tate mock gasped.

"I think he's nothin' but a cad," Kaylee said. "I'm thinking about throwing my stapler next."

"Conroy! Your employees are harassing me!"

"A coward's move." Savannah turned to her and squeezed Kaylee's shoulder. "Us girls never take the easy way out, right?" She hit the button under the counter to admit her fiancé.

The kiss Tate gave her made Kaylee blush and turn away. It went on long enough, Conroy finally cleared his throat, which made Mia giggle.

Kaylee smiled at her computer screen as she continued to read the case file for Gina Harrelson, and Tate passed behind her on his way to meet with Conroy. She heard him pause, and he planted a kiss on the top of her head.

"Playa."

Tate chuckled and moved on.

Basuto's notes were linked. Kaylee clicked through to them and noted he'd found Gina's car, abandoned on the highway. A single, bloody partial fingerprint had been left on the underside of the steering wheel. One that had never been matched to anyone in the databases they had access to. So unless they found a suspect not in one of those databases to try and tie the print to, they had nothing. It was a dead end.

Gina had vanished, possibly—or, probably if Kaylee was honest with herself—under suspicious circumstances. It had been right after Kaylee moved to town, and Gina had been two doors down at the motel. *Too close.*

"I'm out." Tate stacked a pile of papers beside her, tapping them on the counter to straighten them. "Mia needs another set. I'm taking these."

Kaylee frowned. "You're looking into Gina's case?"

"You knew her?"

"I'm in there." She pointed to the pages. "Basuto interviewed me. I was staying at the same motel."

He shifted toward her. "It's all in here?"

"I didn't really see anything that night." Just so he wasn't disappointed when he read that she'd told Basuto nothing of value. "But I heard about it. Saw her a couple of times." In fact, Kaylee had been the one to tell the cops what color Gina's car was.

"Okay." His gaze softened. "Everything else okay?"

Ugh. The man had a sixth sense for when things weren't right for someone. Hollis had been trying—unsuccessfully—to convince him all was well in her world for weeks. He still didn't believe her.

Kaylee didn't believe her either.

But now Hollis had been on a date with this new guy in town, some straight-laced salesman named Phil. Maybe he would figure it out.

As for Tate, Kaylee might have a package from her special ops brother that she was guarding until he reappeared, but that didn't mean she was going to involve a man who'd just found the love of his life. Tate deserved to be happy. She had no intention of letting him get hurt.

Which meant she needed something good to convince him she would never be "okay."

"I saw my parents both get shot. They were murdered in front of me." She glanced at the calendar. "Ten years ago next month."

Savannah and Mia both gasped. A second later, they were both standing right next to her.

"It's never going to be okay, but I deal with it as best I can." She shrugged. "I can't stop living my life." No matter how much it haunted her. Or how much she wished her brother would *come home* already.

Tears filled her eyes. *Where are you, Brad?*

30

Kaylee said, "I'm still here." It would be selfish to do anything other than make the best of things, after all her parents had lost.

"Honey." Savannah had never called anyone that. Not that Kaylee had heard, at least.

Kaylee shot her a sad smile. "I know." She sniffed and said, "Can I ask you something, Tate?"

She'd tried Dean. That hadn't worked. Maybe Tate could ask around about Brad. After all, he was a private investigator and former FBI agent, and he still had contacts there.

He nodded. "I heard about Stuart in the kitchen at the diner. Probably freaked you out, right?"

Before Kaylee could tell him that wasn't it, he continued. "Steer clear of that guy. I woulda said that before you told us what you just shared, but now I'm more than sure. You don't need that in your life."

Savannah nodded. "It's not worth getting hurt. And Dean is already helping him."

Tate said, "Don't get me wrong, the man makes the *best* guacamole. But you don't need to get in the middle of his mess, along with all that stuff with his friend he doesn't remember. It's not worth it. You really should stay away from him."

Apparently, that was the end of what he needed to say because Tate kissed his fiancé and headed out.

Kaylee clicked through to print another copy of the file. Everyone else was reading it, so she figured why not print two?

Maybe her career reading mystery novels would make her see something no one else had.

She didn't want to stumble into danger. There was enough of that in the book she was currently reading. But the chance to help someone *and* get her mind off everything else?

Kaylee printed herself a copy as well.

Stay away from him.

Dean might think Stuart could help her, but Tate was right. The man had way too much danger in him.

Sure, he was seriously attractive, and she had a slightly obsessive crush.

But that didn't mean she was going to do anything about it. Stuart Leland was not a safe place.

Five

Stuart stood in the corner of Kaylee's room, surrounded by the warmth of her comfortable living space. But he couldn't let himself be distracted by her things.

Voices in the hall drifted to him, and a shadow moved under the door frame. Maggie, the owner and operator of Hope Mansion, said, "...spray down the showers. I'll tackle the toilets. Is that okay with you, hon?"

Another woman replied. "Sure thing, Mags. We just really appreciate everything you've done for us."

The voices drifted away.

Stuart needed to leave. Kaylee's things had already told him everything he needed to know. This wasn't about invading her privacy, just getting a feel for the kind of person she was. People thought their material belongings didn't say all that much. That too many people had the same things. But he'd found the opposite to be true. Plenty could be learned in how someone used what they accumulated.

He avoided the cameras he'd found and made his way to the window. Outside, two young boys ran across the yard.

Stuart ducked back behind the curtain and watched them play. Not brothers, just friends, the two boys wrestled and laughed. He stared for longer than necessary, just watching them, enjoying the sight of their carefree playtime. Not many residents of this house could claim a carefree life.

Stuart knew how that felt. He'd lived close to the wire his entire life and didn't think there had ever been a time when he had laughed like that. As though nothing else mattered except the fun. Instead, he'd only known the dark side of life. Pain. Destruction. Those things had been honed in him, creating the man he had been before he and Brad were captured.

Set-up.

Destroyed.

Stuart didn't know what he was now. Except for a man who needed to get out of this room.

But someone was watching Kaylee. The person Stuart wanted to be was the kind of man who would step up and protect her if she was in danger.

Without considering it too much, he moved to a camera. Was there audio? He didn't know. It was possible they could see, but not hear, her. Unless she got on her phone—which he assumed had been cloned by the same people who set up cameras in her room.

There was no way it was Maggie watching her residents. That meant this was external.

Stuart turned the camera so it pointed at his face. "This woman is under my protection." He spoke slowly, in case they would have to read his lips. After they captured his picture and ran it.

The boys were gone now. Stuart replaced the camera and climbed back out the window.

He jogged across the lawn to the cover of trees. *Stupid move.* He'd exposed himself to whoever was on the other end of the feed. But if his gut was correct, and Kaylee was guilty, then it made no sense that someone had their eyes on her whole life.

She would need protection when they decided it was time to make their move.

They were obviously still waiting, otherwise, they'd have extracted her for interrogation already. Or he'd be dealing with the fallout—the result of some other conclusion to this situation. But they hadn't. So, what were they waiting for?

Him?

His suspicion that she was involved was correct. Not just because Brad had mentioned her name, though he had considered that meant she was dirty. Part of the problem. Could she be the solution? He wanted to talk more with her. Because she drew him to her in a way no one had. He thought about her way too much, but that didn't mean he was going to do anything about it. After all, he was no better than the people watching her. He'd intended to clone her phone just like they had.

An itch on the back of his neck interrupted his thoughts. A latent instinct that had saved his life many times before.

All his training and experience, the many missions he'd been on. The ugly things he'd seen—and done. It fired like synapses in his brain, heightening his senses so that he could tell someone was holed up twenty feet to his left. Hiding.

One of the boys, or a bigger threat?

Kaylee had someone on her, and not just eyes on her life. There was a man watching. Waiting. For what?

Stuart wasn't going to hang around until something went wrong just to find out. He knew he could protect her. Certainly he had the skills to do it, and if she was absolved of being a party to the betrayal that led to Brad and Stuart being captured, then he needed to keep her safe until he got to the bottom of this.

Instinct flashed across his vision like a flash of lightning. Stuart ducked against a tree. A chunk of wood splintered a hair's length above his head, and in the second later, he heard the rapport of the gunshot.

Sniper.

Stuart ran. He circled wide, ducking through trees. Changing direction every couple of steps to make himself a moving target.

One harder to hit than someone going in a straight line, in a single direction.

Another shot rang out.

Someone screamed. Stuart's insides flipped over and bile rose in his throat, but there was no time to be sick. He had to get that shooter.

He pulled his gun and continued his wide circle around to the spot where he'd have hidden if this was his assignment.

The shots stopped. The screaming did not. Stuart saw a blur up ahead and knew the guy was on the move.

He spotted him again a quarter mile into the trees and sped up his sprint until he was moving as fast as he possibly could. In a running tackle, he took the guy down. They rolled.

An elbow missed his nose but glanced off his cheekbone. Stuart caught the guy around the neck with one arm.

With his gun hand, he shot the guy point blank range in the foot. But when he shifted at the last second, the shot missed him.

The sniper elbowed him in the stomach. Stuart coughed and sucked in a breath, but didn't let go of his grip on the man's neck. His other hand wasn't the same. The gun tumbled from his fingers to the ground. A knife glinted, and he realized the man had pulled it out.

Darn. Stuart shoved him away and rolled as the knife swiped toward him.

He hit a tree and got up, grasping a rock as he lifted to his feet. He flung the rock toward the man and caught him in the head.

They faced off with each other, Stuart's gun on the ground between them. If he dove for it, the other guy would do the same, and he'd end up sliced. Stuart did not like knives. Unless he was the one using it and the only thing in danger were the vegetables.

It was his least favorite weapon in a fight. Always had been, even before the men who'd held him and Brad captive sliced up his back just for the fun of it.

"Who sent you?" Stuart studied the man as they circled each other, pushing thoughts of holding a knife from his mind with as much force as he could muster. He didn't want to think about Brad.

About what had happened after their captors have given up torturing them and forced them to turn on each other.

Then, the moment Brad had cried out.

"I said, *Who sent you?!*" The scream from his lips echoed through the trees.

A voice from behind him said, "Leland, stand down."

He spun to see Basuto approach, followed by his partner. When Stuart turned back, the sniper had put away his knife. "That's his gun." Stuart pointed out the sniper rifle on the grass, then at his weapon. "This one is mine."

Basuto's partner, Donaldson, swiped up both.

The sniper shifted. "It okay if I reach for my ID?"

Sergeant Basuto said, "Slowly."

Stuart was waiting for Donaldson to hand his gun back to him, but the younger officer did not. He held onto both. Stuart said, "He shot at me. And he was watching Kaylee's room."

He didn't mention the surveillance equipment, as it would be difficult to explain how he knew about it without having been in her room.

"Actually," the sniper pulled out a leather wallet. "It's *his* rifle." He pointed to Stuart, and then let his wallet flip open. "Adam Eckles, Homeland Security. Please cuff this man."

"Stuart?"

He turned to Basuto. "What is going on?"

"I'd like to know the same thing." The sergeant glanced between Stuart and the Homeland agent.

Stuart said, "Why does Homeland Security have Kaylee under observation?"

Eckles shook his head. "We don't. I think the pertinent question is why did you have a sniper scope trained on that house over there? Don't you think you've hurt enough people in your life already, without targeting a home of innocents just trying to escape trauma? All you'll do is further terrify them. Like those two boys. And the woman who got hurt because of the shot you fired."

"A woman is hurt?" Stuart set off toward the house.

Basuto slammed a hand against his chest.

Every instinct in Stuart wanted to shove the sergeant away from him. His whole body jerked as he fought the urge to attack a man who didn't deserve to be hurt just because Stuart had been taught that touch meant he'd need to defend himself.

"This man is dangerous and unstable," Eckles said. "I was sent here to bring him in. There's an outstanding warrant with his name on it. I can show you."

Stuart looked at Basuto. "If there was, you'd know about it."

Basuto nodded, almost imperceptibly.

"I have questions to ask him," Eckles said. "The first of which is why he had a sniper rifle trained on that house."

Stuart was never going to get information out of this man now. Not unless he got the guy alone in a spot where he could ask a few poignant questions. Which meant they needed to be away from the two cops.

The sergeant pulled cuffs from the back of his belt. "Leland?"

A wealth of questions were contained in that one word. Would he submit? Was he going to do so quietly? Stuart held Basuto's gaze. The Homeland agent—if that was even true—wanted to take him. The sergeant didn't like that at all.

It wasn't unusual for Stuart to see so much in a person's gaze. He'd been trained to read people, and Basuto wasn't used to having to shield his thoughts in order to save his life.

He moved quickly, probably wanting to do it fast, walking behind Stuart.

Stuart's instincts fired, and he spun around. He shoved Basuto back so that the sergeant fell to the grass. Donaldson dropped both weapons and pulled his stun gun. "Stand down, Leland."

"You know I can't do that."

After all, the "agent" didn't need to know that Stuart's plan was to go with him. That if he was going to be cuffed and stuffed in this man's car, it would be because he wanted to be. So he could interrogate Adam Eckles.

Stuart launched himself at Donaldson. As though he didn't care what might happen, because there was no way he thought

Eckles would capture him. He saw Donaldson's eyes flare a half second before he squeezed the trigger on the stun gun.

The barbs hit Stuart in the chest.

He could have fought it, but what was the point? That just prolonged the situation. He clenched his teeth and let his body fall, submitting to the twitching voltage that coursed through every muscle in his body.

The second the voltage quit, a knee planted itself in his back. Given precisely where Eckles placed that knee, it was impossible to not suspect Eckles knew something about his captivity and the injuries he'd suffered.

The Homeland agent pulled Stuart's hands behind his back and secured his wrists. "I'll take him from here."

Six

Kaylee hopped off her bike before it came to a stop. She jumped a couple of steps and leaned the bike against the side of the house. Maggie turned when she ran over. "Kaylee."

The home's owner/operator had a young, dark-haired, dark-skinned woman nestled under her arm.

"Is everyone okay?" She looked at the woman, a newcomer. "Are you okay?"

The woman had tears in her big, brown eyes. She blew out a breath and rolled her eyes. "Yeah, freaked me out, but I'm okay."

Kaylee squeezed her elbows. "And the boys?"

Maggie said, "We sent them inside with Salena."

"Okay." Kaylee let go some of the tension she'd been holding. "No one was hurt? I heard it being called in just as shots were fired."

She'd pedaled over here as fast as she could. The second black and white car, and Savannah, had both beaten her here, but what else was she to do? She'd needed the time spent biking to get her reaction under control. The shakes were about gone, but it felt like they might resurge at any moment. She had to fight her natural reaction. Fear, born out of trauma.

The last thing Kaylee wanted was to show everyone here exactly how much her parent's deaths had affected her. Or prove to them that she really did need to speak to a professional. She'd read plenty of books, and she journaled on her computer. She was dealing with it fine.

"I'm going to go check with the police officers, okay?"

Maggie and the young woman with her both nodded, though there was a knowing look in her landlady's eyes. Okay, so she was more than just a landlady, but when Kaylee didn't want to accept that Maggie may have a point, she thought of her that way.

The reality was that the older woman had proved to be so much more than "just" a landlady. Mentor. Friend. Bible study leader. Thankfully, there were plenty of other women who lived in Hope Mansion. Kaylee could fly under the radar as much as possible.

Until she was called on it.

Kaylee took two steps, turned back to Maggie, and hugged her. She whispered, "I'm glad you're okay," in the older woman's ear, while Maggie gave Kaylee a reflexive squeeze.

Kaylee headed for Savannah and Basuto, huddled in conversation on the lawn. She swiped away the tears from her cheeks as she approached. Hopefully neither would notice. Or, if they did, that they didn't feel the need to comment on it.

"What happened?"

Savannah spun to her. Beyond the police detective, Kaylee spotted Stuart. What was he doing here? He seemed to have his hands behind his back, walked along by a clean-shaven man in jeans and boots and wearing a thin jacket over a T-shirt.

"What—"

"Back up, okay?" Basuto didn't give her a choice. He moved toward her and pressed in close without actually touching her, causing Kaylee to step back so he didn't bump her.

Of course, that only irritated her. He'd used his size to intimidate her into doing what he wanted her to. Kaylee planted her hands on her hips. "Someone tell me what happened." She spoke loudly enough so the two cops and the man she didn't know would hear.

"Kaylee," Savannah started.

She cut the detective off with a hand raised. "I live here. I want to know what happened. There were shots fired?"

And Stuart was the one in cuffs. She wanted to believe that wasn't possible, that though he might be reactive, he'd never seriously hurt anyone. But she didn't know that. Not for sure.

Basuto said, "There was a rifle shot. No one was injured."

"Okay."

Savannah lifted her chin. "Forensics will tell us who fired the weapon."

Stuart perked up then. Kaylee noted he looked a little flushed. He said, "You're right." He almost grinned, but not in a happy or fun way. Satisfaction, maybe? Why, she wasn't so sure. It should prove Stuart hadn't done this.

"He'll be booked and in the closest federal holding facility by then." The man holding Stuart's arm shrugged one shoulder. "You can call me, let me know. But I doubt it'll change much, considering everything this guy has done."

Kaylee frowned.

Savannah shifted a hair closer to her. "He's a Homeland Security agent." To the agent, she said, "I'm going to need to see that paperwork before you take him anywhere."

The man's lips twitched. "I'll show you whatever you want, sweetheart."

Savannah scoffed.

Basuto said, "That's not necessary."

The agent was looking at Kaylee now, and she didn't like the intent in the man's eyes. What was that about?

She said, "I'm going to regret asking, but is there something I can help you with before you leave?"

White teeth flashed in a sinister smile. "Kaylee Caldwell?"

Yeah, she was going to regret this. "Yes."

"There are some questions I'd like to ask you, as well."

"About Stuart?" She knew nothing about him. They'd barely even had a whole conversation, and he scared the pants off her. What did a Homeland Security agent want to know?

"Among other things." He worked his jaw side to side. "If you could come with me as well, I'll endeavor to clear this up quickly."

She turned to Savannah. "I have to go with him?"

There was something in the man's body language she did not like. All cops weren't saints, just like all criminals weren't mean. People were people. The hope was that they did the best they could, but that wasn't always the reality.

The sense she got from him was different than the one she got from Stuart. But the conclusion she drew about both was the same. She wasn't sure she wanted to be alone in a car with either one. Both together? That could be even worse.

Kaylee shivered.

Savannah said, "Not if you're not under arrest. This was about your room." She pointed to the back wall of the house. "Your window was accessed, though there's no sign anything in there was disturbed. Aside from the shot, that's all it appears happened here. And no one was hurt."

Someone had broken into her room?

She fought the surprise, even though that would be expected. She didn't want to seem resigned, or nonchalant. What was she supposed to do? And why was keeping secrets so hard?

She realized they were expecting an answer. All she could think was one thing. *Someone was touching my stuff.*

Kaylee turned back to the federal agent. "No, thank you. I'm declining your invitation."

Something like approval stretched across Stuart's face as he gazed at her. Kaylee spun around, memorizing his expression, tucking it within her mind. She would use it as a good memory to combat all the awful ones from her past still tucked away in her head. Those few captured good moments in her life were what held her together in the dark when the past threatened to tear her open.

"Ms. Caldwell!" The federal agent called after her.

"Looks like she doesn't wanna talk to you," Stuart said.

Kaylee heard amusement in his voice. She didn't look back, though. Approval and amusement? That was good and bad, considering she didn't need more fodder for being distracted by him. She had enough to deal with right now. She could also admit that attraction was better than continuing to be scared of him, but that took energy as well.

A car door slammed. When she looked, Kaylee spotted Trina rushing over with her long-legged stride and heels. Kaylee's friend had a flushed look on her face.

"Hey."

"Hey?" Trina glanced at the cops, then at Kaylee. She launched into Kaylee's arms and gave her a tight squeeze. Crossfit was working, apparently. "I thought you were hurt! They said a gun went off!"

She let go, and Kaylee hid the wince. "Who did?"

Trina leaned back. "The police band. Duh. I can't believe you didn't call me!"

"I wasn't here. I only just got here myself."

"But your room was broken into!" Her voice was higher now; so shrill Kaylee wanted to wince.

"Savannah," Kaylee called back over her shoulder. "Can we go look at my room?"

"I'll come with you."

The three of them used the front door, and Trina went first. Down the hall to Kaylee's room, where they'd watched a movie on her laptop a few times.

Trina stopped outside the door. "I can't believe you didn't call your best friend. This is so scary!" She was taller than Kaylee, and thinner. Athletic in a way she got plenty of attention and probably didn't need to hang out with a boring, single woman, like herself, who thought the book was better than the movie. Every single time.

It didn't matter which book had been turned into a movie. The book was always better. Literally *every* time.

Savannah twisted the door handle and went first. "I didn't know you guys were close."

"We've been best friends since Kaylee came to work at the bank."

Kaylee smiled. Sure, she liked Trina, and she was flattered. She just hadn't even contemplated calling the woman when her home had been threatened. There was too much going on. What made Trina so put out that Kaylee hadn't called?

Trina nudged her into the room. Kaylee stumbled, then looked around. "You came in here already, right?"

Savannah nodded. "It looks neat and not like anything was disturbed. But you're the only one who can know that for sure."

Trina circled the room, looking at the low bookshelf where Kaylee kept the stack of library books she had checked out. She crouched, her skirt pulling tight as she shifted things on Kaylee's shelf.

Kaylee pulled open the drawer by her bed.

"Do you have a computer?"

She glanced at Savannah. "Yes." The desktop was empty. When Savannah pointed that out with a wave of her finger, Kaylee said, "Backpack in the closet." She straightened and moved to it. "I never leave it out. I don't like the idea someone could access it, so I shut it completely down after I'm done."

She didn't like TV as a general rule. So much of it was mindless drivel designed to addict the watcher into passivity as the next episode cued itself up automatically.

Sure, some of it was "good" entertainment. Wholesome, or informative. But the whole system was designed to manipulate the user with suggestions, the same way social media did—timing their notifications for maximum dopamine hit.

"Are you okay?"

She shook her head in answer to Savannah's question. "I need to focus. Sorry." She pulled out her backpack, much lighter than it should be. "It's not here." She glanced over at Savannah. "My laptop is gone."

"When was the last time you used it?"

"I don't know." She thought about it. "Maybe last weekend?" She'd been busy, and the series she was reading was just getting good.

"I'll put it in the police report."

Trina bumped into Kaylee's side, then clutched her arm and gasped. "Obviously, whoever broke in stole it! I can't believe this. They've invaded your privacy. Now there's going to be a police investigation, and all your secrets will be spilled all over town. You'll be ruined!"

"Um…I don't know what you keep on your computer, but all that's on mine is my budget spreadsheet," Kaylee said. "It's hardly damning."

"What about your journal?"

Kaylee said, "It's on the cloud and has multiple passwords. I'll just restrict access from anywhere other than the IP address at the police station until I get a new laptop."

Trina rolled straight to the next subject. "Dad said you should come back to the bank and eat lunch with us. You're probably distraught, and the police department isn't safe."

She regretted telling Trina about the bikers who had stormed the place. Truth was, she'd long grown tired of being scared of what *might* happen.

"All righty then." Savannah flipped her notebook closed. "I'll check in with Mia, and we'll get you secured in here. Okay?"

Kaylee nodded. "Thank you."

Savannah headed for the door.

"Detective!" Trina wailed, rushing after her.

Kaylee sighed. *That was close.* A sniper rifle and a Homeland security agent? Whatever happened here, it had to be about what Brad had sent her.

Good thing she'd kept it safe.

She strode to the hall, an idea forming. If this was about Brad, then she needed to be sure. "Trina!"

Her friend broke off the conversation with Savannah and spun.

"Let's go to the bank," she said. "Lunch sounds good."

Seven

"Let's go." Adam shoved Stuart toward the back yard again where a path led off into the wooded area surrounding Hope Mansion. The secluded location of the mansion was a positive for any residents trying to keep a low profile somewhere safe. But, as they'd discovered just recently, it also made it possible for a sniper to get off a shot while hiding in the woods.

"Why fire that shot and draw attention to yourself?" Stuart glanced over and looked at the man following him, holding a pistol pointed at his back.

He didn't recognize the guy…or, at least, he didn't think so. They were about the same age. Same lean build under slightly oversized clothing to hide the definition of his muscles, which would inevitably give away what he wanted to conceal.

Covert tactics had become second nature years ago. Now it was intrinsic. Like the way Stuart could hear a squirrel about fifteen feet to his right, and how he knew it was just him and Adam Eckles right now.

Stuart might have his hands secured behind his back, but he was far from subdued.

"Might as well tell me." Stuart slowed his pace, just a fraction. He needed Eckles a foot or so closer than he was. "Otherwise this doesn't make sense. Or does it? I'm already out of the room, closing in on you. Why take that shot and scare a woman?"

"People need to know." Eckles's voice had a conversational tone. "No one's safe. Not anywhere."

"Agreed. Most of them, nothing but sheeple. Am I right?"

Eckles snorted. "Now we're bonding."

"Worth a try. I'm supposed to get you to sympathize with me. Then I'll use that rapport to get you to doubt your mission here. After that, you'll be distracted with the worry over your life choices, so you won't see me slide the knife from your belt and stab you with it. You'll be bleeding out on the ground before you even realize what's happened."

Eckles started to laugh.

Stuart's next step was a foot plant and a spin. Hands behind his back, he had to settle for a shoulder to the other man's gun hand. He tackled the guy. They landed on the ground and Eckles let out an "oof." Stuart shifted his weight, leaned on the man's diaphragm, and pressed down as hard as he could.

Eckles tried to inhale. He slammed the butt of the gun on the back of Stuart's shoulder.

"Who sent you?" Stuart let up for a second, dodged a blow to his head, and leaned on him again. "Tell me."

Eckles struggled. He tried to gasp and Stuart could see he was losing consciousness. How long before he tried to shoot Stuart in the back? Or did he not want to draw attention to them? Now there was an idea. One shot to draw people, and no more—for a clean getaway.

Stuart rolled onto Eckles's arm, the one holding the gun. Now, on his side, he immobilized the wrist and kicked the other man's knee. The pop was audible. Eckles bellowed in pain but took the opportunity to punch Stuart with his left hand. Even though he dodged the blow, it still managed to connect. This time with his upper arm.

Stuart gritted his teeth as his hand went numb. "Enough."

"Cause you know I'll shoot you."

"Isn't that what you came here to do?"

"If I wanted you dead," Eckles said, "You'd *be* dead."

Stuart sat up. "Untie me."

Eckles barked a laugh. "Yeah, right. You'll kill me the first chance you get. I know all about you. Thickest file I've ever seen." He blew out a breath. "Oh boy, some of them things you've done? Man." He shook his head. "You're hardcore. I almost feel bad bringing you in."

Maybe you should just kill me. Anything would be better than listening to this. "Long time ago." Stuart climbed to his feet, rumpled and bruised from the fight. But some of the adrenaline was gone. He knew what this guy was made of. What Eckles was prepared to do, or not do.

He blew out a long breath.

"Keep moving." Eckles swore. "You trashed my knee, you know?"

"You deserved it."

"Like you don't deserve more prison time than you're ever going to get? You deserve more than a quick death, too."

Stuart didn't need to be reminded of all the things he had done. He recalled every face of every person he'd ever killed. Guilty and innocent. Now he walked like a man condemned. Even though he still had a million questions. Had Homeland Security really come after him? He had no idea what they were going to accuse him of, but no doubt he'd be given a guilty verdict and sentenced to prison for it.

Or death.

Wouldn't be the first time. Only, when he'd been re-assigned to that French prison on a mission, he'd been innocent of the crime. All the evidence had been fabricated.

Eckles marched him to the end of the path, where a silver, midsize SUV rental was parked. He was forced to sit on the backseat and twist his hands up. Only when Eckles had used a plastic tie to secure one wrist to the passenger headrest did he remove the cuffs. Stuart twisted around. The gun pressed sharply against his temple. Eckles grabbed his free hand and used a plastic tie on that one also, stacking Stuart's wrists and giving him zero room to move. It was so tight he could feel it cut into his skin.

Eckles fired up the GPS on his phone and set off. He even put the radio on.

By the time he hit the town, another dot had appeared on the screen of his phone. Now there were two, and one was following the other. The first dot pulled into the parking lot behind the bank. Eckles slowed to take the same turn but instead stopped the car on the far side in a spot obscured by a huge truck with deer antlers on the front and tires that were level with the passenger window.

He put the car in park and sat back, muttering about his knee. Folded his arms. Closed his eyes.

"What are we doing here?" Stuart looked around. "What are we waiting for?"

Eckles said nothing.

A crackle came through the phone's speaker, then the sound of a door closing. "Kaylee. I heard what happened." He paused. "How are you, my dear?"

"I'm fine, thank you, Mr. Nigelson."

Stuart glanced at Eckles. "You're the one who cloned her phone." And hacked her GPS *and* turned her microphone into a listening device. "And she has no idea."

"Soon as she comes out, I'll grab her, and we'll be on our way." Eckles shrugged while Kaylee continued to make small talk with the bank manager and his daughter—her friend Trina. Eckles spoke over them, "No harm, no foul."

Yeah. Stuart had the feeling Kaylee wouldn't see it that way. She was being targeted by a man he was now sure wasn't a legit federal agent. Too many times Stuart had impersonated whoever he wanted and gotten away with it. Why couldn't this guy do the same? Whoever he worked for thought they were above the law. *Been there, done that, too.*

"Don't hurt her. She isn't part of this."

"Ask her that." Eckles still hadn't opened his eyes. "I read her journal. Her brother sent a package, and she's supposed to hide it."

Stuart rocked the car he turned so fast. "Brad's alive?" Was that only wishful thinking?

"Thought you knew what happened. You were there." Eckles said, "He sent the package before that last mission, though."

Stuart wasn't going to tell him captivity had shattered his mind. That there were huge chunks of what happened with Brad that he couldn't remember. Maybe he never would, or maybe his mind kept the secret, knowing he didn't want to know. Like self-preservation.

Maybe his mind was scared of him, the way everyone else was.

Scared of himself.

Stuart said, "So you're supposed to bring the two of us to…whoever."

"And the package."

Which contained who knows what. Eckles obviously had no idea what it was, or he'd have said. It had to be the person who'd set up Brad and Stuart—the betrayal that led to their capture. No one else would even care. He'd been burned. Brad was who-knew-where—maybe not dead, as he had always believed. Maybe laying low until things calmed down.

"We're loose ends then. Is that it?" Stuart studied the man's profile.

He opened his mouth to reply, but Kaylee voice sailed through the phone's speaker, "I'm just going to take a look at my safety deposit box before I wash up. Then we can eat. If that's okay with you guys?"

"Of course." The bank manager sounded so solicitous.

"I'll pour drinks." Trina sounded… Stuart didn't know her at all, so he couldn't say how she sounded. But it didn't seem all that genuine, or friendly. All he could glean from was the way she bounced around the gym in tiny shorts and a tight tank top. And how did that tell him anything? She knew all the men only wanted to watch her. Stuart always just looked at the TV instead.

"Thank you." Kaylee's voice was polite. Overly polite, as though there was a lot she wanted to say but didn't feel comfortable enough with them that she could. And Trina was supposed to be her best friend. Seemed like, from Kaylee's tone of voice, that they weren't nearly as tight as Trina thought they were.

Worlds apart. Different values and interests. They might have gotten along fine with each other working at the bank, but in life they were two completely different types of women. Could a relationship like that even work?

"Showtime." Eckles cracked the door. He slammed it behind him, and Stuart watched him tuck the pistol in a holster at the small of his back.

Stuart had to help her. Eckles was going to want to see what she was hiding in that safety deposit box. What on earth had Brad sent to Kaylee anyway?

Kaylee.

Her brother had said her name. Stuart remembered that much. He'd assumed it was to implicate her as one of the people who'd set them up.

But what if the opposite was true.

Stuart's paranoia might have led him to completely the wrong conclusion. He'd thought she was in on it, and all this time she was the answer. The one with the evidence Brad had collected.

He couldn't believe he'd been that consumed with his issues that he'd missed the fact she was in danger.

Kaylee needed his help.

Stuart twisted, pulled his foot up to his bound hands, and tried to move his fingers. He winced.

The phone in the cup holder crackled.

"Thank you." Kaylee's voice drifted to him as though she spoke to him.

It took a minute of strain and tugging, but he got the pocket knife from his running shoe. He twisted the blade out with his teeth and cut the plastic securing his hands.

The knife tumbled to the carpet by his feet.

"I don't think—" Kaylee stopped speaking. Through the phone he heard a shuffle, and then, "What are you doing in here?" Fear laced her tone.

Stuart hissed and worked his fingers straight, then made fists. *Ouch.* "Kaylee." He shoved the door open and ran to the back door of the bank with the knife in his hand.

He had to get to her.

There was nothing good in him, nothing redeemable. He knew he was too far gone. But if he could save even one innocent that he had put in danger, then it would help his remaining days. He'd be able to gain just a little more peace.

Feet shuffled from both sides. *Surrounded.* Stuart spun around and came face to face with four cops: Basuto, his partner, another uniformed guy, and Conroy.

"Drop the knife."

Stuart let go of it. "I have to get inside."

Conroy said, "Need to make a withdrawal?"

Eight

Kaylee had been about to lift the lid of her safety deposit box when she sensed movement.

"Well?" Trina stood in the doorway.

"I don't think you're supposed to be in here."

"I figured you could use some moral support." Trina shrugged. She leaned against the wall and pulled out her phone, as though this was an everyday occurrence.

Kaylee opened her mouth but decided against saying anything. How could she just tell Trina to get out without it sounding rude? She didn't need *moral support*. And why was Trina acting so clingy all of a sudden? Maybe if Kaylee didn't need to keep the contents of her safety deposit box such a secret, she wouldn't be so weirded out about Trina suddenly showing up.

"I'll be okay," Kaylee said. "You don't have to stay."

"It's fine." Trina didn't look up from her phone.

Kaylee had to remember that this was the plan. She'd been the one to text Ted on the secure messaging app he'd set up on her phone months ago and tell him to let the chief in on her idea. The cops were outside, and so everything would be fine. Right. She just needed to keep telling herself that.

She just had to open the safety deposit box. If there was a target on her because of the flash drive Brad had sent, then it would zero in on her right here. Surely. When she was nice and protected.

Why else would a man from Homeland Security show up today? Not just to take Stuart into custody. She'd figured there was more to it than that, which was why she'd reached out to the cops. They were more than happy to protect "one of their own," which felt good, even if she was afraid to waste their time when it turned out to be nothing—*if* it turned out to be nothing.

Which it very well might. That federal agent could have taken Stuart out of town, back to his office. Arrested on whatever charges there were.

She didn't want to feel bad for him, but she did.

Kaylee sighed. She was going to have to tell them all what was going on, particularly the parts that *might* have to do with Stuart. She still wasn't completely sure about that. She didn't have evidence or anything, but nothing else made sense.

She needed protection. Someone had been in her room, and they'd taken her computer. Despite what she'd told Trina and Savanah, that did freak her out. Brad's package put her in danger.

But what these people didn't know was that she had a whole police department to protect her. And regardless of how she felt, they wouldn't care if this did turn out to be nothing. Though, given the sniper shot, it probably *wasn't* nothing.

She shook her head. "Trina. Can you give me a minute, please?" She used the voice she utilized when kids were being too loud in the library.

Her friend glanced up, something like belligerence flashing on her face for a second. She pushed off the wall and turned to leave.

A man appeared and stood in the doorway. The Homeland agent who'd wanted to talk to her and Stuart earlier. "She can stay, and I'll join her. As you said, it'll just be a minute."

Trina planted one hand on her hip, suddenly prepared to go to bat for Kaylee despite feeling jilted just a second ago. "I don't think so…"

The agent lifted a gun.

"Trina, back up."

Her friend didn't listen. "What do you want?"

The agent said, "For you to back up against the wall and stay there." He motioned with the gun. "Both of you against the wall."

"There are security cameras. You'll be on video with a gun," Kaylee said. "I don't think your bosses at Homeland Security will like that. If that's even who you work for."

She saw Trina shift at the mention of the federal agency. Surprise that this man wasn't just a normal bank robber?

He took a step in. "None of us are who we seem, right?" Before she could answer, he said, "Open the box. Give me the contents."

"I will not. Those are my personal things. Irreplaceable."

"Kaylee," Trina hissed. "Just give it to him before he shoots us."

"I know what you want," Kaylee told him. "I know why you're here."

Trina twisted to her. "Then give it to him!"

"I'm not going to do that." Kaylee folded her arms. "Shoot me. I'm not breaking my promise."

He lifted the gun.

Kaylee braced. He'd do it. He really would shoot her, and she'd die never knowing who she was supposed to have given the flash drive to.

She'd never know what had happened to her brother.

What the package had been about.

"Just give me what's in the box."

Kaylee had thought Stuart was the scariest thing in her life right now. She'd been so wrong. She knew deep down his being here would make her feel better. Not worse. She could feel it in her heart.

She said, "You can't leave without it, can you? Can't return to whoever sent you, not with just Stuart. You need both of us. Or, at least you need him and the…package." She wasn't going to tell him what it was, just in case he didn't know. She might be able to have Ted help her fake him out with something else.

How long would it be until the cops moved in? Hopefully before this guy—

She couldn't finish her thought. Not before he twisted around, gun in hand, and rushed her friend. He brought the weapon down on Trina's face.

She screamed, crumpled to the ground, and started to cry. "Why are you doing this?"

Kaylee didn't look at the blood. She kept her gaze on the doorway, her stomach clenched. Everything in her tight. Unmoving.

He waved the gun again. Her whole body flinched, and she saw his lips move but didn't register he was speaking.

Her world zeroed into focus.

"..in that box. *Now!*"

Kaylee didn't move.

He reached for the box, ripped the top open, and started to grab what was inside.

"No!" She screamed the word, detached enough from what was happening that she could hear how terrifying it sounded. "Don't touch that! It's all I have left of them."

But this man didn't care.

Stuart stepped in. "Enough."

The gunman spun towards him, but Stuart moved to her faster than she'd have thought he could move. Then men in uniform spilled in. Cops. More cops. Everyone shouting for the agent to put down his weapon. Stand down.

Trina cried. Someone pulled her to her feet, and Kaylee saw the blood running down the side of her face as she wailed.

Kaylee wanted to move. Her body was frozen, encased in enough shock and fear to restrict even a twitch of movement.

Stuart's face came into view. His lips moving as the other man's had done.

He touched her cheek. A soft gesture, his skin rough. "Hey."

She flinched and sucked in a breath. Everything spun around her, so she grasped his elbows for support.

He glanced back over his shoulder. "Call Dean."

"No." The word sounded like a croak. "I'm...I'm okay."

Stuart dipped his head to look in her eyes. "Sure?"

She nodded, then realized tears were rolling down her face. Kaylee swiped them away, and he handed her a tissue. Where he'd gotten it from, she had no idea.

"I thought you got arrested."

Stuart glanced at the "special agent" and shrugged. "He's not a real federal agent. Conroy told me that Ted figured it out right before we came in here. He's ex-military. A mercenary for hire, or so Ted thinks."

That wasn't good. Someone had hired this guy to come here. To shoot a rifle, steal her computer, arrest Stuart, and try to get her package from Brad. "There's something I need to tell you."

A shadow crossed over his eyes. "Me, too." He held out his hand. "Should we go somewhere else?"

Conroy came up to them. "Neither of you are going anywhere except for the police station."

Kaylee gasped. "Are you arresting us?"

Stuart shifted to stand slightly in front of her. A protective gesture.

Conroy said, "When you contacted one of my people for help, you chose to involve me and this department. We care about you. That means you fill us in on what's happening, and we do everything we can to keep you safe until it's resolved."

"I'm not in danger."

Stuart didn't react to her dumb statement. Conroy shot her a look.

"I mean, I didn't *think* I was," Kaylee said.

"I don't think that's true either."

"I'm not a liar."

Stuart took her hand in his. "No one thinks you are. But we should tell Conroy what's happening."

She caught his gaze, over his shoulder.

Kaylee nodded. "I know."

She did need Conroy's help. That way she'd know it was being taken care of, and she wouldn't have to worry. She'd have backup if she was in danger.

Plus, she was still holding Stuart's hand, and that was nice. He was strong. He made her feel safer, even if a lot of the threat she'd felt recently was from him.

Am I really going to do this?

She'd been avoiding what was going on up until now. It appeared she wasn't able to do that any longer.

The fake federal agent was slammed against the wall and cuffed. He struggled, but it did no good. They escorted him out.

Kaylee saw the safety deposit box, pictures spilling out. She rushed over and righted them, breathing a prayer of thanks that nothing had been damaged.

"Who are they?"

She didn't look at Stuart, and she didn't want to look at the photos either. She only wanted to put them away. Where she'd know they were safe. "My parents."

She put the lid back on and returned the box to its place.

Both Conroy and Stuart had sympathetic looks on their faces. She spun away and walked out.

The bank manager, Silas Nigelson, was occupied with Trina who was currently being assessed by an EMT. Kaylee slipped past them, thankful she didn't have to try and figure out how to apologize for everything.

First her room. Now this, and Trina was hurt on top of it all.

What did you get yourself into, Brad? Normally she'd pray, as she always had. Find her peace in God. This time, it seemed to make more sense to direct her question to her brother. Wherever he was.

"We can take my car." Conroy pulled keys from his pocket, shifting his suit jacket in the process.

She took comfort in that familiar move she'd seen many times before.

Stuart was on her other side, scanning the street. Cars passed. A couple biked together, a trailer behind them with a child inside. A normal day.

Making her wish she could have a day like that.

Did Stuart ride a bike?

"Come on."

She nodded to Conroy and followed him across the street to his car. "Thank you all for coming. I don't know what I'd have done if…" She couldn't finish.

"I'm glad you contacted us," Conroy said. "Though, a little more warning would have been good." The grin he shot her was new, full of boyish charm. He was a nice guy and a great cop. Lately, now that he had a fiancé, he seemed softer somehow, without the rough edges he normally wore. Mostly because he was happy now. Life was good.

Stuart scanned the parking lot, then glanced back at the bank. Then he looked at the roofs of the buildings around them.

"What is—" She couldn't finish.

Stuart yelled, "Gun!"

Kaylee flinched, and before she could make sense of what was happening, he was tackling her to the ground just as a gunshot went off. A sound like a firework cracked across her.

She hit the asphalt and cried out as he landed on her. Kaylee's entire body jarred and her head slammed against the ground.

"Sorry." Stuart shifted off her. "Stay down. Do *not* move."

Kaylee didn't know if she could.

She glanced around though, trying to figure out what had just happened. Under the car, she could see someone on the other side. Covered in blood.

"Conroy." Ice washed over her. Kaylee yelled, "Conroy!"

Boots pounded toward her. A car horn honked. Kaylee forced her vision to focus and saw Basuto, his face pale with fear.

Kaylee screamed. "Officer down!"

Nine

Stuart couldn't leave her. He touched his palms to Kaylee's cheeks and looked into her eyes. Fear blinked back at him, but she focused just fine. She'd hit her head pretty hard.

Another shot rang out.

Basuto, who'd been racing toward them, hit the asphalt in the middle of the street. Someone screamed. Stuart winced. He knew pain like that. Not only what it felt like initially, but also how to live with the repercussions of injury day in and day out.

Kaylee shifted, letting out a small moan of pain. "Conroy."

Stuart wanted to go after the shooter. He tugged on her arms. "Stay low. Go left."

They moved around the front of the car, to the other side where Conroy lay.

"Stuart!"

He glanced back, over his shoulder.

Dean hugged the corner of the bank building. "Talk to me."

Everyone over there was pinned down. Cops. Pedestrians. Stuart saw more than one person with bloody knees and palms. An older man had been propped against the building, one of the cops pressing a cloth to his forehead.

Stuart peered around the front bumper to see Conroy.

Kaylee shifted beside him. "We need to put pressure on that."

"Conroy!" Mia's scream echoed from the bank against the buildings on the far side. Someone grabbed her around the waist. She kicked out, screaming for her fiancé.

Kaylee gasped a breath. "I can get to him."

Dean yelled, "Stuart!"

He assessed Conroy as fast as he could, then turned back to Dean. His friend's face was pale in a scary way. None of them wanted to lose the police chief. Stuart yelled out, "He's breathing and conscious." But there was a lot of blood.

A shot pinged off the street, kicking up asphalt.

Stuart tugged off his sweater, balled it up, and handed it to Kaylee. "Careful and slow. You keep your head down, yeah?"

She nodded and started to crawl toward the police chief.

Stuart assessed the rooftops to try and figure out where the sniper had set up his perch.

Conroy moaned. Kaylee had her arms straight, pressing down with the sweater on his wound.

Stuart said, "Shoulder?"

"It's too low."

He prayed it wasn't so low it had hit Conroy's heart, though he suspected it hadn't. With a large caliber bullet from a rifle, it would have done significant enough damage that the police chief would probably be dead by now if that was the case.

Kaylee's phone started to ring.

"Pick up the phone, Kaylee!" Dean called out across the street.

She nodded at Stuart and put the phone to her ear. "Hello— wait. Stuart."

He stopped backing up, still scanning the rooftops and looked at her.

"Where are you going?"

"I need to get the sniper."

"Kaylee," Dean called out, sounding frustrated.

Stuart left them to it. He needed to solve the bigger problem of how the sniper had them all pinned down so they couldn't take care of Conroy the way they needed to and get him to the hospital.

He spotted a glint of sunlight and sent up a prayer of thanks. Stuart didn't even have a weapon. Didn't matter. He wouldn't be able to hit the sniper with a gun from this distance.

He needed to be closer.

Stuart trotted down the buildings, the opposite side of the street from the bank. He kept parked cars between him and the sniper's scope. Hiding as he sprinted low toward the movie theater where the man—or woman—had set up shop.

He had to push everything from his mind, except the task at hand—taking care of this threat. Otherwise, emotion would cloud his judgment, and he'd be fighting shock instead, demanding things from his body that adrenaline would deny him. The first rule he'd ever learned of covert operations was to give up everything he was and be the "asset." Otherwise, personal traits and opinions crept in. If he hadn't learned how to do that, he'd have been dead years ago.

Unfortunately, that "unmaking" he'd gone through now meant all he had was fragments of the person he'd been in the past, with no idea of the kind of man he was now.

Only who he maybe wanted to be.

He breached the side door and raced for the stairs inside. He'd been in the movie theater once, but during the entire movie, instinct had found him cataloging escape routes and noting the location of all doors and hallways.

The roof door had been padlocked at one time. That padlock lay discarded now, cut with the bolt cutters that lay beside it. He grabbed them and pushed the door open, keeping his body out of sight.

A gunshot—a pistol this time—sang past the doorframe beside his head.

Stuart didn't flinch. He waited.

Would the guy get inpatient and come looking for him? He couldn't know Stuart's only weapon was the bolt cutters the guy had left behind.

A minute passed. Nothing.

Stuart picked up the busted padlock. He tested the weight in his hand, then fielded it out the door. Impact.

He heard a low exclamation and whipped his head to look out.

He'd hit the leg of the sniper tripod and knocked the thing down. Stuart moved out the door, throwing the bolt cutters. It was a risky move, but his arm was pretty accurate, even left-handed.

The bolt cutters caught the man's outstretched hand holding the gun. He cried out and Stuart slammed into him. He tackled the guy, and they both hit the ground, kind of like the way he'd done with Kaylee.

Only this time it wasn't to save someone's life. He slammed his arm under the guy's chin, nearly snapping his neck back as he forced the man's skull against the roof of the movie theater.

"I need him alive."

Stuart didn't turn, but he was pretty sure it was Basuto. He knelt on the sniper's wrist. The man cried out and punched Stuart's thigh. His entire leg went numb.

Stuart hissed and tried to shift his weight to get some feeling back in it.

Basuto knelt beside him. He grabbed the sniper's free hand and twisted it back. "Roll."

They got the man onto his front, and Basuto put cuffs on. Stuart shifted to stand, and his leg gave out. He tumbled onto his backside and breathed against the pain while the sergeant hauled their sniper to his feet.

The man who'd shot the police chief glared at him.

"You shouldn't have done that." Stuart was content to stand when his legs would hold him up, but there was no way he wouldn't speak his mind. "If the chief dies, there's nothing you can do to talk yourself out of this. No deals."

This guy had to know small towns weren't like the warzones he was probably used to. It drove Stuart crazy how insular they were, but that would come in handy right now.

Basuto said, "He's right. You're done."

The sniper's expression changed, eyes narrowing. He didn't give away much in his expression, but it was clear he didn't think much of the sergeant.

"Who sent you?" Stuart got up, leaning most of his weight on the leg that was still numb. He closed in on the sniper and patted him down. The sergeant didn't need to be caught by a weapon no one had known this man carried.

Basuto motioned to the rifle, now laying on its side on the gravel. "I'll have Donaldson pack up all this stuff."

He found a knife at the man's ankle and a photo in his back pocket. "It's Kaylee." Stuart showed the picture to Basuto.

Then he squared up in front of the sniper. They had to learn this man's name. And Stuart would.

After all, it could be he wasn't in any database. He might be a mercenary. Or he'd been in the military and now worked contracts for hire. An assassin. Government, or freelance? Whoever had set up Brad and Stuart was here, cleaning up their mess.

Stuart had no idea who that was. He didn't even have any theories. "Kill, or capture?"

The man stared him down.

"Tell me what I want to know," Stuart said. "What's your assignment here?"

The sniper's nostrils flared.

"Let's go." Basuto led the man toward the door. "We'll get answers, one way or another."

Stuart followed them, more to see if the man said anything. Though, considering everything, he intended also to provide backup to the sergeant if necessary. "How's the chief?"

Basuto studied the sniper as they headed down the stairs, not taking his attention from the man who'd shot his boss. "Dean said it's bad, but he could pull through. Told me to pray."

"Good idea."

"Yeah?"

Stuart said, "Sure. Can't hurt, right?"

The sniper huffed out a breath.

Stuart didn't need his opinion on matters of faith. "Whether or not you or I believe Someone is up there, prayer is helpful. If it turns out there isn't Someone up there?" He shrugged. "I've lost nothing asking for help since just doing so has slowed me down enough to give me peace in the middle of insanity."

Basuto opened the door at the bottom and led the sniper out to the lobby. "Mmm."

Stuart had fallen back on faith several times in his life. This situation was bad enough he'd be tempted to do it again. He knew Kaylee believed, so why not pray? What he'd told Basuto was true. Praying hadn't ever been a bad idea before. Why would it be now?

They approached the movie theater front door.

"Watch your step." The sniper smirked.

Stuart grabbed him from Basuto's grasp and shoved him against the wall beside the door. The man winced. Stuart said, "Who else is here?"

His lips twitched.

"Your buddy, the fake Homeland agent? He's in police custody. Now you are too."

"Uh…" Basuto didn't continue.

"He's dead?" Stuart asked without looking at the sergeant.

"First person this guy killed."

Stuart spoke to the sniper. "Tying up loose ends?" When the man said nothing, he continued, "Making it so no one can talk."

"Guess that means I'm next, right?"

"And it doesn't matter how much pressure we put on," Stuart said. "You aren't going to talk. We won't be able to ID you, and the minute you hit the system, you'll be killed in some incident or another."

"You'd know."

Stuart pressed his lips into a thin line. They'd get nothing from this guy.

He wanted to ask again what interest they had with Kaylee. Why this man had her picture on him. But what was the point? He wasn't going to talk. They'd never be able to do enough to get him to go against his orders. Or offer him enough to betray them.

"What do they have on you?"

The man's eyes darkened.

"Don't you know vulnerabilities are what gives them that power?"

"So, you care about nothing," the man said. "Is that it?"

At one time, that would have been true. Now? Not so much. Stuart said, "These people are under my protection."

Basuto shifted closer to Stuart with a limp and a slight wince. "I don't know what you're gearing up to do, but I'm not letting this guy go. I don't care if you're wanting him to relay a message back to whoever sent him here. Not when he shot Conroy."

"Understood." Stuart walked away, shoved the door open and stepped outside. If there was someone else here, he couldn't tell. He didn't feel that familiar sensation of being watched right now.

They were keeping their distance.

He waved over a couple of uniformed cops, just to make sure Basuto would have backup. The police here could do whatever they wanted. Stuart had never operated on a local level. He'd cleaned up national problems. Changed the course of a government. Even, once, started a war. Conflict was inevitable, so it may as well happen for a good reason.

He sighed. The man he'd been was still in there.

No matter how much he attempted to convince himself otherwise, he was still that person deep down. He didn't belong here where he put everyone in danger.

Stuart needed to make sure Kaylee was safe, and then he was leaving. He would trace this man to the source, whoever that was.

And then he would take them out.

Ten

"Kaylee!"

She spun to see Basuto in his sergeant's uniform striding toward her, hauling a shorter man with him. The sergeant was five-nine, so the man with him had to be five-six or seven. Stuart was closer to six feet.

Basuto looked down, his eyes widening for a second.

Her body flinched and she stopped herself from looking down at her hands. She already knew they were covered in the chief's blood. She didn't need to see that again.

"I'm taking this guy in. You need a ride—because I want you at the police station ASAP."

She nodded.

"I'll drive you." Ted squeezed her shoulder.

Kaylee tried not to flinch. Stuart was now approaching as well. All of them determined to rally around her. As though she might fall apart at any second.

She sucked in a breath through her nose. *No way. I won't fall apart.* It didn't matter what anyone thought. She wasn't going to do it.

"Okay?" Stuart's eyes darkened, his gaze seriously unhappy. She nodded.

He turned to Ted. "Anyone else around?"

The younger man shook his head. "I was in the bank, looking at surveillance."

"What about the man from inside?"

He answered Basuto's question, saying, "Dead before he hit the ground." Ted motioned to the man Basuto had in cuffs. "This guy killed him before hitting Conroy."

Before either of them could ask, Kaylee said, "Dean got him stable, and he went with Mia in the ambulance."

A muscle in Basuto's tanned jaw flexed. "How bad is it?"

She bit her lip. Ted said, "The bullet passed through him, but he's going to need surgery."

The sergeant nodded. "I'm taking this guy in. Ted?"

The younger man said, "I'll bring Kaylee."

"Get Jess, too. Kaylee needs to be under protection until we figure this all out."

She frowned at the sergeant. There was something he wasn't saying, but he didn't explain what it was. He simply walked the sniper off to his car.

She spun to Ted, about to ask him what that was—why she needed protection—when a woman cried out. Not a word, more like a noise of distress, Trina flew toward them, colliding with Stuart in a sort of tackle. He stepped back with one foot to steady her, so they both didn't go down.

Kaylee spotted a flutter and saw a piece of paper land on the sidewalk next to him.

"I was so scared!" Trina made the same distress noise again and continued gushing over Stuart, glancing at Trina out of the corner of her eyes. "And then you were there, striding in like some hero." She fluttered her eyes adoringly at him and then glanced around, seeming to just now notice they were all standing around, even the guy in cuffs. "Is that him?" Her voice raised to a shriek and she yelled, "That's the man who killed Conroy!"

Kaylee's whole body flinched. Ted moved close so their arms touched.

"He's not dead." Stuart patted Trina's shoulder awkwardly, looking like he'd rather be anywhere than right there.

That was the only thing that redeemed him at that moment. Kaylee saw it in him. This experience with Trina's emotional outburst was no more enjoyable than torture. Given the fact she'd seen the scars on his arms, and under his collar, she knew he'd suffered firsthand. And yet, this ranked right there at the top.

"Trina, please let him go." Kaylee folded her arms. She didn't need Trina to see her blood-stained hands and freak out even more.

"I was so scared." She didn't know who Trina was talking to at this point.

Kaylee walked over, picked up the paper Stuart had dropped, and something caught her eye. Her stomach flipped over.

She took a step back, bumped into Ted, and wound up dropping the paper.

Kaylee spun around. She found who she was looking for and made a beeline for where Jess stood talking to Savannah. Two cops were better than one, right?

They broke off their conversation as she approached.

I need a ride to the police station. But that wasn't what she said. When Kaylee opened her mouth, she blurted out, "He has a picture of me."

"Who?"

She was about to answer Jess's question when Ted said, "It was from the sniper. That's what Stuart said."

She saw Stuart detach Trina from his arm in a no-nonsense way the woman couldn't argue with. Kaylee had no intention of talking to her friend right now. For one thing, she didn't believe Trina's over-the-top reactions were sincere. And as much as she wanted to have compassion and empathy for her, Kaylee couldn't descend into that or she would fall apart.

Something that would take her far too long to come out of.

"She needs protection, and Basuto wants her back at the office."

Savannah, the detective, nodded. "Ted, Jess, you guys take Kaylee."

"I'll come too." Stuart jogged over. "I'd like to speak to the sergeant."

She didn't look at him. Kaylee stared straight ahead as they moved to the car. She wrestled with her mind. She didn't want to remember the trauma that happened the last time they'd tried to go to a car and then back to the office.

Her mind flashed a picture of herself, pressing Stuart's sweater into Conroy's chest for far too long while she waited for help.

The crack of that gunshot echoed in her head. Her whole body flinched.

Stuart took her hand. He held it in his as they crossed the street. He seemed to know and understand what she was going through at that moment. She still didn't look at him, though. She didn't think she could handle it. Tears blurred her vision, but she sniffed and stared at the clouds, willing them to not fall. Once they came, it would be hard to stop them.

Please don't let Conroy die.

Mia didn't need to finally find the man she loved, only to lose him before they could even start their life together.

There was plenty in the world that was senseless. But Kaylee couldn't lose her hope. Since the night her brother showed up at her back door, bloody, and told her it had been done. Things had been fine for years, ever since she'd gotten the word from the state police that the man who'd destroyed her life was dead.

She was silent all the way to the police station, sitting with Stuart still holding her hand. When Jess parked outside the police station, she and Ted got out. Kaylee tightened her hold on Stuart's hand. He didn't get out and neither did she.

Jess leaned back in the open driver's door and handed Stuart keys. "Lock up when you get out."

Then the police officer stood on the sidewalk out front, hand on her gun. Watching.

Protecting them.

"We should go inside."

Stuart shifted on the seat beside her, turning so he was partially facing her. "Are you okay?"

Kaylee squeezed her eyes shut. "I don't want to talk about it. If I do that, then it's real. And that would mean Conroy is really hurt. Mia's life could be destroyed. Conroy's niece and nephew could lose their uncle."

"No one wants that." His voice was gentle. So gentle, it hurt to listen to.

Kaylee pulled in air, but it didn't make it past the lump in her throat.

Stuart groaned and tugged her against him, sliding his arms around her. It occurred to Kaylee that she didn't know him. Like, at all. Now she was hugging him in the backseat of a car like they were on a middle school date. It should feel weird.

There were plenty of worries in the back of her mind. But the fact was, Kaylee felt safe. She hadn't felt safe for *years*.

She wanted to tell him what had happened to her the night her whole world ripped apart. But she needed to ask a different question first.

So she took a few deep breaths to help get a handle on her emotions. Enough to ask, "Why did you have a picture of me?"

"The sniper had it." He gave her a squeeze, then shifted back. "You were the target of that shot."

"But Conroy…"

Stuart shook his head. "You're the one in danger here."

"Like, with the Homeland agent?"

He nodded. "I need to lay it all out for the cops, so they understand. Your safety is our priority. I also need you to tell me what you know. *All* of what you know."

"What does this have to do with you?" She wanted him to tell her, straight out, what connected him. Even though she suspected what it was from all she'd gathered so far.

He studied her for a minute, then said, "Okay. Fair enough."

"I know this has something to do with you. After all, that fake agent was at my house, and then he arrested *you*."

"I figure they tried to implicate me. But he wanted both of us, as well as something from you to take back with him when he left town."

"They know Brad sent me a package."

Stuart worked his mouth side to side. "I knew your brother."

"*Knew?* Like past tense?"

"I don't know where he is. I can't all the way remember what happened to him after I saw him last. Neither of us was in a good way. Things had gotten hot." Pain lanced through his gaze, and he winced. "We were betrayed."

"Can I ask who you both worked for?"

"You can ask, but I don't have clearance to tell you." He paused, thinking, and then said, "I'm sorry about all that with Trina, if you thought she and I had history. Which we definitely don't. I honestly don't know what her deal is, or why she seemed so intent on making sure you saw her hanging all over me."

"She's my friend." Kaylee said, "Only why does that not ring true when I say it out loud?"

"How about I make sure you stay safe, and then you'll have time to figure out the answer to that?"

"Why would you do that?"

What reason could he possibly have for wanting to protect her? They'd barely spoken to each other before. This was probably the longest conversation they'd ever had.

Stuart looked away. "I have my reasons."

Honor. Because he was a nice guy. This was a small town, and people looked out for each other here.

Several couples had gotten together over the past few months. Conroy and Mia were the first. Then Tate and Savannah, who had plans to head to the city to elope soon. Lately, Dean had found Ellie, Jess's big sister. Kaylee wasn't interested in the crazy drama that accompanied those stories. She liked her quiet life.

Only now there was a fake agent, a conspiracy to drag Stuart into it, and a sniper all in the mix. Conroy had been shot and now fought for his life in the hospital.

"I wish I could give you what Brad sent me." She glanced at him, wondering if he'd been the person Brad meant her to give it to. He'd written that someone would show up. She would know to give it to them.

She couldn't shake the niggle of disquiet in her heart. Maybe Stuart wasn't the one. He was supposed to know the code word. So, it might not be him after all. Despite her wanting it to be.

"I just want this to be over."

"I know," he said.

"I don't want to be in danger. I don't want to see blood anymore." She looked down at her hands and sucked in a breath.

The EMT had given her a couple of wet wipes, but Conroy's blood still stained her hands.

"I can't do this again."

Stuart cracked open the door on his side. "Let's go in and get you cleaned up. You can tell me what Brad sent you, and we'll get all this figured out." He was back to that gentle voice again, but it didn't make her feel any better when by all accounts, it should. "I promise I'll do my best to keep you safe. Okay?"

He held out his hand to her.

Kaylee stared at it.

Was he the right choice, or the wrong one? And how could she even tell? Her focus had been all about the flash drive lately, and for good reason. Stuart may be the intended recipient with a better idea of what to do with what was on it than she would. But Kaylee knew full well this was no longer just about the flash drive. And trusting him was a whole other challenge.

She wasn't going to risk her heart.

Eleven

The minute they got out of the car, she'd started to pull away from him. Jess was the one who'd taken her into the bathroom and helped her wash her hands. Sergeant Basuto had ordered Stuart into the conference room, as though he was one of Basuto's underlings.

"Talk." Basuto dropped a paper file on the table.

"That my file, or the one you're starting on the man you have in custody?"

"I should have two men in custody. Now there's only one and the first one is dead. How long will this guy last before he's gunned down or we find him dead in his cell?"

Stuart lifted his eyebrows. "You think he'll commit suicide?"

"I think there's a whole lot more going on here than anyone knows, and I'm not planning on taking any chances. So, you best start talking. Because I'm in charge right now, and my chief is in surgery fighting for his life."

Stuart pulled out a chair and sat.

The door opened, and Ted stuck his head in.

"Come in." Basuto motioned with his hand. "I need you to take notes so we have a plan."

Stuart thought taking notes was a misuse of Ted's extensive computer skills, but maybe that was code for something else. After all, he hadn't brought a pen and paper. He'd brought a tablet.

"First things first," Basuto said. "I'd like a rundown of everything from your point of view. Start with why you were in the woods outside Hope Mansion."

Stuart told him what'd happened with the fake Homeland agent. In return, Basuto gave him some answers about what the man had been doing at the bank. Then Stuart asked, "Do you know who he was?"

"The fake Homeland agent—though that's not been entirely confirmed, yet—has no ID. He had a driver's license on him, but even I saw through that." Basuto shook his head. "Worst ID I've ever seen. He wasn't even trying to pretend it was legit."

"Which means he wanted you to know he wasn't who he said he was. Or didn't care."

Basuto nodded. "I assume so. Ted?"

The computer tech said, "I'm running his photo and fingerprints the medical examiner collected. Nothing yet, but I'll let you know when the search concludes."

"And the man in custody?"

"Same thing."

Basuto said, "What about our friend here?" He motioned to Stuart with his pen.

Stuart said nothing.

"Same. No ID yet."

Stuart said, "Have you tried looking up Bradley Caldwell?"

Ted lifted one dark brow above where hair drooped down to his eyes. "Kaylee's brother?"

Stuart nodded.

Basuto shifted in his chair. "Does her brother have something to do with this?"

"He and I worked clandestine operations together." Stuart was going to have to tell them who he was eventually. Might as well do it now and save them the trouble of running a search that would come up with nothing.

"CIA?" Basuto asked.

"Not officially." Stuart sat completely still in his chair so as not to give away his discomfort. "It was more...off-book than hiring college graduates to spy on other countries." Their job had involved high levels of foreign governments, mercenary groups, and international organizations they could get in with in order to gain access where tourists could not.

"So, this is about you and Kaylee's brother?"

Stuart couldn't help remembering Brad's face. "He had told me about her...something important that I can't seem to recall...so I moved here with the goal of recovering from my last mission and regaining cognitive recollection. My hope is that I remember what she has to do with all this. Now it seems clear they know he sent her something. Once I figure out how that package plays into all of this, I'll have a better idea of who these people are and what secret they're protecting."

"Her brother put her in jeopardy."

Stuart didn't like Basuto's tone. "Her brother was a good man, the best operative I've ever worked with."

Then why did you cause him so much pain?

Stuart shut off his thoughts. He couldn't get sucked down into the past again. Not when Dean wasn't here to monitor him. If he thought about the last time he'd seen Brad, then he would get sucked back there and end up stuck in his trauma, unable to function.

Basuto said, "No man worth his salt puts a delicate, fearful woman like that in danger."

Stuart nodded. He knew Kaylee had suffered, too. She understood what it felt like to see someone you love hurt.

Brad's face flashed in his mind. Stuart massaged his temples, trying to remember past the last point. The feel of that knife in his hand.

Brad had cried out.

Stuart didn't know what happened next. Did he even want to remember? He'd been out of his mind with pain, considering everything they'd been subjected to. But did that excuse the fact he might've hurt Brad?

He would have to tell Kaylee what he knew.

Basuto leaned forward in his chair. "She needs protection. They're trying to eradicate loose ends, right?"

Stuart nodded.

"So, safe house it is."

Stuart didn't want to think about her being taken away, and or that he would be denied access to her. They had things to talk about. "You're right to have the sniper under close guard." He didn't want anyone here to get hurt. The cops were motivated to see justice done since their police chief had been shot. "Any word on Conroy?"

Basuto's face paled.

Ted said, "They're going to let us know when he's out of surgery. Dean's with Mia, as well as a lot of folks from the church. Which means it's our job to figure this out."

Stuart had to wonder if he was just regurgitating the explanation he'd been given for why he couldn't be with his brother, Dean, right now, waiting for word about his boss. Stuart had only lived with Ted for a few months, sharing the house with a group of men, some of whom were a private security team. It had seemed to Stuart that Ted held a lot close to his chest. He didn't let people in easily, something Dean had said had to do with their father and the way they'd been strung along by him.

"Did you find your dad yet?" Stuart knew Ted had been actively looking for the man. He was a founder of the town of Last Chance, and as such, a possible suspect in the police's active search and investigation into a local bad guy known as "West."

Ted winced. "I'll tell you about that later."

Stuart figured that was fair enough. They were all guilty of the same thing—deflecting. Saving the pain for later.

Too bad that wasn't a tactic that would produce good results.

As much as they might all want to avoid the past encroaching on their future, the truth was that it needed to come out. And it wasn't until that happened that they'd be able to deal with the fallout.

"You'll find him."

Ted scrunched up his nose like a shrug.

Basuto said, "Let's figure out a safe house for Kaylee. Ted, can you have Savannah set that up? She needs to work up a schedule for who is going to stay with Kaylee and keep her safe."

"That'd be me." Stuart stood up, needing to go see her now. He didn't like that she was out of sight, considering all that had happened. But could he convince himself that she would be safer with him?

He wanted her to be. Still, would Stuart's skills put her in more danger? Not to mention his history and the trauma he lived with. Kaylee might be better off with cops watching out for her. But he couldn't help wanting to wade into it.

Help out.

Basuto said, "You want in on the protective detail, that's one thing. *After* we clear you for that duty. You've forgotten we don't know squat about who you are. Just that Dean vouched for you, and Ted is one of your roommates. But for all we know, you could be working for the same people as these men."

"I'm not." Stuart folded his arms across his chest. "Kaylee is safe with me. No one knows these guys, and how they think, like I do."

Because he'd been one of them. Different teams, maybe. Different entity signing their paychecks, yes. But Stuart knew their kind, and he was the only one who'd be able to stop Kaylee from being hurt next.

And she would be a target until she gave him the package— whatever it was Brad had sent her.

He had to get her to trust him, so that she would give it to him as she'd said she would. And if she found out too soon what he suspected had happened with Brad, she wouldn't give him anything.

She would probably try and kill him. Or kick him out and run to the cops for protection.

Maybe that was for the best.

She was a downhome, small-town woman. He was an international criminal on paper and worse underneath all the official stuff. Too many people wanted to question him. Those who could vouch for him had discarded both Stuart and Brad like yesterday's party trash.

If what she had in her possession could point him to the source—the root cause of Brad's suffering—then he would do what he needed to.

Find justice for his friend.

Answers for a woman who had suffered enough already. Who wasn't equipped to deal with undue attention, let alone snipers, fake federal agents, and broken-down clandestine agents.

She was never going to trust him.

He went to find the woman herself. Hopefully she would just hand it over straight away, and he could get on with this latest mission. Not an official one, just the most important one he'd ever undertaken.

The person Stuart had been, up until the day he showed up in Last Chance, was a man with no honor. A man who did whatever was necessary for the right amount of money. It was who he'd been brought up to be. Raised. Trained. Honed. He hadn't known any other way of being.

Until he saw her at the grocery store that one day. She'd spotted a bundle of cash in the parking lot and chased down a young woman with two little kids just to give it back to the rightful owner.

That kind of person would never be able to handle the man he had been.

Unless Stuart finished the work he'd been doing to become the man he *wanted* to be now. A man who did the right thing, despite what had gone before. Kind of like the new creation that the pastor had been talking about a few weeks ago. The idea had stuck with him. It made him want to be one of the good guys.

Someone worth caring for.

"Hey."

She started and looked up from the file she was reading at her spot. Her smile was tentative.

"Sorry, I didn't mean to scare you." That was what a good man would say.

"It's okay. I just got sucked into this case." She lifted the file. "It's a missing person's from right after I moved here."

"You aren't supposed to be…writing a statement, or something?"

A guarded look came over her face. "I don't want to talk about that. Not until we know Conroy is going to be okay. I just can't do it."

Stuart had held her hand before. But something told him if he tried to touch her now, she'd only shrug him off.

He had an idea and said, "How about a slice of pie and some ice cream?"

One eyebrow rose, and he saw a glint of humor. "Are you trying to butter me up?"

"You have no idea." He did need her in a good mood. Trusting him, when he asked for the package. Willing to give him the benefit of the doubt, when he told her what he thought he might've done.

"Okay, so it's working." She grabbed her purse and stood.

Stuart felt a smile curl his lips. Probably it looked scary, but she seemed to appreciate it. "Let's see if Hollis will deliver. Until we know you're safe, I think it's best if you stay here."

She looked at him with such trust. It nearly broke his heart.

The way he was going to break hers.

Twelve

Kaylee opened the to-go carton and looked inside. "Did you get this from the restaurant on the highway?"

"No, I called Hollis's diner. She sent it over."

"Oh."

"Problem?"

Kaylee shook her head. She picked up a plastic fork and sat back in the conference room chair so she could dig into what looked like cherry pie with ice cream *and* whipped cream. There was even a cherry perched on the whipped cream.

Basuto had cleared out and was now behind the chief's desk in his office. They still hadn't heard a word about Conroy's surgery.

"I hope he's okay."

Stuart swallowed a bite of his ice cream. "The chief?"

She nodded and dug in. Most of the time she embraced distractions, looking for any way to deny her mind the chance to spiral into despair and fear. But things had become entirely too real.

Even if she wanted to read a book right now, she doubted she'd be able to concentrate enough to get into the story.

Which was why she'd been reading the case file and had brought it in here with her.

She flipped open to the first page.

"What's that?"

A distraction. Because you're a distraction. Reading the dry notes in the file was better than staring at Stuart's profile while he ate pie. He had nice features, though they were rough and rugged. She also didn't need to think about how he could use a haircut. The curls of his dark hair had fallen over his forehead and covered his ears.

"Kaylee?"

Right. She slid the file over so he could read it as well. "Not long after I moved to town, this young woman went missing. I was staying in the motel, and she was a couple of rooms down from me." Kaylee didn't want to think about the past, but it was always right there. "I guess it just hit close to home. I always wondered what happened to her."

"She just disappeared?"

Kaylee nodded. "I heard her door slam and then voices. No one ever saw Gina again."

"Has there been a new development?"

"No." She shook her head. "Since I started working here, I asked. Conroy said I can read whatever cold case files I want. Just in case a fresh pair of eyes is what's needed. If I have an idea, they look into it." She shrugged. "Probably they're just indulging me, and I shouldn't waste police resources with random ideas."

"Unless you come up with something that might solve a case." He shrugged one shoulder. "Who knows?"

Kaylee stared at him. Then she realized what she was doing and concentrated instead on eating her dessert without dropping any on her shirt or her lap.

Stuart pointed to a piece of notepaper she'd inserted. "These are your notes?"

Mostly it was a list of questions she wanted answers to. "Just a couple of ideas I was going to ask Savannah."

"They're good ones." He traced his finger down the paper.

"The police department doesn't have time for unsubstantiated hunches. Not when they have so many open cases, and now they're trying to identify West so they can stop the flow of drugs into town." There were other crimes involved, but those were things she didn't like to think about. Who wanted to be sucked under by the tide of evil that people insisted on perpetrating against one another?

Selfish people with their selfish actions. Most folks didn't hurt anyone, so their selfishness often went unnoticed. Others bought and sold destructive substances. Weapons. Drugs. Then there were those who sold innocent people just to make money.

The whole industry made her want to vomit. Kaylee didn't want anywhere near it.

"Are you okay?"

Kaylee set her fork in the container. "Trina told me I'm burying my head in the sand not wanting to hear about all the details. That I need to be *informed* about what's happening in the world."

"But you'd rather have strong, healthy boundaries."

She wanted to collapse against him and weep out of relief. "Yes! I know what I can handle, and what I can't."

"Do you want to tell me about your parents?"

"I do." And that was the truth. She realized it after she said it. "I just don't know if I *can*."

Stuart laid his hand on hers. "That's okay, Kaylee. It was a painful experience?"

She nodded.

"I've had enough of those to know that reliving it isn't always the best way to move forward. Unless, like me—" He seemed almost hesitant. "—you're trying to remember what happened."

"You've forgotten?"

"I was with your brother." Stuart poked at his pie, not meeting her gaze. "We were betrayed and captured. The whole thing was a setup." He looked at her then. "What was in the package he sent you?"

"You don't know?"

He shook his head.

"If you're the one I'm supposed to give it to, then you're supposed to know the code word. Otherwise, I have to hide it. Until the right person comes along."

Or until her brother showed up.

She said, "Where is he?"

Stuart squeezed his eyes shut.

"Is he dead?"

His chest jerked as though he'd been punched. It was like the bubble popped. Any tension, good or bad, between them dissipated. Stuart got up. He paced the length of the room and then turned, facing her from across the table. The farthest distance apart they could be with him still in the room.

"Stuart, is he dead?"

"I don't know." He hung his head. "Brad was there with me. When I escaped, he was gone. I don't remember what happened. Yet." The last word was squeezed out, an awful secret. A determined promise.

"You don't remember." Her heart sank. If her brother was alive, he'd have contacted her.

Kaylee closed the lid of her container, her appetite gone now. Sickness rolled through her stomach instead. *He's dead.* Her brother. A hero, a protector. He hadn't been able to save their parents any more than she had. A fact which tore him up. Then one day, he'd shown up at her doorstep, blood on his cheek.

It's done.

He never told her what happened exactly. Not in so many words. But instantly she'd known he'd killed the man who had taken their parent's lives, as she stood helplessly watching. From that day, things had been strained between them. She knew he'd thought the tension was because he hadn't protected their parents in the first place. The truth was, she was almost as scared of her brother as she had been of the man who'd murdered a loving couple in front of their sixteen-year-old daughter.

A tear rolled down her cheek. Kaylee swiped it away, trying to get rid of both the droplet and the emotion that came with it. Like she could just flick it from existence. Dismiss it forever.

"You should have told me earlier."

He straightened. "I didn't want to do that to you. The only reason I'm telling you now is because I want to keep you safe."

So he'd kept it from her to protect her. Considered her so fragile, he couldn't possibly tell her the truth about her brother. She'd even gone to Dean to ask him to inquire around to find people who might know where Brad might be.

Kaylee didn't want to feel like a fool, but it was inevitable. He'd kept the truth from her. Because he was trying to spare her feelings? It wasn't like she liked the way she was. It was the way she had to be, and how she needed to order her life.

His memories were fractured. Because of what he'd been through when he was captured? And now she knew her brother had been through it as well. Her mind could barely handle the global problems she heard about in the news, let alone what she or someone she cared about experienced firsthand. So what if she lived most of her life buried in a novel? What was so bad about that when she liked her life?

"You don't need to baby me." She stood, needing to be on the same level as he was. "I want the truth about my brother, even if it's hard."

She might not be able to handle the awful things strangers went through—though she did often pray for innocents. But this was her brother they were talking about. She *had* to be strong enough for this. *Even if it was hard to hear.*

Stuart winced. He didn't agree with her. That much was plain to see on his face. He thought he needed to protect her.

It could be he was telling the truth and honestly didn't remember anything. But she suspected he would continue to withhold the whole truth from her. Which was basically lying.

"I guess now we know you're not the one I'm supposed to give the flash drive to."

His eyes flared.

"Because you would have said so before now." And he'd never have kept her brother's fate from her, the way he was doing now.

He knew what happened to Brad. He just didn't want to tell her.

Kaylee took her pie container and tossed it in the trash. She'd been so close to sharing something meaningful. Developing affection for someone she could've seen herself being friends with. Probably growing feelings for, if attraction was anything to go by.

That wasn't going to happen now.

"Kaylee."

She turned back, already halfway out the door.

"I am sorry." To his credit, he looked genuinely broken. In spirit and, as he'd said, in his mind. Maybe it was true he couldn't remember all of it.

"I know." She walked out, praying he'd find a way to get better. That Dean would be able to help him.

At least now she'd answered the question of why they were being dragged into this together. The men who'd come here for the package obviously knew of Stuart's connection to her brother. Kaylee didn't think he was part of their crew. But, then again, maybe he'd forgotten that as well.

It could be he was the one who'd betrayed Brad, and he simply didn't remember.

Yes, she was right to not give him the flash drive.

One day, someone would show up. She would know to give it to them so the wrong could be made right. Justice could be served.

But it wouldn't be Stuart.

The second she entered the main office area of the police department, the conversation died down. Tate stood beside Savannah. Both of them turned to look at her.

Kaylee lifted a hand and headed for the reception counter. She didn't need anyone asking her if she was *okay*. She'd rather be alone with her thoughts while they worked. "If there isn't any news about Conroy, I'm going to go to the break room and sit down."

Savannah's expression softened.

Tate said, "Is Stuart back there?"

"I'm right here." He stood at the end of the hall.

Kaylee went to her desk.

"Wanna tell me why I got an email from you instructing me to get the man who shot Conroy out of holding, take him to a secluded spot, and put a bullet in his head?"

She spun back.

Tate's expression was thunderous, red-faced and frowning. She'd never seen him so angry. Savannah didn't look much happier, and neither did Basuto who stood at the door to Conroy's office. Other cops in the room had stopped what they were doing.

Kaylee wanted to run, not stay and hear what this was about.

"There's also a nice ten grand that was just deposited into my account." Tate folded his arms. "Came from you. I'm guessing, payment for the job you wanted to hire me to do."

"I'd like to say I know what you're talking about," Stuart said. "But I have no idea."

"Revenge. That's what I'm talking about." Tate looked ready to explode. "You want that guy in custody murdered."

Thirteen

Stuart stared down the private investigator. Tate tended to be a law unto himself, and despite his recent relationship with Savannah, still had that renegade air about him.

Stuart said, "You're gonna have to explain this to me."

Tate was talking like Stuart understood any of this.

"Agreed." Basuto stepped out of Conroy's office and waved an arm inside. "Both of you, step in here."

Stuart moved when Tate did, both of them headed toward the sergeant. Basuto didn't have authority over them—neither were cops. But the sergeant had earned their respect. He was a good guy, one Stuart saw at church on occasion. He didn't throw his weight around or fly off the handle.

Basuto dipped his head to the side, his directive for Savannah to go to Kaylee. When Stuart reached the door to Conroy's office he said, "She shouldn't leave."

"Savannah won't let anything happen to her." Tate's voice was hard. Cold.

Stuart had no choice but to trust them. Kaylee was one of their own, and they would take care of her. She knew the truth now. He didn't remember what had happened to her brother. But to be fair, he knew more than what he'd shared.

Maybe fear, or shame, kept him from opening up to her.

Either way, Kaylee had shut him out. She'd determined he wasn't the one she should give the flash drive to. No way would she accept him in her life now. Not beyond this. Whatever it was that Brad had left her, he needed it—whether she was going to turn it over or not.

Which meant he might have to steal it.

"Okay." Basuto shut the door. "Tate?"

"I got an email from Stuart and ten thousand in my account."

Basuto moved to his cell phone.

Stuart said, "And you assumed it was from me? That I'd hire you to kill someone?"

He didn't want to argue that if he wanted a man dead, he'd do it himself. Stuart didn't need to spend ten grand to hire Tate. Plenty of others would do it far cheaper. He had so many options available to him. He'd hire any one of those guys before even considering Tate. He was a good guy; a private investigator who'd eloped with a cop. But he wasn't going to explain that to these men. They already considered him to be an outlier they couldn't control. A wildcard.

Still, they knew about ten percent of what he was capable of, and then either made up the rest or assumed he was so broken he'd never be able to truly function in this community.

Tate pulled out his phone.

"Send it to Ted," Basuto said. "I'll get him to take a look and get us the origin where the email came from."

"Good." Stuart lifted his chin. "Because it wasn't from me. Not only would I never do that, but I've also been here the whole time."

"You couldn't have sent an email from your phone?"

Stuart drew out his cell and flipped it open. "Calls. Texts. No email or photos." He waved it at Tate. "Means no, I couldn't have. So that email didn't come from me."

"And the money?" Tate asked.

"I'd have to log in to my accounts. Or Ted can since he has full access."

They needed to know the extent to which Stuart had no secrets from the men he lived with. That level of accountability was part of his healing process and the reason he was making so many gains.

Tate seemed surprised.

Stuart didn't know how to explain everything without sounding belligerent. And why did he need to anyway, since it was none of this man's business? "I didn't do this. End of story. There's nothing else to explain except that—whoever is behind this?—they had a guy pretend to be a federal agent so convincingly it passed a cursory check and you guys let him arrest me. Then there's the sniper. If you think there aren't others already in town, you're kidding yourselves. And they have a computer expert on their payroll."

"So, you're being set up?" Basuto set down his phone. "I'm sure Ted can confirm if that's the case."

Stuart pulled over a chair and sat down. He should just go. Grab his bag and take off. That would be safest, right? The people after him knew he was here. Until his mind healed enough to remember what happened, he wouldn't know who to trust. So why hang around and wait to be picked off.

He ran his hands down his face.

If he could get Kaylee to give him the flash drive, he could take it with him, and then he'd have it when he was ready to take them down.

The people here were more than capable of protecting her.

But why did the thought of leaving her—maybe never seeing her again—make him feel like he was tearing his own heart out?

"If they're implicating you," Tate said. "That means you're a threat to them."

"They don't know that I can't remember what happened. But they know Brad sent his sister a package, and they're right that it contains incriminating evidence." He motioned to Kaylee with a finger.

He'd come here initially assuming she was part of it, intent on uncovering *that*, first, and then "dealing" with her, second. Whatever that would have looked like.

"So, we need to flush them out. Right?" Tate glanced between Stuart and Basuto.

The sergeant laced his fingers over his flat stomach. "How do we do that when we don't know how many there are? If we lay Stuart and Kaylee out as bait and jump too early, we'll get a few, but not all of them."

Stuart nodded. "What if we let Tate take the guy you have in custody, make it look like he's going to do what I supposedly asked him to. I'll lie in wait and see how many there are."

He figured the others would rescue their friend. Though, maybe they wanted him dead since the sniper did his own thing and killed the fake Homeland agent.

He asked, "Has the guy in custody said anything?"

Basuto shook his head. "He hasn't even asked for a lawyer."

"He won't."

"He's said nothing."

Stuart dipped his head to the side. "He likely won't. Even under torture." After all, he knew he wouldn't bend in that same scenario. The men who'd held him and Brad had figured that out. Then they'd plied them with drugs to try and trick them into talking.

He lifted a shaky hand and shoved hair back from his forehead. It immediately flopped back into place.

"Whatever we do, I don't want Kaylee in danger." Basuto said, "And I'm not releasing the man who shot Conroy. So, figure out a different plan if that's what you want to do."

"I don't mind being bait," Stuart said. "We can make it look like I'm getting whatever Brad sent to Kaylee."

He *needed* to know what was on the flash drive. Then he'd have a better idea of who these people were.

He continued, "I'll pretend I'm taking it and leaving town. They'll swoop in—"

"And you'll be dead a second later." Tate leaned against the wall. "They'll take the flash drive off your body and come back to kill Kaylee as well."

"That's where you come in," Stuart said. "Saving my life, all our lives, and bringing these people to justice."

Last Chance had its own team, but they were barely back from their last mission—even though they'd started their renovation project already.

Stuart needed to figure out how they were going to solve this without Zander and the boys' help. "The fewer people involved, the better. Means less risk."

He didn't trust Tate, but he figured the man didn't want to deal with a dead body. He was close to an FBI agent, as the man was his brother-in-law.

Tate nodded. "If you've got a plan, I'm all ears. We'll get this cleared up so no one else ends up in the hospital like Conroy."

Stuart looked at Kaylee, sitting at Savannah's desk. The two women spoke with their heads close. He wanted to know what they were talking about. Then he'd be able to help her.

Live a life where he'd be a part of her world. Help her figure out if she could, or should, really trust Trina. Stuart knew which way he leaned. The bank manager's daughter was one of those people who said one thing and did another, who showed a face to people based on what they thought others wanted to see. And she wasn't even good at it. Though, truth be told, he was measuring her against some of the world's best covert operations tactics.

Trina was small town, small time, and Kaylee should let her go from her life.

He wanted to help her try to solve the case of that missing woman. To be there when the police found who West was, and support her through anything else she faced.

Stuart didn't even know what a healthy relationship looked like. He didn't know anyone personally who had a marriage that'd actually lasted, though there were some older couples at church who'd been together for years.

Could he make it work with Kaylee? Would she let him?

Maybe they were too far gone. Too much deception and mistrust. Most of it was understandable. He'd withheld information from her. She didn't trust him.

They might never be able to work through those things and get to the other side where life was supposed to be good. And was, if Conroy, Tate, and Dean were anything to go by. Things weren't perfect, but he'd seen the transformation in those men. They were happy.

Something Stuart didn't think he'd ever experienced, not once in his entire life. He had very few good memories beyond the last year; zero traditions, no family to speak of, and nothing in his history, as far as romantic relationships. He'd been about the job, and downtime consisted of hiking and rock climbing. Alone. Usually in a country where he didn't speak the language—which was entirely on purpose.

Kaylee loved her brother, and she was a part of this community. She didn't need his barren wasteland of a life invading hers and dragging her down. Sure, he'd made friends here. He might be building something. But how did he know if he was capable of carrying it on beyond a month from now, let alone years or the rest of his life?

The desk phone rang. "Sergeant Basuto." Basuto twisted in his chair, the phone to his ear, listening for a second. "Thank you." He hung up. "The chief is out of surgery. His injury was extensive, but it's looking good."

Stuart's head filled with memories of Brad, gasping for life. Pain. Both of them bleeding. The world swam in and out around him, and he swayed as he got up.

"I'm going for a walk."

He didn't need these people, not for permission to do whatever he wanted and certainly not for protection. If there was a team here gunning for him and Kaylee, then Stuart was going to draw them away from her. He would take care of them. *Before* they got anywhere near her.

Stuart pulled the door open and stepped into the main office. Kaylee looked over, eyes wide. Surprise and concern there in her expression. She wore it all right there, out loud for all to see.

No way they'd get *anywhere* near her. Not again.

She started to speak, but he ignored her and crossed the room. He opted for the back hall since that was where Ted's office was located. Plus, then he didn't have to have Kaylee let him out the front door. Stuart didn't knock on the door. He strode in and faced down his younger roommate.

"I need you to do something for me."

"Will it save someone's life and put a bad guy out of commission?"

"Yes."

Ted grinned. "Then shut the door."

He shoved it closed, but a blue canvas shoe shoved its way between the door and the frame.

Fourteen

"Not so fast." Kaylee didn't think about it. She just went on instinct, shoving the door open and waltzing into Ted's tiny office where she stopped, folded her arms, and stuck one foot out. "What are you guys talking about?"

"Nothing." Stuart's expression was flat. Not exactly dead, just completely neutral in a way that gave away precisely the word he'd just used.

She changed tactics. "Ted?"

He opened his mouth, but his attention was snagged by his computer monitor. One of them, anyway. The man had three, one turned vertical. Kaylee hadn't even known they could do that.

"Everything okay?"

He'd been very busy lately, trying to identify all the men in an old photo from Vietnam. A group of soldiers, all local. Men who had founded Last Chance.

One of whom was his father. A man Ted had been looking for.

Ted shoved his chair back and stood, muttering a word he probably shouldn't have said. He dove for the wall and hit the power button on the extension cord. Then ran to a shelf on the far side and unplugged the modem. Or the router. She wasn't sure which was which, or what they did, and every time he'd tried to explain it to her, he wound up getting frustrated.

Stuart watched him. "Ted?"

"The phone we took off the guy in custody."

"The guy who shot Conroy?" Kaylee asked.

Ted nodded. "There was a worm on the phone and when I connected, it activated." He scrubbed his hands down his face, and then back into his hair. "I hope it didn't get into our network." His face had paled, and he looked like he wanted to be sick. "I have to go talk to Basuto."

Ted squeezed past them, glancing at Stuart as he moved. "I'll be back."

Stuart nodded.

When Ted had gone, Kaylee said, "What was that about?"

He shrugged. "What?"

"You want to take on these guys, right?" That had to be it. "You're shutting me out so you can go in single handedly and what...eliminate the threat?"

He said nothing.

Kaylee let out her frustration in a groan. "You were going to leave without me. Leave me here, and go put yourself in danger."

She didn't want to get sucked down again, mired in the past and all those fears she lived with every day. Like they were a parrot on her shoulder or something. There was no escape. No matter how she wanted to be free of it, those memories and experiences were part of her.

"Kaylee—"

"No." She shook her head. "What did I expect? You're a lone wolf, right? Just like Brad, you want to fix all the problems yourself and no one else needs to help. It's how you protect people. By going off on your own."

"Protecting people is a problem?"

"You think I can't handle what's happening." Maybe she couldn't. She didn't know. And yeah, she'd lived her life in a way that was safe and protected. But this was as good of a time as any to face down those fears and see if she could get free of them.

To make her own choices as to what her destiny was going to be.

Right?

He studied her, his expression still giving nothing away. "Isn't that what you want?"

"I don't want to be afraid." She sucked in a long breath. "I don't like being afraid."

Stuart shifted closer. "No one is without fear. It can keep you safe and help you make better choices. You have to use the fear."

"Even when it's paralyzing."

He touched her elbow. "I know what that feels like, and I don't like it either. My mind was so fractured. I still don't remember exactly what happened. Sometimes, right as I wake up, my mind tricks me into thinking I'm still there. Or I wonder if all this is a dream. That I'm still there, my mind broken, living in my head in this delusion."

"And you made up me?" She shook her head. "I'm sure you could've thought up someone better than me to be your friend's sister. Someone brave and beautiful."

"That's how I know it's not a dream."

"Because I'm a hot mess?"

Stuart touched her cheek then. "Because I'd never have been able to dream up someone as beautiful as you."

Kaylee's mouth dropped open.

"That's why I want this done, so you're not in danger any longer." He dropped his hand and took a step back. "I need you to give me the flash drive."

She frowned.

"I want to flush out these guys first, but then I need whatever is on it."

"Do you even know the password?"

Stuart started to speak, then hesitated. "There's a password on it?"

"The note said if you don't enter it within thirty seconds, the whole flash drive wipes, and everything is gone."

He scratched his jaw.

"That's why I haven't looked at it. And why I've been waiting for the right person." When Ted had tried to access that phone, he'd run up against a similar problem. "Do you think they're related?" She motioned to the phone. "Is that type of security something you guys do?"

Stuart said, "You can buy whatever computer program you want online if you're willing to pay for it. Or you hire someone to write it. But it stands up to reason that Brad would want to keep the information safe."

He didn't look super happy, though.

She said, "You don't know the password, do you?"

His brow furrowed. "If Brad told me, I might've forgotten."

"True." He had said his mind was fractured. "Maybe you'll remember." And, in the meantime, he had plenty of things to take care of. She didn't exactly want to be part of it. "I just don't want to sit here doing nothing, feeling useless and being too scared to live my life."

"So, you decide now to stand up to it?"

"I want to make my own choices." She shrugged. "It sounds hokey, but I really should be in control of my destiny."

"A sniper shot Conroy."

She winced. "I know."

He shifted closer to her. "I don't want anything to happen to you. I *want* you to stay here, where you're safe."

"A biker gang stormed in and shot the place up a few months ago," she pointed out. "It's not a foolproof plan."

"Maybe Basuto was right, and you do need to be in a safe house."

"Nowhere is safe." Kaylee lifted her chin. "I know that better than anyone. And it means I need to learn to live with it."

"It's hard to say no to you."

She waited.

He chuckled. Before he could say anything, her phone buzzed. Kaylee pulled it out. "Trina. She's outside, in case I want to make a break for it. Get out of here."

She shook her head and tried to figure out what on earth Trina was thinking. The woman made no sense sometimes. She'd been distraught about what had happened at the bank but still hadn't managed to figure out Kaylee had only gone there to see what would happen if she checked her safety deposit box.

Maybe she shouldn't expect Trina could figure that out. She wasn't a cop, or some kind of secret agent.

"You wanna go with her?"

As he asked the question, the back door popped open. Kaylee braced. Stuart moved in front of her. Protecting her with his own body. A shield.

Trina came in. "Kaylee." She ignored Stuart, which was odd considering how she'd thrown herself at him earlier.

"Hi." She looked around his shoulder but didn't come out from behind him. "I'm fine here, Trina. But thanks for thinking of me." Kaylee worked here and was surrounded by law enforcement, so why Trina would think she wanted to "escape" and leave this building, especially when there had been a sniper on the loose…she didn't even try to understand. "We're waiting to hear a word about Conroy."

Stuart shifted. "He came out of the surgery, and he'll recover."

Kaylee touched his arm, squeezing it for solidarity as relief rolled over her. Conroy was going to be okay.

Trina stood kind of stiff, her back very straight and her arms by her sides. Fingers flexing. Like she didn't know what to do with her hands. "This has all been so crazy, right?"

Kaylee nodded. "Are you okay? Did you get hurt earlier?"

"No more than you, I figure."

Wow, was Trina actually considering Kaylee first above herself for once? "I'm all right. Thank you," Kaylee said, genuinely meaning it. "And now that I know Conroy will eventually be okay as well? That's a relief."

Trina smiled. Something about it was off, as though she didn't mean it. "That's good news."

She blew out a breath, feeling some of the stress bleed away.

Stuart didn't want anyone else to get hurt, any more than she wanted that to happen. That was why he was determined to protect her. Not necessarily because she couldn't handle it. The last thing she wanted to do was face down gunmen and snipers and fake federal agents. No, thank you. She'd seen enough blood to last more than one lifetime.

"We should get going, you know?"

Kaylee said, "I think I'll stick around here, where it's safe. Let the cops—" and Stuart "—take care of the people responsible for shooting Conroy."

There was someone behind the shooting, and clearly they wanted what Brad had sent her.

Trina said, "No one will suspect you didn't already give whatever you're hiding to the police. That means we can grab it and take it somewhere safer. Keep it under wraps so it doesn't fall into the wrong hands."

Why did she suddenly want to be a part of this? "Thanks for offering to help."

Before she could say more, Stuart cut in. "The flash drive is already safe where it is, or it would've been found already." He turned to her. "Right?"

Kaylee nodded. "It's safe where it is."

"Okay." Trina chuckled, though it sounded strained. "But it could be *safer* as well. Right?" She glanced between them.

Stuart reached out and took hold of Kaylee's hand, so she was tucked even more securely behind him. She couldn't even see her friend over his shoulder. She tried to move so that she could stand next to him, but he wouldn't move aside. Realization dawned on her. He thought Trina was a threat? Her fingers stilled on the back of his shirt.

Under her fingers, she could feel ridges. Raised lines in his skin. Scars.

He said, "Trina, thank you for offering to help but the flash drive stays where it is, and Kaylee is safer here at the police station than she would be if she left. There are too many variables to risk her being out and around town."

"It's not like I would take her out for ice cream or something like that!" Trina's voice was almost a wail. "No one will expect Kaylee to be with me. That's why it's perfect. Let's go, Kaylee. Dad is waiting in the car, and we can find somewhere safe to be."

Trina wanted her to go with her, if only to have a welcome distraction. But, just as Stuart had said, she didn't want to put anyone in unnecessary danger. Conroy was shot because he'd been standing with her. She was sure that even if he had been the sniper's target, it was only because of Kaylee—and Stuart—that he'd been hit.

Whether it had been a miss, or a hit, by the sniper, she didn't know. Either way, though, she'd brought this on the police chief.

It was her fault.

"As Stuart said, thank you for offering, Trina—" She shifted to look around his shoulder at her friend. Her argument died at what she saw.

Trina had a gun and her voice suddenly took on a menacing tone.

"Let's go, Kaylee. Now."

Fifteen

Kaylee shifted. Stuart did the same, keeping her behind him. "She's not going with you."

"Then I'll kill you." Trina shrugged. "Same result."

She thought she could take him out? She likely wouldn't be so stupid as to fire a weapon in a police station. That would be far too obvious.

"Who are you?"

He felt Kaylee shift at his question. Trina said, "The person who's going to get that flash drive. That's who."

Behind him, Kaylee grasped a handful of his T-shirt.

"Let's go."

"You aren't going to shoot us in a police station."

"Kaylee?"

Stuart pressed his lips together. Behind him, Kaylee said, "I'll go with you. Just don't shoot anyone." She pushed against him.

Stuart could have held his ground, but moving closer to Trina served a purpose. He'd seen the woman around town enough. She was a gym bunny whose primary purpose was picking up guys who caught her eye. Her secondary purpose was working out. But everyone knew that having good cardio didn't always equate to strength when it counted—like, at a time it could save your life. Or someone else's.

Trina backed up until she stood partway out the door.

Stuart was tempted to rush at her and shove her back. Would she drop the gun? The way she carried herself wasn't that of a small town, bank manager's daughter. It was something far different. That gave him pause, wondering what this Trina woman was capable of exactly.

"Pretty gutsy move, abducting someone from inside the police station."

She motioned with the gun for them to walk outside and stepped back to hold the edge of the wood with her free hand. "Walk."

She obviously was used to doing what she wanted and didn't feel the need to explain herself to anyone.

Stuart reached back as he walked. He needed Kaylee to let go of him, so he could resolve this situation. He got her to release her grip and stepped forward.

"Not so fast." A man held a gun over the roof of a compact car. The bank manager, Silas Nigelson.

"What's—" Kaylee didn't get to finish.

The bank manager said, "Get in. All of you. Before someone sees us." Silas let out an expletive. "Way to keep it low key, Trina."

She didn't respond to her father's criticism. Instead, she pulled open the rear door and shoved Kaylee in. When Trina spun back around with her arm out, Stuart was poised, ready to grab it. Take her down.

Silas shifted his aim to point the gun at Stuart.

He froze, staring at the barrel of a gun while his mind flashed an image of a buried memory. Who had pointed a weapon at him before? *When* had it happened?

"Get in, or die. Your choice." The bank manager shrugged. "I don't care either way."

Stuart got in, figuring that meant *either way* they planned to kill him. He wasn't certain he'd delayed Trina long enough for someone at the police station to notice what'd happened in the back hall. Hopefully, Ted would discover they'd gone missing soon.

Then the cops would be on their tail.

Trina nearly slammed his foot in the door when she closed it.

The doors were child locked, so they wouldn't be jumping out, and Stuart had nothing to use as a garrote if he wanted to restrain Trina by strangulation while also forcing her father to pull over and let them go.

Other options flitted through his mind. He dismissed most of what he considered. There weren't many ways he could get out of this, and less that meant Kaylee was both protected and released unharmed.

"Where's the flash drive, Kaylee?" Trina's question was hard. Her tone was that of a stranger, not someone who claimed this woman as her best friend.

Beside him in the backseat, Kaylee reached out and took his hand. None of the four of them had put on seatbelts. That might not end well. Maybe he should get Kaylee to buckle up.

She glanced at him, determination blazing like flames in her eyes. The set of her chin was one he'd seen before. But never in a situation like this.

She shouldn't be here.

You shouldn't have dragged her into this, Brad.

The memory rose, bringing with it a pain that sliced through his temples. Stuart sucked in a breath and squeezed his eyes shut.

"*Where is it?*"

He opened his eyes. Kaylee's mouth opened, then shut again, but she said nothing. Stuart knew how they were going to play this. He said, "If she's going to give up the one thing that's keeping us both alive, then there will be some compensations."

"Yes, that's right." Kaylee nodded. "You're going to let Stuart go."

"No, they're not."

Trina laughed. "No time to make a plan." Her gaze zeroed in on Kaylee. "You give me the flash drive, I'll think about not killing both of you."

"Why are you doing this?"

"Money. Fame." Trina shrugged. "Does it even matter? You'll be dead, and not around to be all offended up on your moral high ground."

"Then you should tell me." Kaylee lifted her chin. "I'd like to know before I die."

Stuart's teeth hurt from clenching so hard. "*If*—and that's a big 'if'—she gives you the flash drive, you're never going to show up in Last Chance again." He paused. "Either of you."

Trina snorted.

In the driver's seat, Silas said, "Done."

Stuart heard a catch in his tone. It registered on some level he knew but didn't understand. Not unless Silas said more than one word. Stuart was the one making demands right now. "We get a copy, and you get the flash drive."

Kaylee shifted.

It was password protected. Given what she'd said, he wondered if he had been given the code by Brad and had simply forgotten it. Or, if he was never supposed to have worried about it in the first place.

No, he had to believe her brother had sent him here to protect her. To safeguard her well-being, and get the flash drive to the requisite authority to get justice. Bring down whoever was responsible for betraying them. Figure out what happened to Brad so Kaylee would know, and he would have peace of mind he'd done what he needed to.

None of which had squat to do with Silas and Trina, who had just erupted with laughter like they were reveling in the worst prank that had ever been committed. The kind where some poor unsuspecting soul got hurt.

"I didn't say you get the copy." Stuart lifted his chin. "You can have the original. No one will know I also have it. Whoever you are, and whatever you think you're going to gain by getting your hands on it—"

"Is our business." Trina shot her dad a look.

"I think you're in over your heads, but I don't know you." Stuart paused. "Maybe you've been pulling covert operations from Last Chance for years."

Trina sneered. "Your team buddies aren't the only ones with skills."

Kaylee squeezed his hand.

Stuart said, "They're professionals. Former military, private security specialists. Contractors with friends all over the world. In all branches of government, international police, and multi-billion-dollar companies."

She had to know that was a far cry from where she was—working for a bank, thinking she was hot stuff. That she had even a slight clue as to what she was doing.

"Where will you even take the flash drive?"

Trina didn't seem concerned. "Once we see what all the fuss is about, we'll know what to do. Right, Dad?"

Stuart saw his jaw flex, but the older man said nothing. Out of the two of them, Silas was the one that concerned him. Trina thought she knew what she was doing. And, he'd have to give her credit, she did seem to. However, her father had that old school coldness about him. A man who could smile at you one moment, and then drink a shot of something stiff and shatter your legs with a baseball bat the next.

Mafia, maybe. In a former life.

Trina twisted all the way around in the passenger seat. "Where is the flash drive?"

Up ahead, on the street, Stuart saw movement on a side road. It was gone too fast to figure out what it was. Help? There had to be a reason neither his nor Kaylee's phones had rung.

Were the police right behind them?

"It's mine." Kaylee's voice was full of hurt. Betrayal by her best friend, and the knowledge she would betray her brother's wishes if she gave away what he'd given her to safeguard.

He squeezed her hand. "Brad gave that to her for safekeeping. She isn't supposed to share it with anyone. No matter what."

Maybe Trina would shoot him, but he was pretty sure she wouldn't shoot Kaylee until she got what she wanted. What he needed was for Kaylee to *not* mention the password on the storage device, or the fact it had safety features. They'd know it was even more valuable then. And they'd need more than what she could give them.

As far as he was concerned, the simple approach was always the best.

For the first time in his life, Stuart wanted the police to come and save him. It was a strange feeling. Still, that was the life he lived now. The man he wanted to be, inspiring others to help. To do their sworn duty in a time of crisis, because they all cared about the people in their town. And maybe they were more there for Kaylee than for him. But that was fine by Stuart.

He had been about to let her go with Trina, right up until the moment Trina pulled that gun. He actually would've thought he was doing it for her good, letting her leave with a woman who was supposedly her friend. Had she not shown her true colors first, Stuart would have believed she was taking care of Kaylee.

Thank You. It could only be God's hand that had allowed him to see the truth of Trina's intentions—the fact she'd shown all her cards entirely too early—and Kaylee was still with him.

Where he could keep her safe.

There but by the grace of God…

Once he got Kaylee back to a safe place, Stuart needed to finish this. She just wasn't safe around him. His judgment was compromised, and he couldn't be trusted to keep her out of harm's way. Not when he'd been about to send her into danger and then had had to get into the car as well, in order to avoid a confrontation, to make sure she didn't get hurt. Or taken somewhere he couldn't get to her.

"Just tell me where it is." Trina shifted the gun to point it at Stuart's knee. "Or he doesn't walk for the rest of his life. Don't think I'm joking, because I am *not*."

Kaylee whimpered. A tear rolled down her cheek.

He wanted to tell her she was *so brave.* She was seriously holding up great. Amazing. Then his attention was snagged by the road again.

Silas let out a grunt. "Hold on."

Trina twisted around. "What—"

The car hit a spike strip, bumped over it, and shuddered. The tires had blown.

Stuart grabbed the gun and Trina's arm. He twisted both, giving her a burn on her skin. She cried out. He got control of the gun and pulled her arm back next, twisting it as he squeezed his finger onto the trigger and fired a shot. It narrowly missed Silas and exited out the side window next to him.

He swerved the car. It barreled between two cop cars that had been parked nose-to-nose.

"Keep going." Trina's voice was pained. She shoved a foot down onto the driver's side floorboard, and Silas cried out.

The car accelerated.

She jerked the wheel to the side, and they rounded a corner. Two tires left the ground.

Kaylee screamed. "Jesus, help us."

Sixteen

She had barely gotten the words of her simple prayer out when the car slammed into another parked vehicle, a delivery van. The airbags deployed, and they were all jerked forward.

Kaylee slammed her face into the back of the driver's seat. She had to catch herself before she fell to the floor.

Stuart slammed into the door frame beside the passenger door. She heard the sickening thud as his forehead hit the interior. He leaned back and groaned.

Trina shoved the door open and dove out, stumbling onto her knees. Moving faster than anyone rightfully should right now. "Go, Dad!"

Silas Nigelson only grunted.

Trina, the gun still in her hand, made a run for it. Still in her bank clothes. Low heels on her feet. She raced past the delivery van blocking the side street.

Kaylee heard a yell.

Three cops in uniform raced past the car. She heard a gunshot, and one flinched. They all kept running, calling out for Trina to stop.

Kaylee's world spun. It took a second for her mind to realize she needed to breathe. Then she was sucking in air that smelled like tangy smoke. She coughed it out.

Someone opened her door.

Donaldson crouched beside her. "Hey, Kaylee. You okay?"

Another officer pulled open the front door and cuffed Silas to the steering wheel while he moaned.

Kaylee looked at Stuart. She scooted toward him on the backseat and touched his shoulder. "Stuart?"

He moaned. Blood trailed down from a cut on his temple.

"Hey." She gave him a tiny shake, just in case. Then she asked Donaldson, "Did you call Dean?"

"He'll be here in two minutes," the younger officer said. "What do you need?"

"A cloth, or rag. Something to press against his head."

"Head wounds bleed a lot, you know?"

"Okay." Why was that relevant? Maybe he was telling her so she didn't freak out at the sight of it as it kept coming. And coming.

She refused to think about blood on her hands. Conroy. Her parents, lying lifeless in the street. She wasn't going to freak out. Nothing would be solved by it.

Like when Trina had been yelling at her. Waving a gun around. What would it have benefited her to scream about all the lies Trina had told her? To complain, as loudly as possible, that Trina had betrayed her. Kaylee had fallen for it. But the satisfaction she'd have felt making a ruckus would've been hollow.

So, she'd kept her mouth shut. Done what her brother had instructed her to do, what her favorite fictional spy would do. Even Stuart had seemed to agree—he'd even squeezed her hand in solidarity.

Now he just needed to wake up.

A sob worked its way to her throat. She swallowed it down. *No. I'm not going to dissolve.*

Instead, she told Donaldson everything. She'd have to tell him all over again so he could write it all down, but she needed to say it. To have him react like that—eyes flaring and his face turning red—it gave away the fact she was holding something important for her brother. But she no longer cared.

These people were her friends. Her family. They would give their lives for her, as Conroy had almost done.

That was what a good life was about. And she would never again take any of them for granted.

Stuart moaned.

"It's okay. Trina's gone, and Silas is cuffed. We're safe now." He had saved her. That was the truth.

In a time where she should have, by all rights, dissolved into a mess of traumatized emotions, losing the ability to think straight, she hadn't. She'd kept her cool. Stood her ground.

Kayla didn't think she would ever get over the fear. Maybe that wasn't the goal. Just as avoiding all possible situations where she might feel fear probably wasn't the healthiest way to move on with her life. She would never be "cured" of her trauma. Despite trying to ignore it, or deal with it, the memories would forever be there.

Now she had new ones.

Maybe life was just about finding good in the bad. Moments of peace and joy. Where she felt safe, despite what was happening.

Because Stuart was with her. A man who cared enough he didn't want her to be scared. Who didn't let her get kidnapped alone. Who thought she was beautiful.

"Stuart." She needed to look into his eyes and see those things for herself. To see all the feelings she had for him reflected in his gaze.

She gave his shoulder another gentle shake.

He moved before she realized what was happening, so fast she couldn't even track his movements. His hand slammed against her throat and his fingers wrapped around her neck, cutting off her air.

"Stuart," Donaldson yelled his name like an order. "Let her go, man."

Kaylee couldn't speak.

He opened his eyes just as hers bugged out. Only paranoia and fear were there, not everything she'd been expecting just moments before. That he knew her. That he felt safe.

She patted his arm and squeezed it, willing him to realize where he was. That he was hurting her.

Inhaling through her nose didn't work. Spots exploded around his head, obscuring her vision. She was starting to pass out.

Donaldson grabbed her arm and tried to pull her away from him. "Stuart, let her go!"

In one last ditch effort, she shoved at his chest.

He let her go. She fell toward Donaldson, coughing and gasping for air. Her throat felt like the worst infection-like swelling she'd ever experienced.

She looked at him. He had both hands over his face. When he pulled them away, he looked grief stricken.

"Stuart." She couldn't get his name out without coughing, and it was barely audible.

Donaldson tugged on her arm. "Let's go."

Across the car, Officer Allen pulled out Silas Nigelson. He'd been shot during the past few months, in a raid by gunmen on the police station. Now he was back to full duty.

The bank manager had a very red nose, but it wasn't bleeding. Donaldson walked her to the back of the car while Dean passed them, heading for Stuart.

"He's disoriented. He hit his head."

Dean glanced at her and nodded, then got in the car.

"He didn't mean it."

Donaldson tugged her away. "Come on. Let's give them some room."

"He wasn't trying to hurt me. He thought I was a threat." For some reason, she continued, "It's what people with trauma do. They get flashbacks. Especially in intense situations, and when they get hurt."

"I know what happened to you," Donaldson admitted. "What you saw…with your parents."

"I don't want to talk about it. But you know that means I understand Stuart. More than a lot of people might."

"Doesn't mean he gets to hurt you."

"He couldn't help it."

Yes, she was defending him. "He didn't mean it," wasn't a good defense. There wasn't much that would excuse what he'd done, nearly choking her. He could have killed her. But that didn't mean she couldn't offer understanding and forgiveness. Wasn't that what the pastor was always talking about?

This wasn't an offense. But the principle still stood.

Donaldson said, "Did you forgive the man who murdered your parents?"

"He's dead."

She'd figured that settled the matter, given the eye-for-an-eye policy. Justice had been served. It didn't heal the devastation caused. Maybe it made Brad feel better. Kaylee just tried to move on.

Now she had just discovered that she could withstand a whole lot more fear than she'd imagined. "Trina pointed a gun at me."

"You told me that." He was a younger man, and he'd been there with both Conroy and Mia the day they faced down the man intent on destroying their lives. Seemed like Donaldson was having a hard time with all this—probably the fact his chief was in the hospital, fighting for his life. He was now falling back on the fact he was one of the good guys. The "bad guys" were those who didn't fight on his side. And he didn't count Stuart as one of the good guys.

She took a moment and prayed he would find peace soon.

Kaylee said, "I looked Trina in the eyes, and she told me she would make sure that Stuart never walked again. And not once did I freak out. I just stared her down and kept my cool."

"Good for you."

"You don't get it," Kaylee said. "This is huge. I never thought I'd be able to handle something like that. And I stood my ground." She couldn't help the smile that stretched her lips wide.

"I'm glad you're super happy you got kidnapped."

She rolled her eyes. "I'm glad you guys intervened. Who knows what might've happened if you all didn't show up." She lifted on the balls of her feet and planted a quick kiss on his cheek. "I appreciate you, Donaldson."

He blushed.

"Where's Basuto?"

"Right here." The sergeant jogged over.

Dean backed out of the car, and Stuart climbed out after him. Neither looked happy. In fact, it kind of looked as if they'd been arguing in the car.

She said, "Everything okay?"

Neither said anything. Basuto was the first to speak. "Trina is in the wind. She's fast, and our guys lost her."

Kaylee's stomach flipped over. She was gone? That meant she was out there, maybe even watching.

She spun around.

Silas struggled against Officer Allen. "It was all Trina! She's crazy, and she dragged me into this for some payday. I didn't know what was happening!"

"He's lying."

She spun to see Stuart's attention was on Basuto. The sergeant nodded. "Nigelson isn't getting out from under this until she's brought in and everything is squared away."

Stuart nodded.

"But we also have a separate problem." Basuto's shoulders were tense. Kaylee's shoulders followed suit and a chill ran through her. With Silas in handcuffs, she'd thought their only problem was Trina, but there was more? "We got word there's a tactical team inbound from the State Department. They want to talk to you—" He pointed at Stuart, then glanced at her. "—and they want whatever you have. Apparently, it's national security."

Stuart took a step back.

Dean glanced at him. "I'll call *our* team. See if they can get in the middle, stir up some distractions."

Stuart nodded.

"Seems like the two of you have solid targets on you," Basuto said. "Might want to lay low somewhere under the radar. Get whatever you have and go to ground until we figure out what all this is about."

Kaylee had been so relieved at how well she'd done facing down Trina, she wasn't prepared to be blindsided by this new development. "We need to run?"

She'd thought her life was safe. Now it was certain it very much was *not*.

Stuart said, "I know a place we can go, but I need to do something first." He glanced at Dean. "Can you help me?"

The former SEAL said, "You wanna try one more time?"

Stuart nodded.

"I'll call Ellie. She can help me get set up. Ted, too."

"Don't bother Ted. He needs to be at the police station," Basuto said. "He has plenty to do, and he's been worked up about finding your father."

Dean frowned but said nothing.

Stuart turned to her. "I know you didn't want to tell Trina where the flash drive is, and that was the right thing to do." He nodded. "You did good."

"Thanks." Why did she feel like this was leading up to something?

"Now I need you to tell *me* where it is so we can go get it. The thing needs to be kept safe and secure."

Kaylee had been doing that this whole time. Obviously she had, or someone would have found it by now. "The note said not to give it to anyone who doesn't know the password." Before he could argue, which he was gearing up to do, she continued, "Brad said it's my job to keep it safe. So, if you don't have the password, then I can't give it to you."

Instead of arguing that point, he turned to Dean. "You're up."

The former SEAL nodded. "Let's get you your memory back."

Seventeen

"Can you stay here please?"

He wanted to do this quickly, but Kaylee was making it difficult. She hadn't stopped wandering around in circles, staring at everything around her, since he brought her through the front door of his house. She also didn't seem to care that he'd all but strangled her. The way she could endure hardship, and then brush herself off and keep going, was something that continued to astound him the longer he knew her.

"This place is huge."

Stuart said, "Kitchen is over there. The bathroom is down the hall. I'll alarm the system, so you don't have to worry about anyone sneaking up on you." The team was here, but he didn't know what they were doing.

He glanced back at Dean. "Where are the boys?"

Dean looked up from his phone. "On a run. The shortcut gets them back in an hour, and they're good to help with whatever you need."

"An *hour*?" Kaylee gaped.

Stuart said, "Dean and I will be downstairs. If a bunch of sweaty guys suddenly walk in, it's all good. We know them."

She nodded. "They live here with you guys. I've seen them around town, so it's fine. I'll be fine. You don't…need any help?"

He shook his head. "We're good."

There was no way he wanted her walking in on one of his therapy sessions. Not when that meant recreating as much of the experience as possible—including the fear and pain. But he needed to do this now. He needed to remember.

Stuart touched her shoulders. "You're safe here."

She gifted him with a small smile. "It's been an insane couple of days. I'd love to just sit somewhere quiet and have a few minutes of peace."

"Whatever you want in the kitchen, just help yourself. Okay?"

"Thank you."

Stuart couldn't resist. He leaned close and touched his lips to her forehead. He squeezed her shoulders, then headed for the hallway, figuring he'd likely never get the chance to be that close to her again. Doing this might get him the result he wanted through resurfaced memories, but the damage to his psyche could be irreparable. And that was really saying something, since even he could admit he was already damaged.

Kaylee seemed to have completely forgiven him for squeezing the breath out of her and putting those bruises on her neck, but he would do it again. That was inevitable. He could never completely trust himself not to hurt her. His damage, coupled with her vulnerabilities, made for a stormy combination that meant he *had to* keep his distance.

"Wanna tell me about that?"

Stuart's head pounded, and not just from the bump he'd received when the car stopped. "Doesn't matter. Doing so won't make it all go away, so what's the point?"

"Says who?"

Stuart descended the basement stairs. Other people's opinions were the least relevant thing in his life. He would never have chosen to come here if he actually cared what people thought. He'd be living in a shack on the beach in Thailand, spending next to nothing and speaking to no one. It would be the best way to experience beauty he'd never found anywhere else and the only way to know he wouldn't ever hurt anyone else again because of his trauma.

Instead, out of his mind, he'd assumed Kaylee was a threat and had put her in danger. A good woman who didn't deserve that.

He stopped at the door. "Let's just do this. Remembering the code word makes Kaylee safe. I finish this, and we can all move on with our lives."

"Why does that not sound like a good thing?"

Stuart lifted his chin. "Doesn't matter what it sounds like. Kaylee will get her life back, and I'll be far enough away that I won't hurt her."

Dean said, "You don't think it might be possible you could have a relationship with her and not hurt her?"

"I already did hurt her. You saw the bruises on her neck." He shoved the door open, tugged his shirt off, and tossed it back into the hallway. "Let's just do this."

Dean used his phone to adjust the temperature, making it far warmer than the rest of the house. Stuart laid on the floor against the wall for twenty minutes while sweat beaded on his body. Then a crackle sounded through speakers mounted high on the walls. Yelling in a language he spoke, but not fluently. He could recite the words at this point. Music played, as though the neighbors had cranked their favorite retro Afghani tunes, determined to serenade the whole neighborhood.

Stuart closed his eyes and let his mind go back there. He didn't want Dean to have to use pharmaceuticals to alter his mental state. He even prayed that he'd be able to do this by himself. Kaylee deserved answers. She deserved to be safe.

After all, that was why he'd done the work he had. For years. Fighting the world's tide of evil for the innocent people who didn't even know it existed. Or maybe it was all a façade and they were happier pretending to not notice what was right in front of them.

And then there were people like Kaylee who knew what it meant to be a victim and yet still carried on.

His mind continually wanted to suck him back to that place, so there wasn't much effort required to remember the parts he could. Pain. Terror.

His heart rate kicked up. Dean recorded all his vitals through sensors Ted had placed around the room.

They knew we were coming.

"I know," Stuart had said. Across the room, his friend had been steadily bleeding from a wound on his leg where he'd been caught by a bullet. *Just a graze.*

Neither of them had wanted to admit the depth of the situation they were in.

Made worse by the one memory he would never forget.

Do it. The kidnapper had screamed the accented words in his ear, spittle landing on Stuart's cheek. *Do it now.*

His breath came fast now, the world spinning. He tried to sit up and bile rose in his throat. Stuart coughed and gasped.

Brad gasped. "Stu...don't let them kill me. Promise me... Promise me you'll do it before they do."

He stared at the wall. "I'm sorry."

Stuart squeezed his eyes shut and drifted.

He gripped the knife, feeling his hand slide against the base of the blade. A sharp pain cut at his skin.

Laughter echoed against the walls and filled his ears. "Do it. Hurt your friend."

One captor held Brad on his feet in front of Stuart, his friend's eyes boring into him. Fear. Understanding. He mouthed, "Do it."

"No." Stuart didn't want to hurt his friend, no matter what Brad had made him promise. He wasn't going to do it.

The captor shoved his hand. The knife pressed against Brad's stomach. His friend cried out, the sound tearing through Stuart like he was the one being cut.

Laughter filled his ears, and he choked on a sob.

They tossed him to the floor, still laughing. He rolled and saw Brad leaning against the wall, hands to his stomach. Blood on his fingers. On his shirt.

Stuart screamed out his frustration.

The captor produced another syringe. He jabbed it in Stuart's upper arm and pressed the plunger down while Stuart tried to shove him away. Kick him. Anything. Something. He had to stop this.

But it wouldn't stop.

It was never going to end.

The two captors dragged Brad from the room. His friend screamed, legs sliding across the floor as they pulled him out into the hall.

"Brad!"

Time drifted. Hours turned to days as the sun tracked its way across the floor over and over again.

Brad never returned. That meant he had to be dead, just as they'd said. Tormenting him with the fact that he'd killed his friend.

And then a commotion. An explosion rocked the room. Plaster fell from the ceiling in waves of dust that coated him. Gunfire outside. Two sides, locked in a battle.

Men ran down the hall, outside his room.

Another explosion. The wall of his cell blew out and a gust of wind came with it, filling the room with dirt and smoke.

Stuart clambered to his feet, fell back on his knees, and cried out his frustration.

He wasn't going to die here. He would rather die out there, fighting for his life. Trying to escape, even if he had no weapon.

Visibility outside was near zero, but that might play in his favor. He climbed over rubble and waited. Watched. Listened through the smoke.

On the ground was a twisted piece of metal. Stuart held it with both hands and made his way outside. The compound was only a few buildings, but the wall was high. He wouldn't be able to climb over it.

Gunfire cracked in the black sky.

Stuart flinched, but it was on the far side of the compound. Two men raced across the open space, headed toward it.

They never even saw him.

Stuart raced to the door. It was hardly fortified, even the main entrance. Just a place people could slip in and out, avoiding the vehicles at the other entrance.

A guard stepped out, gun pointed. Stuart swung the metal and the man went down. He took the gun and the man's phone, making the call before he even fully broke free of the compound. Even if he didn't succeed, he wanted someone he trusted to know the truth.

Brad was the only friend he had, but the group of men were those he knew he could count on. He'd always known they lived lives of honor. And though they were hours away on a mission, he'd hide, and they'd find him. Get him out.

Stuart took the phone with him and stepped out of the cover of the compound wall. A pickup truck was parked fifteen feet to his left. Aside from that, there was nothing but shrubs and mountains for as far as he could see.

The second he left cover, Stuart would be completely exposed.

But he did it. He'd driven away, fighting his way out the entire time, and then he had hidden in a neighboring farm until Zander and his team, Dean with them, had picked him up. That had been a battle of its own. So much war.

Stuart was still exhausted, and it had been months since he climbed into the chopper and they took off.

He never wanted to see another desert or scrub bush—or pickup truck, for that matter. Not for as long as he lived.

He rolled to his back and stared at the ceiling, one hand on his chest. The password. He had to go back further, to the days before he'd been forced to shove that knife into Brad's stomach, murdering him.

"Dean!"

The door cracked. "Yeah?"

"Stuart, are you okay?" Kaylee's face was so much like her brother's, he saw there in her eyes the same expression Brad wore when Stuart had killed him.

He rolled away from her to face the wall. That was why he couldn't stay. Every time he looked at her, he would see the gaze of the man he'd killed. He would know that the hurt she lived with was because of him.

And he would keep hurting her. He knew that with as much certainty as he knew she would find someone else.

A man who knew how to love her.

"I'll get my kit." Dean's footsteps retreated.

Stuart pulled in a long breath and blew it out slowly. His entire body was sweat slicked and achy. His head pounded, and his muscles were cramped.

"Are you okay?"

He didn't look at her.

"What is this room?"

Stuart pressed his lips together.

"Why are you doing this to yourself?"

Dean came back. "Kaylee, I need you to wait outside. Everything is okay."

It wasn't, but Stuart understood the sentiment behind Dean's words. He needed to reassure her in a way that was efficient, so they could get back to work.

"I don't know." She even sounded unsure. "I think—"

Stuart needed her to leave. He wanted to get this over with as soon as he could, get the password, and take the flash drive. Leave the town of Last Chance for good, so she would finally be safe.

From him.

He rolled over. "Kaylee, get out."

She glanced around the room. "But—"

"GET OUT."

Her eyes filled with tears, and she ran from the room.

Eighteen

Kaylee fled up the stairs. She blinked against the blur of tears while twin tracks rolled down her face. He'd been distant after what happened in the car, then he'd kissed her forehead, and now he was back to being mean? She turned at the top of the stairs and slammed into a huge body. Her nose bounced off the man's chest.

T-shirt, damp with sweat. She looked down at beat-up tennis shoes and basketball shorts, then up to a clammy face, red cheeks, and glistening hair.

He was huge. Her head didn't even reach his shoulder, and his arms were thick like two ham legs. His T-shirt stretched across his upper body, and his hair was short in a military style. Not longer and flopped down over his forehead like Stuart's.

Kaylee swallowed a scream. *Don't freak out.* She'd done enough of that today.

The man backed up a step and glanced back over his shoulder. "Hit the showers."

Three men trailed past them. All were big, but this guy was the biggest. Kaylee pressed her palm into her chest, willing her heart to quit beating so fast. She looked like a mess.

"I'm Zander." He didn't wait more than a second before he said, "And you're Kaylee."

She nodded. If she spoke, she'd probably fumble her words. Or tell this guy she'd never met that the man she liked had just yelled at her.

"He's downstairs?"

"Yes." Kaylee cleared her throat.

"Let's go to the kitchen." He motioned with a sweep of his hand for her to go in front of him. "Leave them to it."

Downstairs, Stuart started yelling again. Crying out. Asking for help. Kaylee's whole body shuddered. She walked down the hall. "He sounds…" She didn't know how to explain it.

"He's trying to remember what happened, right?" Zander's voice was low. He could probably sound lethal if he wanted. Even being cordial made her want to snap a salute—or pee her pants.

He might be a perfectly nice guy, but for some reason, God had seen fit to make him the most massive, scary-looking man she'd ever seen.

Zander pulled out a stool, and then circled the breakfast bar to the kitchen. He pulled two bottled waters from the fridge, handed her one, and then downed the entire contents of his before he filled it back up at the sink and did the same thing again.

He crushed the water bottle, replaced the lid, and threw it in the recycling bin against the wall. "Do I freak you out?"

Kaylee shook her head.

"I can't make myself any smaller even if I wanted to."

She *almost* smiled at that. "The man who murdered my parents had red hair and freckles, but in my memories, he was as big as you." She tried to shrug off the tension of the past few days. "And the last person to point a gun at me was a woman who was supposed to be my best friend."

"Rough day?"

"I think Stuart's might be worse."

"Is that why you've got bruises on your neck?"

Kaylee touched two fingers to her throat. "I startled him."

"It's good he's with Dean."

"He's trying to remember what he can't, right?" she said, repeating his words.

Zander nodded. The man's expression was flat, and she wondered what it would even look like if he was excited. Or mad. Then again, he was just a distraction right now. Her life was in shambles, and she was latching onto something that had no bearing on her future. Or the level of danger she was in at present.

He pulled the blender away from the backsplash and pulled bags of frozen fruit from the freezer.

She looked away from him and sipped her water, turning to study the living room. It was clear a group of guys lived here. But they weren't slobs. In fact, given the military angle, she figured it was more likely they were hyper clean. Nothing had been left out. The carpet was older but looked like it had been vacuumed recently.

Downstairs, Stuart cried out.

The sound rang through the house. She flinched in her seat, nearly spilling the water on her lap. It was hard to hear. To know he was in that much distress and she was not able to do anything to help. She couldn't take it. He didn't want her help. He only wanted to suffer alone, with Dean supervising.

Zander flipped the blender on, drowning out the sound of Stuart and his therapy session.

The question she wanted an answer to was whether Brad had intended for her to give the flash drive to Stuart. Could be her brother hadn't trusted him, and so she shouldn't either. Which meant she might as well not bother waiting around for the right person to show up. She could just take the flash drive to the FBI, or someone who could break into it without the password. There were people who could do that, and both Conroy and Tate knew someone at the FBI. Agent Eric Cullings was Tate's brother-in-law.

The FBI would know what to do with the information her brother had gathered. Her part in this, done. There would then be no reason for whoever was coming here to want her. And she wouldn't need to fight the urge to throw the flash drive off dead man's cliff. Or flush it down the toilet.

Especially now that she was sure her brother had died because of it.

Whoever betrayed him and fractured Stuart's mind needed to pay. But putting that mission on her was asking for failure. She didn't know how to do this. Stuart was even trained in covert operations, and he was having trouble with all of it.

Maybe this Zander guy could take the flash drive.

The blender's deafening whir shut off. "Want some?"

She shook her head.

He pulled out four cups and filled each one, then pulled out his phone and sent a text. "Need anything else?"

"Uh…no. I don't think so. Thanks."

He shrugged one ham shoulder. "Stuart is a good guy, you know."

"I'm not sure he believes that."

"Who we are and who we wanna be are sometimes two different things."

"That's true," she said. "Then there's Trina. My best friend…or she *was*. She sticks a gun in my face because she wants the flash drive for herself. And how did she even know about the flash drive? That's what I want to know. Like, I literally want to slap her until she tells me. I can't believe she would do that."

Zander sipped from his smoothie cup, his hips leaned against the counter where he had a giant container of protein powder.

He looked thoughtful but didn't seem to feel the need to comment.

Kaylee's phone rang. She slid it from her bag and saw she had a video call coming in from Mia, through an app known to be encrypted. She swiped to answer. "Hello?"

"Kaylee, its Mia." The lieutenant's face filled the screen.

"Is everything okay?" The background of the image was a plain wall and a gold frame around cheap, mass-produced artwork. "Is it Conroy?"

"Actually, yes." Mia smiled. "He's awake, and he asked to talk to you."

"Me?" Kaylee settled back onto the stool. She used the pop socket on her phone case to stand it up so she could take another drink.

The image shifted and she saw him. Pale faced, hooked up to machines.

"Conroy."

"It looks worse than it is."

Kaylee swiped away an errant tear. "I don't believe you. I think it's *exactly* as bad as it looks."

Zander grinned. "You tell 'im."

Conroy said, "Are you okay? I heard about Trina and her dad."

"Don't worry about me." Kaylee frowned, shaking her head. It was weird seeing her own image on the phone screen. She looked like she'd been dragged through a hedge backward. And Stuart had kissed her forehead? Talk about pity affection. He probably couldn't wait to get her out of his life, and that was why he was down there torturing himself into trying to remember what he might never have known. How long would he keep trying until he gave up?

"Just concentrate on rest and healing. Everyone is praying for you." She sniffed, feeling the swell of emotion. "I'm glad you're all right."

Conroy smiled. His eyes drifted shut, and Mia shifted the phone back to herself. "He was really worried about you. The first thing he said when he woke up was to tell me to call you, so he could see for himself you are okay."

Kaylee smiled. "I'm okay."

"And you're safe?"

She nodded, then flipped the camera so Mia saw Zander in the kitchen where he was still standing, within earshot. Another man, freshly showered, walked in and grabbed two smoothie glasses.

"I want updates."

Zander snapped to attention. "Yes, ma'am."

Mia grinned. Kaylee flipped the camera back to herself and said, "Between my new friends, and Dean and Stuart, I'm sure I'll be safe."

"Trina is still at large. Basuto is keeping me posted on the search for her." Mia said, "Zander?"

He lowered his glass, clearly listening to the entire conversation. "I'm on Kaylee until otherwise instructed. The boys are going to do a sweep for anymore fake federal agents and snipers."

"You can find snipers?"

His expression shifted. Kaylee swallowed, unsure if Mia wanted to know how Zander reacted to that question. "Uh… he's looking a little…"

"Affronted?" Mia shrugged. "It's all hands on deck. And those military snipers? You can walk right by one and have absolutely no idea they're even there."

Kaylee felt her eyes widen. She glanced over at Zander who simply shrugged. "We'll look anyway."

"Okay," Kaylee said. "When Conroy wakes up again, tell him thank you for thinking of me."

Mia nodded and they signed off the call.

Zander said, "They'll miss the days when craziness was only about tracking down one of the founders or a murderer bent on revenge."

Kaylee blinked.

"Don't worry. We won't let anything happen to you." Zander folded those ham arms across his chest, his glass empty now and on the counter beside the protein powder. "Ted is looking into the corporation Stuart and your brother used to work for."

"It wasn't the CIA?"

Zander said, "Private company that was supposed to be a contractor for the US government. Ted hasn't found much yet, but I gave him a couple of ideas on places to look. Rocks to turn over."

"Do you think they're the ones who betrayed Stuart and my brother?"

"Possibly." He shrugged one shoulder, very noncommittal.

It was irritating that he gave so little away, and she had a feeling it could get old real fast. As it was, probably he was cognizant of the fact they didn't know each other.

"For the record, not handing over the flash drive to the first person who asks for it is the right call."

Downstairs, Stuart cried out again.

Kaylee flinched. "Are you going to ask me for it?"

"Would you give it to me?"

"Do you have the password?"

He shook his head. "Maybe there is no password. Maybe Brad is the one who betrayed them both, and there's nothing on the device. Or it's all a setup, and they're going to blame Stuart for the whole thing. There are multiple ways this could play out. They get what they want, and good folks are destroyed in the process."

"Are you honestly that cynical?"

"I'm a realist. There's a difference."

Kaylee pressed her lips together. She had incrementally figured out how to handle everything and thought she was coping pretty well. Now she'd had a gun pointed in her face. Trina had threatened to destroy Stuart's legs, and now he was downstairs reliving the worst experience of his life, just so she didn't have cause to withhold the flash drive from him.

Dean strode in, sweat on his forehead. She twisted in her seat, about to burst from wanting to know the result of this crazy experiment.

Her stomach knotted. "Did he remember?"

Nineteen

Stuart had taken a shower and put on fresh clothes. His back was still sticky from not having toweled off all the way, and his hair was wetting the back of his collared T-shirt.

This must be what showing up for your first date ever felt like when the girl opened the door. Or her father. Maybe that was what happened in most young relationships.

Either way, he stepped into the common area and saw Kaylee. Her jaw flexed as she looked at him, probably remembering the fact he'd screamed in her face. When he'd been lying on the floor in a bad way. After she left, he'd had Dean inject him with a powerful, mind-altering drug. It was now nearly out of his system.

"Here." Dean handed him a strong cup of coffee.

Stuart could smell it, and the liquid looked almost thick. "Did Zander brew this?"

The big man looked up from his laptop, open on the dining table. He never sat. The man was on his feet constantly from the time he woke up to the time he laid down to go to sleep. And for the five hours between, he was unconscious. Seriously, one time there'd been a massive storm that nearly pulled the whole roof off, and he'd slept through the whole thing.

"Drink it." He went back to his computer and to a map he'd pulled up on the screen.

Stuart glanced between Dean and Kaylee. "What's going on?"

Dean said, "We'll get to that. How are you feeling?"

There was zero point lying, or pretending. Dean was his doctor. Though, not officially. "Shaky and hungry."

Dean strode into the kitchen. "Like you have the munchies, or you're so hungry you want to hurl?"

Stuart took the opportunity to move closer to Kaylee, who still hadn't gotten up. She didn't need to stand. But she also didn't need to look at him like he might bite her head off at any moment. Then again, he'd strangled her and he'd yelled at her. He deserved her wariness.

He just didn't like being a fresh source of fear for her.

Stuart slipped into a stool so he appeared less imposing. Not the one next to her, but close enough. "Both."

Dean rummaged around in the back of the cupboard and found a packet of plain crackers no one else liked. How long they'd been there, no one knew. He slid it to him across the counter.

Stuart bit into the dry, salt-flavored nastiness. "Yum, thanks."

Dean grinned.

"Seriously," Stuart said. "Thank you."

Dean only nodded.

He turned to Kaylee. "I'm sorry if I hurt you. And I'm sorry I yelled."

She gave him a small smile, but that was all.

"Peppermint."

Her eyes filled with tears. Not the reaction he'd been looking for, but it was something. "I didn't want you to have to go through all that just to get the password."

Stuart turned away from her. "Now we know."

He wanted to ask where the flash drive was but didn't think he'd be able to get the words out. Not with the memory of stabbing her brother so close. He could still feel the knife in his hands, the captor's grip covering his. He looked down and realized he was thumbing the scar on the side of his knuckle, at the base of his pointer finger.

"Drink the coffee."

Stuart sipped enough to clear his throat. He was the one she was supposed to give the flash drive to. That knowledge should've been enough, but it wasn't. He'd hurt her. Physically and emotionally she was battered, probably as much as he felt right now having just gone through an experience as intense as the one he'd forced on himself downstairs. He could say he knew how she felt, but given he'd been the cause of it, he wasn't going to commiserate with her. It wouldn't comfort either of them.

He didn't need to create more of a bond between the two of them when it was only a matter of time before he ended up destroying what they had between them. He'd done a fine job of screwing things up already.

Him and Kaylee? Stuart might care for her, but nothing was going to come of it.

"Yeah, it's me."

Stuart spun to see Zander on his phone, his attention still on that computer screen.

"The images we got of the compound where Leland was held; pull it up for me and then share your screen, so I can see what you've got." Zander paused. "Before that. The five or so minutes right before he leaves." Another pause. "No, the other side of the compound. I wanna know what was happening."

Stuart started to get up.

Dean said, "Sit back down," and rounded the counter to head for Zander.

Kaylee turned in her seat. "What's going on?"

"I second that question." He shoved another cracker in his mouth since the nausea wasn't going away. He didn't like drugs at the best of times—at least, anything stronger than coffee. Mind-altering ones were worse.

"Thanks. That's what I was looking for." Zander hung up the phone. He pointed to something for Dean's benefit. "Right there."

Dean scratched at his jaw. "We missed that."

"What is it?" Kaylee's question was soft.

He twisted to her, sharing a moment in the quiet with both of them out of the loop. Then Dean said, "Stuart?"

He didn't like the look on either man's face. "Just spit it out."

Zander said, "You're in a *fragile* place."

"You'll find out how fragile I am next time we go a few rounds in the ring."

Zander might be bigger with a right hook that made even the best guy feel like he'd been hit by an airplane, but Stuart was fast.

Dean said, "Guys."

Stuart sobered.

"Kaylee," Dean spoke tentatively. "We think Brad might be alive."

Stuart nearly fell off the stool. "We *left him there?!*"

She looked at each of them in turn, a shell-shocked expression on her face. Dean came over to him, but Stuart didn't need his help to stand. He leaned back against the breakfast bar. It brought him closer to Kaylee, close enough she could put her hand on his arm for just a second—before she realized what she was doing and dropped it.

"We didn't leave him there." Zander folded his arms, a power move that showed off his bulk. "He left before you did."

Dean said, "The commotion you described might've been Brad causing mayhem so he could escape. He likely had no idea his actions made it so you got out as well."

"We both got free?" Stuart tried to think it through. He was physically and mentally drained and had been before going downstairs. "They told me he was dead."

"He would never have left without you," Kaylee said. "Not when you guys were friends." She paused. "And if he did escape, why would he not contact one of us. You got out months ago, right? Before you came here."

"I came straight to Last Chance." Stuart motioned to Dean and Zander. "These guys are the ones who got me out." He turned to the two men. "She's right. Why would he be free and not have at least called one of us?"

Zander shrugged. "I'm not a mind reader." He brought the laptop over, showing Kaylee and Stuart the screen. "Brad walked out of that compound. He was in a firefight, and he was injured. But he got out."

Kaylee gasped, covering her mouth with her hand.

Stuart stared at the image of his friend on the screen. Even if it was a satellite picture, he knew it was Brad. "Why would he not have called?" The question was barely above a whisper.

Kaylee jumped off her stool and paced to the far end of the living room. The lines of her body were tense, but more than that, she was hurt. The people she cared about had either been killed or had abandoned her. Then Brad had gone and done his own brand of damage.

Stuart crossed the room, trying to figure out what he was going to say. He settled on arguing, "Maybe Brad isn't able to contact you. He could've been captured again after that photo was taken."

Only that meant Stuart had walked away from his friend when Brad still needed him and after he made it possible for Stuart to escape. And all that, after he'd stabbed the guy.

He didn't like the idea, but it was possible.

Kaylee glanced aside, tears in her eyes. She didn't even want to look at him right now.

Stuart turned to Dean. "We need to stay on point."

Zander said, "I'll put in a request, get my guy to comb this footage, and figure out where Brad went. Work out where he might be now." He snatched up his phone and left the room.

After he'd gone, Dean said, "I need both of you to remember that you're fragile right now. It's not the time to lose sight of what needs to be done."

Stuart turned to Kaylee. "We need that flash drive."

She lifted her chin, but he saw it quiver a second before she pressed her lips together.

"Please." He'd told her the password, but he needed her to give him her trust in return.

Finally, she said, "Peppermint was my mother's favorite flavor."

I want to help her. Only You know if that's even possible. They were both hurt, but he knew down to his soul that God could heal anything. After all, he was standing here. Right? The fact Stuart was able to function on any level was a testament to the healing power God had, and the work He'd done through Dean's assistance.

Stuart would be forever grateful to his friend and his Heavenly Father for helping him.

Would Kaylee ever let him in enough that Stuart could pay it forward with her? She deserved so much. He wanted to be the one to give it to her, but he couldn't guarantee he wouldn't hurt her in the process.

In the end, he realized he cared about her entirely too much. It wasn't worth the risk.

Kaylee moved to the stool, gathered up her purse, and slipped both her phone and the file she'd been reading—the one about that missing girl—into it.

Zander came back in. "Okay, we're on the Brad thing. The boys are on the sniper team, flushing out anyone else in town. Dean?"

"I'm headed to check on Conroy, and then I'll go see Ted. Find out what's happening there."

Zander nodded.

Kaylee said, "Can you give me a ride back into town?"

Stuart started to move before he realized she was talking to Zander. He opened his mouth.

Zander cut him off. "Good idea." He pulled a set of keys from a hook that Ellie had Dean mount on the wall near the kitchen doorway. Since then, their keys weren't misplaced nearly as often.

"Kaylee?"

She turned to him. "Zander can keep me safe, right? He's trained like the rest of you."

Zander sucked in a breath, affronted.

"More so." Stuart figured the guy could use a little ego stroking once in a while—until they got in the ring. "Am I not invited?"

"I think it's better if I just go and get the flash drive." She lifted her chin, her bravado undercut by the fact she hugged her purse to her front. "You probably need to rest. And I could use some space. I'll be fine."

He took a step toward her, not even knowing what to say. She was probably right. Truth be told, he could use a nap. But at a time like this? He wasn't going to clock out before this was anywhere near over.

She scurried two steps toward Zander, and he realized she really was afraid of him.

Stuart froze.

He shifted his gaze to the big man, not needing to say anything to communicate his concern.

Zander nodded. "We'll be good."

Stuart hoped that was true. He trusted Zander, but this was Kaylee. Her safety meant more than any of theirs.

Kaylee didn't even look at him. She followed Zander down the hall, and Stuart watched her do it. He just stood there and kicked himself as she walked away. Letting her go was for the best.

So why did he want to chase after her so badly?

Twenty

"You probably think I'm just being childish, ignoring him and latching onto you."

Zander held the passenger door of a huge SUV open. He hadn't even rolled up the garage door, which comforted her. She figured, as a protection specialist, he knew what he was doing.

"Why are you trusting me?"

Kaylee raised her eyebrows in surprise. He really didn't know. "You live with them. They respect you." Kaylee shrugged. "That's good enough for me. Especially considering we won't be gone more than half an hour."

Zander tipped his head to the side. She figured that meant, "fair enough," and then she asked, "How much do you charge for this kind of thing anyway?"

That got her a reaction. As she hauled herself onto the front seat, Zander said, "Five hundred an hour."

He shut the door on her coughing and sputtering. When he got in the driver's side, she said, "Five *hundred?*"

"Saving lives doesn't come cheap."

"Wow."

"My insurance rates are a nightmare."

Kaylee just blinked. "Well, thank you."

"You're welcome."

"Are you going to send me an invoice later?"

He hit the button on the visor for the garage door and started the engine. "Not to you."

She twisted to stare him down, her fingers freezing on the seatbelt buckle. "Who is paying for my protection?"

"Stuart." He shot her a look like she should've figured that out.

"Great." She straightened. He pulled out of the garage. "Now I feel even more like a jerk."

"You stood your ground, and it made you feel like a jerk?"

She shrugged one shoulder.

"Huh."

Kaylee watched the roadside as he drove. Even though she was probably completely justified being mad at Stuart, she couldn't help feeling sympathetic. He'd gone through something insane. It had nearly broken him.

Of anyone, she knew what that felt like.

One night, after a movie, her parents had been shot by a man who had left her alive. To this day, she didn't know why. She never would, considering he was dead now. Brad had killed him. If he'd found the reason she'd been left alive, he hadn't told her what it was.

She pulled out the cold case file, trying to settle her thoughts with facts that encompassed zero emotion. After reading for a minute, she glanced at him. "I just don't like this whole Trina thing. I mean she's gone off the deep end, and for what? A shot at the flash drive? There's no way I'm going to give it to her, and now the cops are looking for her. Where is she going to hide?"

"If she has half a brain, she's in Mexico by now."

Was Trina that smart? Kaylee had the feeling her "friend" was a completely different person than she'd previously thought. And now she was faced with the reality that maybe she didn't know one single true thing about her, even though they'd known each other ever since Kaylee first started working at the bank.

"Maybe it's her dad," Kaylee said. "Hopefully Basuto questions him and figures it out. Because if he did something to her, that's important to know."

"You think all evil is a result of people who have those actions forced on them. Like they can't help it?"

"Some of them. But I still think people are responsible for their actions, and they should be held accountable." Kaylee shrugged. "But she was supposed to be my friend. I want to understand why she suddenly turned around and pointed a gun at me. How did she even know the flash drive was valuable anyway, and who would she have given it to? It's not like she knows who to sell it to on the black market. It's covert operations, international stuff. Right?"

"Guess we'll find out." Zander turned a corner into the neighborhood she'd entered into the maps app on his phone. "Maybe she does know some black-market players. Or some friend of a friend who has connections."

"This is insane. It makes no sense." She flipped a page and blinked. "Huh."

"What's that?"

"A cold case. I don't even know why I'm reading it right now, but it's a distraction, and my brain wants to be occupied so I don't freak out regarding my present circumstance."

"And the 'huh'?"

"A photo of the victim." Kaylee glanced at him. "Basuto put a note in here that says her mother insisted she'd been wearing a necklace the day she went missing." She brought the photo closer to get a better look at the necklace.

She explained why she cared as much as she did about this missing girl, given her proximity to the young woman at the time of her disappearance and what had been going on in her life at the time.

"Easier to try and help someone else. Especially when your life is going crazy. You can control your feelings about a missing young woman who might never be found. But your own life? Who knows what's going to happen next? *That*, you have no way to control."

"So I just want to manage my whole life." Kaylee shut the file. "I already knew that."

"It's not a bad thing to keep your world simple. Control the variables as much as you can, so that you know what to expect."

She wasn't sure that made it sound like a good thing. Some people might not want anything to do with a life as narrow as hers was. But that was their choice. She was entitled to choose whatever life she wanted to have. One she could love that gave her peace and supplied her with the contentment she needed.

Kaylee spotted what she was looking for and pointed up ahead, the sidewalk on the north side of the street. "Right there."

"One of those 'little library' things?"

She nodded. "One sec." Kaylee pulled out her phone and sent a text. "The kid who lives right here—" She pointed to the white house they were parked in front of. "—watches the library. He has a camera pointed at it from his bedroom window, and I have the password to access the footage from the cloud. So if anything has happened, we'll be able to see who was here."

Zander looked impressed.

Her phone buzzed with a reply. "Everything is good. Lewis said he checked this morning, and the envelope is still there."

"You stay in the car."

"Open the little door, and it's taped on the inside lip of the roof closest to you. The envelope is half the size of one of those old floppy disks."

"Copy that." Zander kept one hand close to his gun. He jogged across the street to the mailbox-sized birdhouse that had a collection of old books inside. She'd read most of them, had purchased half of them herself, and kept a list of recommendations taped to the inside of the door.

Kaylee glanced at Lewis's house. The blind in the front window shifted, but she didn't see anyone watching. Probably the cat.

Zander got the tiny envelope—barely big enough for a couple of dollars worth of coins—and turned to make his way back.

A bang sounded. Kaylee glanced at Lewis's white house. The front door opened, and Lewis strode out. Kaylee opened the car door before she could even register his strained expression.

Behind him, Trina's face was set. Determined.

"Lewis!"

His gaze flicked to her. "Kaylee!"

Trina shook him, her arm grasping his bicep. The kid was twelve, but so gangly and short that he barely weighed ninety pounds. As an avid reader and gamer who spent zero time on his physique, he wasn't exactly strong enough to fight off a grown woman who worked out regularly.

And especially not when she had a gun pointed at the back of his head.

Trina looked at Zander. "I don't know who you are, but give me that flash drive now or this kid dies."

Zander took slow, measured steps toward them. He was in the middle of the street now. Trina was at the corner where the front walk hit a right angle and then turned to the driveway. Kaylee wasn't close enough to do anything since she was at the curb still.

She moved around the SUV door and took a few measured steps of her own.

"Both of you, stop!" Trina screeched the words.

Lewis whimpered.

Kaylee put her hands out. "Everything is fine." She tried to speak calmly...to distract Trina from the fact Zander was still inching toward her while her attention was divided. "Everyone is going to be calm, and we'll get this figured out."

Where the clarity was coming from, Kaylee had no idea. There was a well of stoicism inside her that she could draw from in times of intense stress. Maybe it was that she had lost so much, and nothing could ever be as bad as what she had already been through.

She'd survived terrible things.

Trina said, "The flash drive, or he dies." She jerked Lewis again.

The boy's terrorized, tear-filled eyes bored into her. "She hit my mom."

"I wouldn't have had to if she hadn't fought me." Trina said, "Just give me what I want."

"Let the kid go." Zander sounded as calm as Kaylee had, only his was real. Cool and collected. "And I'll consider not killing you." And lethal.

Kaylee saw Lewis's reaction. She mouthed, "*It's okay.*"

Zander was closer now. Kaylee moved as well. Both of them, closing in on Trina and Lewis. Was she really going to hurt him? Who would do that to a child?

Kaylee continued distracting Trina so Zander could do what he needed to, "Why are you doing this? You work at a bank. You're not a child murderer." She paused only a split second before adding, "That's what this will be. And then you'll go to jail for the rest of your life."

"Not if I get that flash drive first." She waved the gun. "Now give it to me. I know you got it from the little library."

Kaylee wished she was close enough to grab a book from it. She'd have literally thrown the book at her former friend. Lewis was going to be scarred for life by this. Kind of like the way Kaylee had been. And Trina didn't care at all.

She didn't get it.

"Let him go." Kaylee tried to sound strong and unafraid.

Her friend's attention shifted a fraction, and Zander made his move. Kaylee did the same, aiming for Lewis.

Zander slammed into Trina, grabbing her wrist—the hand that held the gun. Kaylee saw the second Trina let go of her hold on Lewis and reached her arms out to him. He slammed into her like he'd just escaped the clutches of a bear.

She heard Zander grunt and saw that Trina had scratched his face.

He seemed surprised for a second and then twisted her arm and rolled her to her front. He pulled the arm back behind her and slapped on a pair of cuffs from the back of his belt. Then he sat back on his heels. "Yeesh, where did you find this woman?"

"She's supposed to be my friend." Kaylee turned to Lewis. "Let's go see to your mom, okay? We can call an ambulance, and they'll check her out."

Lewis nodded.

"Some friend," Zander muttered.

"I know, okay? I made a bad choice. You think I have poor judgment. I'm doing the best I can."

He hauled Trina to her feet and something around her neck glinted. Kaylee turned to Lewis. "Go inside. Call 9-1-1, and I'll be there in one second."

As soon as he raced away, she closed in on Trina and lifted the necklace from the collar of her blouse. "This belongs to someone else."

"Whatever. Finders keepers."

Kaylee wanted to be sick. "Who are you?"

"Anyone I wanna be." But her bravado slipped, and Kaylee saw what looked like genuine fear in her eyes. She wasn't going to fall for it, though. Not if it was a ruse.

"I have to go help Lewis." Kaylee glanced at Zander and took a step away. "You're good?"

Zander's eyebrow rose. "I'm thinking, yeah. I can handle her."

She wanted to warn him to not be cocky, but Trina said, "You have to help me, Kaylee. He'll kill me. I didn't succeed."

She walked away.

"Kaylee, he'll kill me!"

Twenty-one

Dean jumped out of the car first. Stuart needed a second. The street was filled with police vehicles, even an ambulance. Zander stood in the center, holding onto a cuffed Trina.

Dean went inside the house where they'd been told Kaylee was with a kid and his mom. An officer took Trina from Zander and started to walk her to a police car. Stuart went to Zander who was talking to the sergeant.

What he wanted to do was go inside so he could see Kaylee, but the thought of getting rejected again held him back. Kaylee wanted "space," and that was exactly what he would give her. The kind of man he wanted to be didn't do whatever he wanted against a woman's wishes. Stuart had to respect her choice.

But then, the man he'd always been knew that protecting her ranked higher in priority than her need for that "space" she'd asked for. The covert agent would haul her off to a safe house and set up a way to take down the threat. She didn't need to be happy about it. She would be alive enough, and she'd realize later it had been the best course of action and then forgive him.

Zander's conversation with the sergeant broke off as he approached, and he lifted a brow. What had they been talking about that they didn't want him to hear or be a part of?

"Stuart!" Trina's shrill voice drew all their attention.

He turned to her, his mind still full of Kaylee. And the two men. People weren't his strong suit.

"Help me, please! I can't go to jail!"

Zander said, "You should've thought of that before you committed multiple crimes." He glanced at Stuart. "Just so you know, you're the fourth person she's tried appealing to."

"Good to know." Stuart folded his arms, holding back the wince. His entire body ached despite the dose of pain meds Dean had insisted he take—not the ones that made him drowsy. Unfortunately, that left the ones that made him nauseous.

"I won't survive jail!"

Stuart glanced at Zander, who shrugged. Then Stuart said, "US prisons aren't that bad. I've been incarcerated in France *and* Russia. Serving time here would be a cakewalk compared to either one of them."

Basuto stared at him.

"Russia?" Trina shook her head. "My *Dad* is Russian." She switched to the language and said, "He taught me everything I know. How to hide. How to kill."

Basuto glanced between them. "You understand that."

Stuart nodded. As for Zander, he wasn't sure if the man spoke Russian, though he did speak several other languages. Stuart used Russian to ask Trina, "Why should that make me consider you any differently? You threatened to take away my ability to walk, all to force your own way and make Kaylee give you the flash drive."

"He made me do it." She scrunched up her face, and he wondered if she was trying to get tears to fall. "It was all his idea!"

Stuart turned to Basuto. "You should probably call a translator, just in case she sticks with this tactic. Since Trina is *Russian* and all." He resisted the urge to grin—that was how unseriously he was

146

taking her. He could translate, sure, but he was also far too close to all of this to be beyond reproach. Especially considering all this would likely end up in court.

Stuart didn't know if he would live that long.

The sergeant lifted his chin. "Get her back to holding."

Donaldson led Trina away while she flailed and screeched. "I can get you in contact with the team that's coming to town! I can hand them over to you. I know who they are."

Zander made a disparaging noise in his throat but said nothing.

Basuto called out, "The DA is the one who will make any deals. That's not my purview. If it was, you'd get nothing. Terrorizing a kid?" He shook his head. "No. I don't think so."

The officer got her in the backseat and shut the car door. Her wailing was still audible, but now at least Stuart could think.

Basuto tipped his head in her direction. "What did she say, when she was speaking Russian?"

Stuart told the sergeant, "Her father taught her how to kill. He put her up to it." His tone gave away how he felt about that.

People should own up to responsibility for their actions. Not seek to drag others down, or blame them. No one had been here, forcing Trina to do this. She hadn't been coerced, and she wasn't under duress.

So exactly how much weight was her defense supposed to have?

"That's interesting," Basuto said. "Considering he's saying it was all her idea." He shook his head, a sardonic expression on his face. "That's why we had to hold onto him until we found her. Now we can sit them both down and unpack it all. We'll finally be able to get to the bottom of this."

Zander said, "You might want to ask her about that missing girl, the cold case Kaylee has been reading about."

Basuto shook his head. "Why?"

"Something Kaylee noticed about Trina's necklace."

The sergeant said, "Copy that." He took a step back. "You guys are good?"

They both nodded. Basuto trotted away.

"Go inside and see her."

Stuart opened his mouth. Zander cut him off before he could say anything. "She asked me to go with her because of you." He lifted a hand. "Because you respect and trust me enough with her life." Zander flashed a grin.

Stuart shook his head. "Trina seriously held a gun to her again?"

"And threatened to shoot a kid."

He couldn't believe it. "There's no way she's Russian, right? And isn't that one giant distraction from the real point here? That someone betrayed Brad and me, leading to our capture. What do I care about crazy Trina and what she might have done?"

"We're almost out of the woods, right?" Zander pulled a tiny manila envelope from his pocket, tore it open, and dumped the contents into his palm.

"That is tiny."

The flash drive was almost flat and so small he'd be scared to push it into the USB port on a computer. Too much force and the thing would be snapped in half.

Zander offered it up.

Stuart's fingers twitched. That one thing contained all the answers. "We need to get it into a computer and get the password in. Brad is as bad as Ted, so there's probably a failsafe of some kind. You know? Like, don't put the password in correctly within a minute and the whole thing wipes."

Zander winced.

"Hold onto it. Take it back to the house with you."

Stuart had surprised his friend. His roommate. He wasn't sure what exactly they were. But he did know that the important thing here was that they were all vulnerable until this was done. There were men, in town and probably more on the way, gunning for them. That meant if Stuart had the device, then he was doubly vulnerable.

"Designated survivor style?"

He nodded. "If they get both me *and* the flash drive, then I'm worth nothing." Trina had tried to use their lives as leverage to get her hands on it. "They won't kill me if I can't hand them everything they want."

"Copy that."

"Check in. Frequently."

Zander nodded. They shook hands, and the team leader strode back to his car. When Stuart turned to the house, he saw Dean walk out. He was followed by two EMTs carrying a woman on a stretcher. Behind them, Kaylee and a tween boy walked out. The boy looked shell shocked.

Stuart hung back while mother and son were loaded into the waiting ambulance.

Dean slapped him on the back of the shoulder as he passed.

The ambulance doors were slammed shut, and Kaylee turned. Relief washed over her face at the realization he stood not far from her. She rushed toward him. Stuart opened his arms at the last second, and she slammed into him.

He wrapped his arms around her. "Kaylee." He crooned her name as he held her, then used nonsense words until she could inhale without the hitch in the middle. When she relaxed against him, not so tense, he said, "You did it. We got the flash drive with no loss of life."

"This isn't over though, is it?"

"No. But we can do it one step at a time. Together."

She stared up at him. "I'd like that. I'm sorry I left."

"It's been intense, and I haven't been at my best." Stuart needed to get rid of the giant elephant out here on the street with them. "You don't need to deal with my problems. It's not fair to drag you down while I'm trying to get past them."

He wasn't sure he ever would.

"I know you didn't mean to hurt me. You never would have done that if you'd been aware of what you were doing."

"It was still my eyes looking at you while I had my hand around your throat."

That was why he wasn't going to make her try to figure out how to live with him. She needed full disclosure of what she would be getting herself into. There was work for him to do before he was fit to be in a relationship. Except that now was not the time to do that because his attention needed to instead be on exposing whoever betrayed them. He needed to bring the person to justice once and for all.

Then there was Brad. Stuart was intent on finding his friend. To finally know the truth of what had happened.

She reached up and touched his cheek. "I forgive you. If you'll forgive me for running out."

He shook his head, gave her a squeeze, and let her go. "Those are nothing alike. You don't need my forgiveness, Kaylee. You've been great this whole time. I'm sorry Brad even dragged you into this, and that your life was turned upside down."

"It's been interesting, for sure." She ran a hand through her dark hair. "I know now that I'm far more capable of withstanding fear than I thought. I figured I'd have shut down and been catatonic or something. But I wasn't."

Stuart pressed his lips together. He nodded, acting like he was glad she realized that. The truth was, he'd rather she never experienced it in the first place. No way did she need to have gone through that. He was so proud of her that she'd not only done it but had found the positive in the midst of it.

"This isn't over, is it?"

Stuart shook his head. "You can stay here, safe, but I have two more things to do. Find Brad. Get the flash drive in the right hands."

"Who do you think betrayed you guys? Was it the people you worked for?"

He shrugged one shoulder and took her hand so they could walk to Dean's car where he was waiting for them. "It's possible. There's no love lost. Assets are valuable, and then they're scraped off. We outlived our usefulness, I guess."

"So they destroy you?"

"It kills our credibility. We were already suspects, given our backgrounds. They only hire renegades. Not the usual Ivy Leaguers the CIA comes up with." Stuart reached for the door handle. "They can discredit anything I say now, even if I do come up with the truth. No one will believe a broken man. Especially if I have no evidence."

"But we do. Right?" She looked so hopeful, it was hard to argue. "We have the flash drive."

Stuart didn't know about, "we," but she was right. He nodded. "I'll get this done. You don't have to worry."

He pulled the door open and held it for her.

The steady whomp-whomp of helicopter rotors caught his attention. He spun around. *Oh, no.* That wasn't good.

"Get in."

She scrambled inside.

Stuart climbed in beside her and told Dean, "Drive."

The last thing he needed was to be caught out in the open when he wasn't ready to face them.

Stuart was going to finish this his way.

Twenty-two

Kaylee scooted far enough over she could see out the window on the far side. She peered out at the sky as the helicopter dipped low.

Dean ducked in the driver's seat. "Whoa, guys."

Whether he thought the helicopter pilot could hear him, or not, Kaylee still agreed with him. "They're flying way too low."

Sure enough, the bottom of the helicopter rails looked close enough to nearly clip the roof of a house.

The noise was deafening. The steady whomp of rotors continued as it slowed and rotated.

"We should get out of here." Stuart shut the door on his side. He'd gotten in the back with her instead of in the front passenger seat. "We don't know what they're going to do."

"No." Dean shook his head. "We're going to stick around. Make sure no one is hurt, and see what they're going to do."

Stuart made a noncommittal noise in response but didn't argue. Kaylee just stared out the window as the chopper, black and sleek and flashy looking, turned in a circle. She spotted a pilot, another guy in the front, and more than one person in the back. Most of them were dressed in black with helmets and wicked-looking, huge guns. Except for one guy in a dark blue jacket and jeans, his back to them.

Kaylee said, "Where's the flash drive?"

"Zander took it."

"Okay. That's good." It should by all accounts be far from both her and Stuart. That way, if something happened and they were taken, these guys wouldn't get their hands on the evidence as well. "Who are they? They don't exactly look friendly."

"They're not." Stuart sounded like he had to bite the words out. "I recognize the chopper. They work for the same company, which means it's my employers trying to find us and the evidence Brad discovered."

Kaylee squinted. "Brad."

"What?"

The man in blue started to fall. Kaylee's breath caught in her throat. The wind roared through her ears as she watched.

He tumbled end over end, out of the helicopter, and onto the grass. His body hit the ground. He bounced once and tumbled over in a heap.

"Kaylee!"

She was out of the car.

Her feet tripped over each other. She fell to her knees, catching herself by her hands on the asphalt of the street. Her breath came in gasps. Finally, she managed to take a whole breath and screamed, "Brad!"

She raced toward her brother.

"Kaylee, get down!"

She ignored Stuart and pumped her arms and legs as fast as she could. Finally, blessedly, she reached his side.

Gunshots smacked the grass around her, kicking up dirt. She screamed and threw her body over her brother's, covering his torso and head. Was he even alive?

Had they thrown his dead body from that chopper?

153

Answering gunshots echoed over the sound of the aircraft. One pinged off metal. She heard more.

None hit her. Or her brother, or the grass around them.

Alarms sounded. She could hear them faintly over the rotors. And then she looked up. The helicopter retreated, angling away from them as it flew off toward the mountains.

"Call Zander. Tell him I want to know where that went!" Stuart landed beside her. "Kaylee, what were you thinking? You could've been shot!"

"Go! Go!" A man she didn't know raced down the street toward her. Kaylee flinched, moving away. But he didn't come toward her. He ran right past, followed by two men. All of them had guns.

She tumbled from her crouch onto her backside, and recognized them. They were Zander's team. The three men jumped into a Jeep. One in the back, the other two in the front. The engine roared, and the tires screeched as they took off in pursuit of the helicopter.

She moved to her knees only enough to roll her brother to his back. She cried out at the sight of his face, bloody and beaten. "Brad."

"Kaylee."

She shook her head. She couldn't handle Stuart's concern, or his attempts to comfort her when he was just as distraught as she was. She could hear it in his voice.

Kaylee laid a gentle hand on her brother's shoulder. It was hard to know where to touch, there was so much blood and so many bruises. He'd been beaten. Maybe even tortured. A whimper worked its way up her throat, and she didn't bother to hold it back.

Dean landed beside her. "Give me a little space."

Stuart came around to gather her up in his arms again. "Should I call the ambulance to come back?"

Dean shook his head. "We need to get him in the car."

"Is he going to live?"

Dean said, "Come on. We have to hurry."

Stuart and Dean gathered Brad up. His head lolled. He was out cold, and it was probably for the best considering how much pain he would likely be in when he woke up. *God, don't let him die.* Her brother had gone through so much. He'd been a captive. Hurt.

New compassion for Stuart and all he'd gone through moved in her. She wanted to talk to him, but that would have to wait. She climbed into the back of the car, and they helped her brother inside. She tried to pull him onto her lap but didn't want to tug too much. Dean folded Brad's legs inside, and she held him while they got in the front.

The doors shut. Stuart turned on the engine, hit the gas and peeled out.

Kaylee swayed with the motion. Dean turned in the front, his knees to the passenger seat. He studied Brad and spoke on the phone. She didn't understand half the words he said but none of them sounded good. It sounded as bad as the dark look on his face.

"He's going to die."

Stuart glanced over his shoulder. "Don't talk like that. We're almost to the hospital."

"I can't lose him." She grasped two handfuls of her brother's shirt. "He's the only family I have left."

"Almost there," Dean spoke low, probably trying to sound reassuring.

Kaylee felt the tracks of tears roll down her face but didn't bother wiping them away. There was no point. *God.* The cry of her heart was a reflex. Falling back on the sovereignty of God. The Father might not have kept her parents alive, but she could ask Him for this. Maybe He would not deny her the answer to her prayers a second time.

Stuart pulled into the emergency bay, right behind the now-empty ambulance that had contained Lewis and his mom. They must already be inside.

Stuart jumped out of the car and raced to the doors. She heard him yell, and while he got help, Dean continued to check out her brother. Kaylee just stared at his face.

One eye swollen and blue. His lip was cut, and the rest of his skin was sticky with sweat, dirt, and dried blood.

The back door opened. Stuart reached across the seat and hauled Brad from her lap, while two nurses helped him get her brother on a stretcher.

"I'll park the car."

She didn't move.

"Kaylee."

They wheeled her brother to the door. Dean got out, trotted around the car, and got in the driver's side. Stuart reached in and held out his hand to her. "Come on."

When she didn't move, he tugged on her hands. Kaylee got her feet under her, and he pretty much lifted her from the car, slamming the door behind her.

Dean drove away.

Stuart tucked her hand in his arm and walked her around to the front door. "Everything is going to be okay." His words were slower but steady. As though he repeated a mantra. Trying to convince himself, make him believe, while his heart probably screamed like hers.

"They had him this whole time."

"But he's not dead. They think they broke us, and him, by doing this." He paused at the front door and studied her face. "Did they?"

She'd been broken so many times. Her parents' deaths. The night she realized her brother had killed their murderer. Kaylee didn't even know if she'd ever actually managed to put herself back together.

Maybe she was still broken and always would be.

"Kaylee?"

"They're not the ones who broke me," she said, honestly.

He frowned, understanding what she was saying. Or what she *wasn't,* maybe. She was too frazzled for a deep conversation.

Stuart led her inside, and they explained who they were, then he had her sit beside him in the waiting area. "Your brother is alive." He sounded relieved. When she glanced at him, Stuart said, "I thought I'd killed him. That I was responsible for his death, and that I'd left him there."

"But they captured him after he tried to escape."

"And they let me escape." Stuart said, "Which means he sacrificed, and I went free." He shook his head. "Why do that? It makes no sense."

She'd seen him at church but didn't know where he was at with things of faith. "Does it have to make sense? I mean, if you can reason it out, doesn't that mean it loses some of what makes it so amazing."

"I'd just be mad at your brother for doing that, not grateful. Like with God." He shifted, holding her hand in his lap, as though he needed it there. "There is *no way* Jesus should have done what He did for me."

"Even if you were the only one."

"That actually makes it worse." He smiled, more self-deprecating than humorous. "Because I would never accept that someone perfect did that for me."

"It was the only way." Now she sounded as though she were repeating a mantra. A meditation. Reminding herself of all God had done. "We have some of those capabilities in us. Something of the divine, that lifts us above other earthly beings. The ability to be selfless is one of them. Though we use it in corrupt ways most of the time, and it's only a shadow of what He put in us, it's still there."

"Not in me." Stuart shook his head. "No one should ever give up anything for me. It doesn't matter if I live the rest of my life doing good things and try to pretend I'm selfless. Caring for orphans, or helping victims. It doesn't matter." The repetition sounded so defeated. "I'll never be worthy of it. Not even what Brad did for me. Knowingly, or unknowingly."

"Isn't that why it's a gift no one deserves?" It was the essence of grace, after all. The gift no one deserved. While some people seemed to have been good all their lives, others fell to their knees, weeping, they were so grateful for salvation.

"That doesn't make me feel better." He slung his arm around her shoulders and tugged her to him, planting a kiss on the top of her head. "But thank you for trying."

A doctor wearing a white coat strode out, spoke with the reception lady, and looked at them when she indicated their spot. The doctor was a new hire. She'd apparently never worked in a small town before. They'd had to bring someone in fast after the last doctor turned out to be a town founder—and a murdering psycho.

The doctor came close, her focus on Kaylee. "You're Kaylee?"

She stood, trying not to be nervous just because of who this woman's predecessor had been. "Yes, Brad is my brother. He'll be okay?"

"Right now he's in a medically-induced coma until the swelling in his brain goes down. He has more than several broken bones, and one of his legs will need multiple surgeries." The doctor reached up and squeezed the back of her neck. "It'll take time, but when he's ready, we'll wake him up. After that, it's a case of assessing his condition moving forward and making a plan."

Kaylee blew out a long breath. "Thank you, so much."

"It's good you brought him when you did. Wherever he was, he wouldn't have lasted much longer."

Twenty-three

Stuart watched her as she sat beside her brother's bed, holding his hand. She was where she was supposed to be. Here in this town. With her family.

He turned, walked away from the room, and strode down the hall. Before she had even stepped into her brother's room, Kaylee had written down the series of numbers they needed to access the flash drive onto a piece of paper.

Her brother was alive.

She wanted nothing more to do with the flash drive.

The elevator opened and Dean stepped out. "You're leaving?" He moved forward, ushering Stuart away from the door to make space for an older couple. An orderly pushed the man in a wheelchair, while his wife walked beside him, holding his hand.

Guilt had Stuart taking a couple of paces back. "She doesn't need me right now."

Unlike this couple, Kaylee and Stuart would never become anything. Together, long into their silver years. Still supporting one another. Still showing love.

"So you're going to take care of all this other stuff instead?" Dean groaned. "I guess that's probably a good idea. Basuto is freaking out because of that helicopter. The boys all got sworn in, so they're with the cops right now."

Stuart winced.

"Yeah, that was my reaction." Dean shook his head. "I'm not sure how the sergeant is going to take it when he realizes that though Zander and his boys might be highly skilled and able bodied, they don't exactly take orders well."

"He'll get over it when they clean up."

"Maybe."

The elevator doors slid shut. Stuart wanted to rush over and hit the button again, but Dean got in front of him. He acted like he didn't realize his friend was barring his way out and said, "Did they find the chopper?"

"It flew off. They followed until it was clear the men inside had retreated. Maybe they'll be back, and maybe not." Dean shrugged. "Could be they'd done what they came to do."

Stuart's stomach turned over.

"Then again, it could be they wanted to send a clear message and are waiting for our next move."

"If they wanted to send a message, then they should have killed him." Stuart shrugged. "Why leave Brad alive?"

"Dead is clean. It's done. With Brad here, it ties up Kaylee which also ties up you. Everyone is distracted, waiting for word of his condition."

Okay, so that made sense. Stuart said, "They want to divide our focus, but you think they know about Zander?"

Dean shrugged. He studied Stuart for a minute. "You want me to stay with her? Make sure she's safe?" He motioned with his chin down the hall. "Ellie can sit with her, and I'll keep them both protected."

Stuart held out his hand. Dean shook it. "The less divided I can be, the better."

"You think they know how much you care for her?"

"I think I should keep my phone conversations sanitized until I know for sure they haven't cloned my phone the way they did Kaylee's."

Dean nodded. "We have to assume they have eyes and ears everywhere."

"You think Ted figured that out?"

"He's meeting with Zander now, and he's bringing an air-gapped computer. They're going to look at the flash drive and see what we're dealing with."

There was a whole lot of "we" going on. Stuart figured it was down to his friends. Men he'd met a couple of years ago when he'd saved their lives. They repaid that favor when they'd picked him up after his capture.

Since then, he'd been Dean's first, true therapy patient. An experiment and a favor to his friend. Helping Stuart get the answers he needed.

Now it seemed these men, and the town as well, had claimed him as one of their own. Maybe when he put all this right—if he was alive and a free man—he might go talk to Hollis about that job in her kitchen.

Dean said, "I told Zander to call you when they get in."

Stuart nodded. "Thanks."

"Don't worry. We'll take care of Kaylee and her brother."

"And if he doesn't wake up?"

"Then we'll take care of Kaylee. *And* her brother."

Stuart shook his friend's hand again.

"One more thing?"

He lifted his brows. There was *more*? Stuart could barely handle what he had so far.

Dean's lips twitched. "Yeah, that was my reaction when Savannah called me."

"What did the detective want?"

"She said to tell you the bank manager, Silas Nigelson, was cut loose. They didn't have any more reason to hold him, and they're not charging him with anything."

"Not kidnapping?" Stuart had been there. Silas had participated.

Now he was out? Roaming free as though he'd done *nothing*? This was insane.

"There's no evidence he did anything more than drive, and he's saying that's only because Trina threatened him. They're both telling the same story, and that gave the DA no room to find a reason to file charges that might get thrown out by the judge anyway. Silas said his daughter is 'touched in the head'—his words—and he was only trying to keep her contained."

"He pointed a gun at me."

Dean winced. "I told her that. Apparently, Silas is maintaining he only got you in the car with them so that you could see the truth about his daughter and aid him in locking her down. He's supposedly mad you didn't. So you might want to be careful."

"Seriously?" Stuart didn't need some small-town grudge. Not now...not even after he got the more serious business out of the way and resolved. "And the Russia thing?"

Dean shrugged.

"What about the missing girl?"

"Trina is saying she found the necklace on the street. Savannah is getting it tested as possible evidence, but that will take time."

Stuart figured Kaylee would want to know she was right. She might have even solved the case. But would that make a difference when it was he and Brad who'd nearly destroyed her life? And they'd also wrecked the peace of mind she'd built for herself.

He had a lot to apologize for. Stuart would make amends if that was what she wanted. But he figured it would be a greater benefit to her if he just left.

And never came back.

Dean went toward Brad's room. Stuart hit the restroom and splashed cold water on his face to shock himself awake. Zander still hadn't contacted him by the time he came out, so he called the team leader.

"You're calling me?" Zander said, "I figured you'd show up any minute now and take the flash drive. I've been waiting for you."

"What are you talking about?"

"Kaylee's with her brother, right?"

Stuart frowned. "Yes."

"So, what's left for you now except getting this done?"

"Would you even give me the flash drive if I came and asked you for it?" He stuck his hand in his pocket, fingering the paper.

Zander huffed. "We both know what you used to do. And you're gonna come here and *ask me for it?*"

"I'm a nice guy now. You didn't notice?"

"Maybe you've lost your edge." Zander was quiet for a second. "She said code word. Is that even the same as the password? Cause there are layers of encryption on this thing. Ted says it looks like there are a series of codes set up to shut a trap door every time the password is not entered properly. If you wait too long or use the wrong keystroke, it sets off a chain reaction."

"Which will dump the contents," Stuart finished for him. "And then we'll never get it."

Everything Brad had done, and all he'd been through—what both of them had been through—would end up being for nothing. Could he handle that? Maybe it didn't matter whether or not he could handle it, because the truth was, this would never be over unless he finished it.

Even if the flash drive was destroyed somehow, the information on it unusable, Stuart would have to run. He'd live the rest of his life looking over his shoulder. Same with Kaylee and Brad. Even if he recovered, they still would never be safe.

Stuart clenched his jaw. "Ready? Kaylee gave me the codes." He'd be sharing it over a line that could be under surveillance, but that was a risk they were going to have to take. Whoever it was couldn't possibly infiltrate the computer being used to access the flash drive. Air gapped meant it wasn't connected to any external network and had no internet capabilities. No one could hack it without direct, physical access.

It was safe.

"You're on speaker. Fire away."

Stuart read what Kaylee had written.

He heard Ted in the background. Each series of numbers was confirmed with, "Copy." Until the end. "I'm in." Ted was quiet for a second. "Whoa."

Stuart would have preferred to be there just then. He could have looked over Ted's shoulder at the screen of the laptop and wouldn't have had to finally say, "Put me out of my misery, Zan."

"One sec." Zander shifted, the sound audible across the phone line.

Stuart backed up and leaned against the wall. A nurse passed, shooting him a look. He didn't know what for.

Zander said, "This is bad." After a century-long pause, he continued, "How much do you know about the most recent appointee to a high-level government director job?"

He was going to be cagey now? Stuart had read the newspaper nearly a week ago, but not since. The latest news was that the CIA had just gotten a new boss. The guy had been CEO of a firm that handled government contracts for weapons research and aerospace engineering. He'd also been a silent partner in the company Stuart and Brad worked for.

Not officially. They'd been contractors, and expendable ones, at that.

Stuart should've known. "It was him?"

"Clean up. New job, new expectations. Take out the trash, so you don't have to worry about it now that your butt's all cushy in the brand-new chair. Just kick back, put your feet on the desk and coast while earning that sweet government pension."

"I'm thinking private jet doesn't need a pension."

"Unless he's broke."

"Can Ted find out?" Maybe he'd scraped off Brad and Stuart because of the upcoming promotion.

Or for another reason, namely the fact captivity hadn't killed them, leaving them as loose ends that needed eliminating.

Stuart squeezed the bridge of his nose. He might not remember everything, but he could remember enough. "I had no idea. Brad had already amassed all this evidence, and I was totally in the dark."

"You said you hadn't seen him for a while. Maybe he'd been working this but didn't want to bring you in until he was certain."

"You don't have to try and make me feel better." The CIA director had men at his disposal now, as well as those who worked for him at the same company that had disposed of Stuart. "We can get him, right? Expose him for kidnapping and holding Brad. He probably wheedled his way into this position. There has to be dirt on him. A threat to his ambitions, or he wouldn't be exposing himself by gunning for us."

"Good point," Zander said. "Means nothing traces back to him. Not if he can help it. Otherwise, he just implicates himself, because it'll come out. There have to be layers of protection so no one suspects."

Stuart sighed. "Find a connection. Hire Ted, and pay him contractor rates." To Ted, hopefully listening, "I'll pay you whatever you want. Just find me evidence to nail this guy with a life sentence."

"I'll let you know what I've got when I'm done going through everything." Ted sounded so diplomatic he should run for mayor or something. "Then we'll make a plan."

"More 'we' from you. Am I a cop? Or are you signing onto my team now?" He glanced at the ceiling. As his gaze shifted, he spotted someone at the end of the hall. The figure ducked out of sight too quickly. He breathed in a sharp breath. "Send the boys here."

"Why? Talk to me!" Zander barked through the open line.

"I need backup. They've breached the hospital." Stuart hung up the phone.

Twenty-four

It took Kaylee a second to figure out what the buzzing was. She opened the big plastic bag of Brad's things the nurse had brought in. His clothes and shoes. There was a phone in there. Everything smelled. She didn't think too much about that, just clutched the bag and spoke silent prayers of thanks.

Brad was here, and he was alive.

No matter what else had happened, or might happen before this was over, that was what she needed to focus on. That way she wouldn't lose sight of the big picture.

Everything was going to be okay.

Thank You, Lord. She had her family back.

Things were by no means straight between her and Stuart. They'd had a sweet moment, but he'd left her to sit with her brother and then just disappeared...to wherever. Now Dean stood in the hall outside her room. Guarding her, and her brother.

Kaylee was safe. Brad had been found. That left Stuart to...what? Finishing what he'd started would be her guess. What it would look like, she didn't know. Though, she'd read plenty of spy novels so she'd come up with some creative solutions if he asked for her opinion. But he hadn't. He'd walked off and left her, like he didn't need her anymore.

Dead weight. No help to put the wrong right again, when he was the one trained in covert operations. The kind of man who would shoot himself up with drugs to relive his worst, real-life nightmare, just to get her the word, "peppermint."

Who did that?

Kaylee leaned against the bed and looked at her brother's beaten face. He rested now. What reason did she have to be anything but joyful that Brad was here, alive. The flash drive was no longer her responsibility. Her part in this was done, and she could rest now. It was over for her.

So what if that the attraction between her and Stuart might have become something? What did that matter now? She liked having him here in town, with her, and just knowing he was still local made her feel better. They'd had a good conversation about the gift of grace. He'd kissed her head.

She wanted more, but it wasn't to be. He would probably leave when he was finally free to go wherever he wanted without having to live under the threat of being hunted. Of course, he would leave when the only reason he'd come here was for the flash drive. Last Chance wasn't his home, and Kaylee wasn't going to live anywhere else.

Therefore, it wasn't meant to be.

Whatever she might have thought? No more. She had plenty to think about. Dreaming of a life like Mia and Conroy—except the part where he was shot by a sniper—or Savannah and Tate, Ellie and Dean, was pointless. She wasn't brave enough to take a chance on something that could fall apart.

The destruction that would cause in her would be catastrophic.

A soft knock tapped on the door. "Hey." Ellie pushed her glasses up her nose and stepped in, as though she might be disturbing them.

Kaylee dropped the bag of clothing and rounded the bed to her newest friend. She opened her arms and smiled as Ellie approached.

They hugged. In the hall, Dean watched his girlfriend with a smile Kaylee decided was adorable. A word she'd never have said aloud to describe any man, let alone a former Navy SEAL.

As she squeezed Ellie with her arms, Kaylee said, "He's alive." She sighed and leaned back. "I thought for a while that he might be dead, and now he's going to be okay."

Ellie smiled. "That's great news."

Kaylee nodded. "I want him to wake up so badly, but I know he needs to rest if he's going to heal properly. The doctor is the one who will make the call." She couldn't help chuckling. "I still want to shake him awake so we can celebrate together. He's here."

Ellie chuckled. "I have a sister, not a brother, but I can say the urge to shake is there too."

Kaylee laughed with her, hoping the sound encouraged her brother to hear and believe that everything was fine now…and then he'd have the wherewithal to wake up. She would look into his eyes. Tell him that he was safe now.

She moved to his bedside, gently laid her hand on his shoulder, and leaned down. She whispered, "You're safe now."

She heard that buzzing again and went to look at the bag. "He must have a phone, or something, in here." Would she have to turn it over to the police?

"I'll leave you to it." Ellie said, "I should go back to work, anyway."

Ellie was a history professor and spent her days at the library researching for the book she was writing. Kaylee loved books, but summers were for reading outside on a blanket at the park. Not being cooped up at the library during good weather.

"You don't have to go. I do like the company."

Ellie smiled.

"But thank you for coming."

"Of course." Ellie wandered out toward Dean. Her love for him was obvious.

Kaylee didn't look while they said goodbye. She didn't need a reminder of what she was missing because Stuart had chosen to leave her here. Protected—which made being mad at him harder because he'd safeguarded her—and looking after her brother.

She sighed and sat up to rifle through the bag on her lap. Jeans and a grubby T-shirt. The jacket he'd been wearing when they tossed him from the helicopter. Her breath caught in her throat just thinking about it again.

Tucked in an inside pocket of the jacket, she found a cell phone. The battery was low enough the notification was the first thing she saw. Then the four missed text messages. Someone was trying to contact Brad?

She unlocked the phone. No fingerprint or passcode ID. Who did that? Even she knew it should be secure. Unless Brad didn't care because there was nothing sensitive on it.

Or it wasn't his phone.

That meant it had been planted. Left here for her to find.

No contacts were listed. No photos. No apps. Nothing that might tell her whose phone it was.

It buzzed again. Kaylee nearly dropped it.

Hello, Kaylee.

She stared at the words. Clicking the home button a few times, she found no other messages in the app history before this one and no numbers saved in the call history.

She glanced up at Dean. Out in the hall, he was still talking to Ellie and smiling now. Whispering close like two people in love.

The phone buzzed again.

Pay attention. Or people get hurt.

"Who are you?" The words were quiet. Brad didn't need to hear the tremor of anxiousness in her voice. Should she type the question back?

Before she could, another message appeared.

I'm the person you're going to listen to.

Three dots blinked at her on the screen. He was still typing.

Like I'm listening to you.

Kaylee got up. "Dean—"

A red flicker appeared on Ellie's back.

He looked around her, into the room. "Everything okay, Kaylee?"

Ellie turned. She couldn't see the red dot of a laser sight on her shoulder.

The phone buzzed in her hand. Kaylee swallowed.

"Kaylee?"

She tried to smile. "It's fine. Never mind."

They didn't look convinced. She turned away and sat, moving her thumbs to the screen to reply. Instead, a message stared at her.

Tell anyone, and she's the first to die.

Kaylee typed back, "What do you want?"

Now you're getting it.

Three dots.

We want the flash drive. Get it from the police station, and bring it to us.

Us? How many of them were there? One of the men was in a holding cell at the station, the one who'd shot Conroy. One was dead. She'd seen others in that helicopter. Was this one of them? She typed back, "They won't just give it to me."

Then take it.

Three blinking dots. Taunting her. She should throw the phone in the toilet and flush it. Or throw it down the hospital stairwell so it shattered into a thousand pieces.

She looked at the hall. Ellie and Dean were still talking, and that laser dot was still there. A sniper's scope, targeting an innocent woman.

If you don't bring us the flash drive, we blow up the hospital.

Then we blow up the police station.

When that's gone, we blow up Hope Mansion.

Those three dots blinked at her, but she didn't care what else there was. She typed, "Okay," by jabbing the screen. Hopefully she'd break it.

Get moving. Or your precious town is in ruins.

She stood, shoving the chair back as she moved. How was she supposed to get across town to the police station, let alone take the flash drive without anyone realizing she'd stolen it? Her co-workers were there, as well as Zander probably. Maybe even Stuart as well. One person might be manageable. But she'd never get past all of them.

This was impossible.

Starting with losing Dean before he realized she'd fled the hospital.

The laser sight's red dot was gone now. A sniper, still watching. Where did he move it? Was it pointed at her now, or Brad?

Fear raced through her, prickling her skin with tiny bumps, causing her hair to stand straight up. Kaylee gathered her purse and the phone that didn't belong to her.

"Going somewhere?" Dean's question wasn't accusatory in tone, but he certainly expected an answer.

There was a bathroom in the room, so she couldn't use that as an excuse. Instead, she said, "Just to get some coffee. I need to stretch my legs, and if I don't get some caffeine in me, I'll fall asleep standing up." She smiled.

Dean said, "If you can wait until my backup gets here, that would be better. Or Ellie can get you the coffee."

Before she could ask why that was necessary, he said, "I'd rather not leave Brad unprotected, and I told Stuart I'd keep an eye on you."

Kaylee didn't have to pretend to be irritated by that. "I'm not a child that needs to be looked after. Stuart doesn't need to worry about me when he has plenty to occupy himself."

And he'd have even more to do after she took the flash drive. No matter what justice needed to happen, it wasn't worth the lives of innocent people in this town. The hospital. The police station. Hope Mansion. No one in any of those buildings deserved to die a fiery death, blown up and torn apart.

She started to walk away.

"Ellie, stay here."

"And protect Brad?" Her voice squeaked.

Kaylee kept walking.

"I'll be back in a second. Just hang on." He didn't want his girlfriend with him? Dean was torn between going after her and doing his job.

She winced. He didn't deserve this, and she'd have to apologize to him later. Probably to all of them. Until then, she couldn't explain why she had to do this.

These people had helicopters. They listened on phones. Snipers. Bombs. Torture.

She blinked back the first sheen of tears. No way was anyone else going to get hurt. There had already been far too much suffering.

Kaylee broke into a run, glanced over her shoulder and yelled, "Stay with Brad!"

She spotted the door to the stairs and pushed the EXIT bar at full speed. She raced down the concrete stairwell while Dean followed her. But he wasn't going to catch her.

No way, not when that would mean an explosion.

"Kaylee!"

He was too far back.

She shoved her way out into the underground parking lot and slammed right into a man.

Her eyes widened, and she screamed.

"You're coming with me."

Twenty-five

Stuart didn't want to admit he'd lost them. But he had.

He twisted around in the lobby and nearly ran into an older gentleman. He said, "Sorry," and ducked around the man so he could stride to the elevators. He got off on the floor where Brad's room was located. The nurse recognized him from when he'd been here only an hour or so ago with Kaylee. She noted his name and waved him to the room.

Once he was able to see Kaylee with his own eyes, he'd feel better. The antsy feeling of knowing there was someone in the hospital he'd instinctually known was suspicious wasn't going to go away until he knew for sure those under his protection were safe.

He wrapped his knuckles on the door jam and stepped in, but aside from Brad in the bed, there was only a nurse inside the room.

The nurse looked over. She was an older lady with a pixie cut of bleached highlights in her gray hair. She grinned, red lips and a brilliant white smile. "Your friend here is doing well."

Stuart's instincts flared again. "There was a woman in here. His sister, Kaylee. Any idea where she went?"

"Can't say I do." She pressed a button on the heart rate monitor, apparently not overly concerned.

Stuart didn't share the sentiment. "There was also a man in the hall, keeping an eye out."

"You're talking about Dean, right?"

"Yes, ma'am." Stuart shifted his weight from one foot to the other. "Any idea where he went?"

"I can look for you if you want to sit with your friend."

Stuart still hadn't looked at Brad. Had she realized that? Is that why she seemed to force the acknowledgement of his friend's presence? Maybe she was hung up on the fact he hadn't. He looked at the man in the hospital bed.

Air got stuck in his throat. Stuart coughed, as though that was the problem. "It looks…bad."

"He's responding to the medicine. Vital signs are stronger every hour." The nurse moved around the bed to where he stood, still by the door, but she continued to keep her distance. "There's every reason to be hopeful, even while we're cautious. And I called the pastor. Had your friend added to the prayer list—anonymously, of course."

Stuart nodded. "Of course." He should have said, "Thanks," instead, but it was too late now. "You haven't seen my friend or Dean?"

The nurse shook her head. "Dean's girlfriend was here for a few minutes. I'll go ask where they went." She moved to the door. "Probably downstairs for some bad coffee."

Stuart followed. Not just because he didn't want to look at Brad's beaten face and know he was at least partially to blame for what his friend had gone through. But also because Stuart had been shot a few weeks ago. The time he'd spent here in the hospital recuperating hadn't been his best. There was a nurse who worked the night shift who'd, in the end, refused to treat him even though he'd apologized—and Dean had explained the particulars of his trauma.

Unlike Kaylee, who had suffered multiple times because of him and still talked to him about grace. Still looked at him like he could solve her problems. As though he was some kind of knight in shining armor. It was hokey, and probably cliché now. Women these days don't want to be rescued. But it was the way Stuart was built. And he thought Kaylee just might be perfect for him.

Which was why he'd walked away to make sure the flash drive and those men would be dealt with.

So he'd be free to make of this thing between him and Kaylee whatever it could be.

Because, if she thought there was something in him that was worth taking the time to get to know, worth caring about, then she might be right. Then again, she could just not know him well enough. She didn't know she was wrong. Or she only thought she knew him—the man he wanted to be.

Stuart would find her. Finish this. Then figure out which it was.

A sense of urgency filled him. He didn't know where it came from, but Stuart didn't intend to dismiss it.

He stepped out of the room and looked both directions.

The nurse spoke with the other nurse down the hall. Behind the desk, the one who'd checked him in, shook her head. She looked like she wanted to say something to him, so he moved closer.

"I thought you were the one coming here to watch Brad since Dean left to follow after Kaylee."

"What does that mean?"

"The one watching the door."

"No," Stuart shook his head. "The 'followed after' part."

"Oh," the nurse said. "She ran off that way, and he chased after her."

"Call security. Tell them to put a guard outside Brad's room. No one goes in or out without first informing Sergeant Basuto at Last Chance PD."

Stuart raced the direction she'd pointed to the end of the hall. Not where the elevators were. Just more rooms…and a stairwell.

He glanced around. Dean had chased after her. But where had Kaylee run off to? This made no sense.

The stairwell door was slightly ajar. Strange, because it was a heavy fire door meant to click closed itself with little assistance.

A brown shoe was wedged between the door and frame. Stuart pushed on it but encountered resistance.

Stuart shoved far enough he could peer around the door. "Dean!"

His friend stirred. Stuart pushed more on the door, knowing he was shoving it into his friend's body, but wiggled through the small gap and moved to crouch by him. "What happened?" He gently, but firmly, shook Dean's shoulders. "Where's Kaylee?"

Dean blew out a breath, his eyes were glassy. What had he been hit with? He said, "Kay..." Then managed to get out the words, "...took her."

The world around Stuart turned a revolution and made him want to throw up. He grabbed the door handle, pulled it open, and yelled, "Dean needs help!"

He saw the nurses react, let go, and race down the stairs. The direction Dean had pointed when he said those two words that changed everything.

Took her.

Who? The men who'd been in the helicopter? But the team was after them. Someone else? He had no idea. It didn't matter. He was going to get her back and there would be a severe price to pay if anyone got in his way.

One floor from the parking lot, he stumbled over two concrete steps and rolled his ankle. Stuart caught himself on the rail and managed to keep from going down. He stumbled again across the landing and shoved at the bar on the EXIT door, pulled the gun from the back of his belt, and scanned the parking lot.

No Kaylee.

He turned back to the stairwell and pushed the door open. A cell phone lay on the ground by the wall. He grabbed it and opened the door.

"Stuart!" Dean's voice rang down the stairwell. He didn't sound healthy, or happy.

When he got back to his friend, Dean was on his feet. "You okay?"

Dean shook his head. "She ran off. He was in here."

"Who?"

"I don't know. Didn't see his face." Dean's skin was sticky, his hairline damp. Eyes red.

The nurse shifted her weight. "We need to check you out."

Dean shook his head. "I'm okay." He reached for the sleeve of his shirt and tugged it up. On the outside of his arm was a red dot.

"We need access to the security footage. Find out what happened."

"He stunned me." Dean worked his jaw side to side like he'd been punched. "She ran through the door, and I followed. The second I stepped through? Zap. While I was fighting off the voltage, he stuck a needle in my arm. Took Kaylee down the stairs and left me here."

"Any idea how long you were out?"

That at least would tell them how much of a head start this person had.

Dean looked at his watch. "Maybe fifteen minutes."

"And you came around?" The nurse clasped her fingers around his wrist and stared at her watch. "That's impressive."

Stuart said, "Any idea what he hit you with?"

"How could he know that," the nurse asked, "unless he was told?"

"Ma'am, with all due respect, some drugs you can just tell. Get hit with something enough times, you come to know how it works on you."

Dean said, "I don't know what it was, but I'm not sure it was for me. Probably it was to knock out Kaylee, and then he realized he'd have to put me down if he wanted her. Which explains why it didn't put me out for longer."

"Stun gun. Quieter and less mess than a pistol." Stuart said, "Let's go talk to the security guard."

They strode down the hall to the elevator.

The nurse went behind her desk. "First floor. I'll call ahead so the head of security knows to expect you."

Stuart said, "Thank you." Even though the comment had been more for Dean than for him, he was still grateful.

They double timed it to the elevator and hit the button to head down to the first floor. Stuart opened the phone.

"Is that your flip phone?"

"I found this on the ground, bottom of the stairwell." He scrolled through to messages and saw the thread. "This is them."

He showed Dean the conversation and said, "Has to be Kaylee. They want the flash drive."

"That has to be why she ran out. But who took her?" Dean said, "This doesn't say anything about extraction, just that she gets the flash drive and contacts them for instructions."

"Zander needs to know she might show up." Stuart didn't want to believe she had known she'd get taken, or that Dean would be hurt. "They threatened to blow up all these buildings?"

She was probably so scared. Now she was gone. Taken.

By them, or someone else?

"We'll get her back."

Stuart ignored his friend. He didn't like false hope, and there was no point talking around and around about this when they needed more information. Dean called Zander, and Stuart went into the security office. The guard had to call Basuto for confirmation, and Stuart spent far longer than he wanted explaining what'd happened, but finally, the guard showed him the footage.

He watched the closed stairwell door in the parking lot as the guard wound it back looking for Kaylee's exit.

"Maybe they didn't even come out this way. Could be they got off on a different floor, and they're still in the hospital." The guard started to twist in his seat.

So what if he didn't believe there had been a kidnapping. Yes, hospitals had good security. But these people weren't your average small-town threat.

The door opened.

"There." Stuart pointed at the screen. The image was black and white and seriously grainy. "That's her."

Kaylee stepped out of the door, led by a man. Shorter than her, but only an inch or so. Suit. Stocky. A frazzled expression on his face.

And a gun pointed at her.

He said something, and she stumbled forward.

Stuart pointed at the screen. "Send this footage to Sergeant Basuto," and then he stepped back into the hallway where Dean was still on the phone.

"One sec."

Stuart said, "Silas Nigelson was the man who took Kaylee."

Dean blanched. "The bank manager? That's who got the drop on me." His focus shifted to the phone call and he said, "Okay." Dean lowered the cell phone and put it on speaker. "Go ahead."

"You said it was Nigelson?"

Stuart answered, "Held a gun on Kaylee. She dropped the phone, and he shoved her into the parking lot."

"He isn't working with these guys," Zander said. "He's on his own."

"Then he's going to ruin everything. They want her to get them the flash drive."

"They'll destroy the town, but my guess is Nigelson doesn't care. He probably wants it for himself."

Dean shook his head. "That was just Trina, wasn't it?"

Zander said, "I'm beginning to think she might've been right about him."

"That he's a Russian agent? That's nuts." Stuart said, "More likely he's another one of those crazy founders." But was that the point right now? "Either way we need to know where he went."

It was his only hope of getting Kaylee back.

Twenty-six

"You can't be kidnapping me! They're going to blow up the town!"

Silas Nigelson drove the car. Kaylee had been shoved into the front passenger seat, her hands bound with what looked like a wire. Too tight for her to even separate her wrists, let alone have any hope of breaking free.

"Why are you doing this?" She practically screamed the question at him. "I dropped the phone, or I'd show you."

"What phone?" He drove, barely distracted by her. Intent on the road and his thoughts, Silas barely spared her a single glance marred by his furrowed brow.

"The one Brad had on him when they threw him out of the helicopter. They texted me. They'll start blowing up buildings in town unless I get them the flash drive."

And she'd dropped it. *Why did you do that?* Aside from the fact someone could find it and realize, at least in part, what had happened. It could have been a subconscious cry for help. But she

180

was also pretty sure the cell phone had just slipped out of her hand in the heat of the moment when Silas had shoved her.

"Forget about the phone. That doesn't matter now."

"Is Dean dead? Did you kill him?" Kaylee didn't want to think about how awful that would be for Ellie and the whole town, losing him. Dean was a force for good. He'd saved so many lives, no one could keep count anymore. "What was in that syringe?"

She'd tried to stop Silas from jabbing Dean with it, but he'd shoved her against the wall. She had slammed her head, and before the sparks could clear, he was tossing the syringe down the stairs.

Silas jerked the wheel to the side and turned a corner. She slammed against the door, and he said, "It was supposed to be for you, but you can't do anything without drawing unneeded attention to yourself. I had to improvise."

"You were going to knock me out." Realization dawned, and with it, a shudder of cold fear moved through her.

"Will you shut up?" He shifted like he was going to hit her.

Kaylee flinched, but he never made contact. She pressed her lips together and tears filled her eyes.

It was like the night she and her parents had faced down that gunman all over again. Cold fear. Paralyzing terror that didn't let go. She'd thought she could withstand so much more now. But the surprise was long gone.

Now she was back to just being scared.

"What do—"

"*Shut up*," he roared. "You don't have to keep talking. Just give me a minute to think."

"Sorry." She poured as much frustration and sarcasm into the word as she possibly could. "I can't believe I've been *so* inconsiderate. How shameful of me."

Silas swung out his arm. She braced for the smack she knew was coming, and tried to lean her head away from him.

Instead of hitting her, he grabbed the back of her neck and slammed her face onto the front of the dash.

Out cold.

Kaylee didn't know how long it had been when she blinked, her eyes adjusting to her new surroundings. The realization that she was awake again slowly spread into her consciousness. Her entire face felt like she'd walked headfirst into a brick wall. She moaned at the pain and tried to shift.

Her movement was restricted. Her hands still bound by the wire and now tied to a pipe. Her body lay awkwardly. Any movement shot pain through her head, and when she licked her lips it tasted funny. Like blood.

A moan escaped her lips. She straightened her legs and hauled her upper body up to lean against the wall. Bare drywall. The floor was dusty, and there was a half-used package of rolled insulation on the other side of the room.

Above her shoulder was a sink. Toilet. Pipes stuck out of the floor in the corner—plumbing for a bathtub?

Where was she? Some kind of abandoned building, apartment, or house? Paper blinds had been stuck up to cover the window, so she couldn't see out. For all she knew, she wasn't even in town anymore.

The door to the room was shut. She wondered if it had also been locked. But it wasn't like she could check since she'd been secured to this pipe. Would she die here, her body discovered by her friends at the police department? She'd be another case number. A reason for them to lose control, grieving but still having to do their jobs anyway.

Ignoring the pain in her face, Kaylee tugged on the pipe with her hands. The cord was tied around the back of it, the knot tight, and she was too close for her fingers to twist and try to untie it. It didn't budge. She wasn't going to be able to get out of this herself.

She breathed through clenched teeth, able to smell the wetness streaming from a knot on her temple. It was on her shirt as well.

Kaylee looked down. Blood had streamed onto her shirt front.

She gasped and let out a terrible-sounding noise. *No. Don't cry.* But it happened anyway, whether she liked it or not. Kaylee had to let out the emotion. Purge it from her body.

Finally, the emotion subsided, and then she cried because the crying made her head hurt even more.

She leaned back against the wall. "Silas!" She called his name several times.

He never came.

Exhausted, Kaylee sagged down farther. Those men who'd held her brother weren't going to get the flash drive. She couldn't save innocent people in Last Chance from being killed, because she hadn't gotten it from…

Where, was the flash drive?

She tried to remember what Stuart said he'd done with it but couldn't remember for sure. Zander? Or Ted? Maybe Basuto had it.

And those men would storm the police station as the bikers had. *What a nightmare that was.* She'd ducked and cowered. Tried to pretend she was strong.

One of the bikers had looked at her, and she'd seen compassion on his face. As though he understood her reaction. Then he'd walked away to deal with his trigger-happy friend. It had been one of the worst days of Kaylee's life.

But not number one.

Nothing would overshadow the terrible preeminence of the day her parents were killed. In her mind, there was nothing worse, and there never would be. Or that was the fear talking. She didn't have anything to lose as bad as that—even if Brad's life was in danger. Her parents…for her, that was the ultimate in loss, and she'd faced it.

Never again would she hold onto something that closely, only to lose it.

Was that what she'd been doing? Pushing everyone away, thinking it was for the best so she would be safe behind her peace-of-mind bubble. Thinking she was protecting herself. Living a happy, closed life that meant she didn't allow anyone in.

Kaylee shut her eyes.

She needed Silas to come in here so she could explain to him how the town was in danger. That the threat to the town was bigger than whatever he wanted. He had to understand its greater importance or nothing could be put right. He should never have taken her. Not that he could've known she was about to leave and make a trade—save the people of this town—but his selfishness could cost lives.

"Silas!" She screamed his name over and over again. "Don't leave me in here! What's happening?" She'd trusted him once. Had respected him as her boss, the way she'd appreciated having Trina as a friend.

What a joke that had turned out to be.

She didn't care why he was doing it. Only that he'd realize the foolishness and help her to put things right.

Finally, the door opened. Silas had a phone to his ear, displeasure written across his face. "That's what I'm doing." He paused. "There's no need for you to get all high and mighty. It's too late for that."

He ended the call.

She wanted him to come close enough she could kick him, but he stayed across the room. Maybe that was for the best. Would she be able to attack him and take him down, or would she only fail miserably and end up in an even worse situation?

This man was nothing like the person she thought she'd known.

Both he and Trina had concealed the truth. And she'd fallen for it like a chump.

But he still needed to understand the threat here. "There are men in town. People Stuart used to work with, and they want the flash drive to save their butts—"

He lifted a gun. "Quiet. You don't need to worry about that now. All you need to be concerned with is sitting in here. I'll trade you for the flash drive and be on my way."

"Why are you doing this?" Kaylee didn't want people to die. Not if there was any way for her to do something about it.

Instead of answering, he smiled. There was nothing funny about it, just cold humor he already knew no one else would understand. "Do you know how long I've been waiting around for something big enough to come along? Now I have a shot at buying my way back home. You think I'm going to let *anything* ruin that?"

"People will die."

Silas shrugged one shoulder. "This whole town can burn to the ground. I just want my ticket out."

Her stomach rolled over. "Who are you?"

"Don't worry about me, Kaylee." Silas stared down the gun at her. "Stuart will trade you for the flash drive, and I'll be gone before he finds you."

Trade her? "He…you can't…"

Her thoughts spun like a dryer, flip flopping until she could make sense of nothing. Silas thought Stuart was going to give him the flash drive in exchange for her life? He wouldn't do that. There was nothing more important than getting justice for him and Brad. Stuart wanted to put the wrong right again. There was no stopping him.

He would never give that up. Not even for Kaylee.

"Don't do this. Please, Silas. Don't put people at risk like this."

He turned to the door, dismissing her. "Nothing is going to stop me."

The sound, when he closed the door, echoed in the hollow room. Kaylee shut her eyes, squeezing them tight until it caused an answering throb in her temples.

She hissed an inhale through clenched teeth. Silas was crazy if he thought he'd be able to get the flash drive. Too many people guarded it. More wanted to get their hands on it. He wouldn't be able to overpower them all.

This was insane.

And why had she been dragged into the middle of it again?

Because he thought Stuart cared enough about her that he would value her life more highly than justice, or his freedom. Kaylee didn't even know if he did care about her that much. He certainly hadn't told her, so she couldn't know for sure. Maybe the basic value of life anyone had—not wanting an innocent to die. But his whole reason for being in Last Chance was to get that flash drive.

He wasn't going to give it up. Kaylee knew he would never be free if he didn't get the evidence to the right person. And he deserved to be free.

Just like the people in this town deserved to live.

Twenty-seven

Stuart hit the button and hung up the phone. "Silas wants the flash drive in exchange for Kaylee."

The men standing around him weren't at all surprised. Zander sat on the edge of an unoccupied desk. Basuto ran his hands down his face, and Tate reached over to squeeze the back of his fiancé's neck. Savannah's lips pressed into a thin line.

"I'm not qualified for this, but I'm still taking point on a kidnapping involving a woman who works with us." Basuto stared him down. "We don't go renegade." He turned to Tate. "Call the FBI?"

Tate nodded. "Good idea." He moved away while sliding out his phone, probably to call his brother-in-law.

Basuto spun back to him. "Did he say where?"

"The old train station. I'm supposed to come alone and bring the flash drive. When he verifies its contents, he'll tell me where to find Kaylee."

Zander shook his head.

Basuto didn't look much happier.

Stuart said, "I don't plan on waiting that long. I want to get her back now."

Detective Wilcox leaned back in her chair. "Hmm."

Basuto said, "What are you thinking, Savannah?"

"We could go, set up now. But Nigelson could have eyes on the train station, and maybe that's why he picked it. So that our commotion would alert him to what's going on."

"I like the idea of an ambush." Basuto asked, "Any indication he's working with anyone else?"

"Other than Trina?" Stuart asked. "No, and we don't know that they're level with each other. Could be she'll jump to betray him, or she'll spin us a line that has us chasing our tails, and then we lose Kaylee because we were too late."

He didn't like any of those ideas. Zander shot him a commiserating look. Stuart didn't need camaraderie now, just as he'd never had it before. Brad was his friend and colleague. They had worked together some, but they hadn't been partners. Stuart never knew what the mission would be. And he never knew if he'd be alone, targeting someone, or working with them.

It was why he'd kept Brad at arm's length. Until they were captured together, and he started to care about the outcome. For both of them.

Emotions weren't good. They only compromised his judgment and made him care too much when what he needed was logic. Logic was what would get Kaylee back and enable him to keep hold of the flash drive for the sake of justice. Justice, and making sure both he and Brad—and Kaylee as well—got to live the rest of their lives in peace.

There would be time for emotions later.

"I want to talk to Trina." Stuart asked Savannah, "Can you take the train station, work with Basuto, and make a plan for grabbing Silas if it comes to that?" He'd rather it didn't, but if he couldn't find Kaylee in time, they would need a Plan B.

Basuto didn't look especially happy but nodded his approval to the detective.

She got up, grabbed her backpack, and strode out.

Stuart turned to Zander. "You and Ted have the flash drive. After I talk to Trina, I'm going to get Kaylee."

Zander said, "When this is done, we need to sit Ted down and make him talk."

"Why?"

"Something's up." Zander shrugged. "He claims he's too busy to talk about it."

"But he's been using that excuse for three months now."

Zander nodded.

Basuto shifted his weight. "One problem at a time?" When they both nodded, the sergeant said, "Conroy needs to get back to work as soon as he can."

Stuart figured the police chief felt the same way, and that was why he didn't say anything but, "Trina?"

"So long as your conversation is in English."

Zander said, "I'll observe with you, Sergeant. If there's any Russian, I'll translate."

Basuto glanced between Stuart and Zander. "Does everyone except me speak Russian?"

Stuart shrugged.

"Let's go." Zander pushed off the desk and stood. "I don't want to leave Ted by himself with those files much longer."

Basuto had them wait in the observation room while he brought Trina in. She looked like a cat locked in a crate who just knew something horrible was about to happen. In a second, the claws would be out, and she would be slashing away. It was clear Basuto had no intention of getting cut.

When Stuart walked in and shut the door so that it was just the two of them—with Zander and Basuto watching through the glass—he didn't move to the table. She was cuffed to a ring on the surface. She didn't look at him. Her hair fell to the sides of her face, disguising her expression.

As he walked to the table, her dark eyes tracked him.

He decided to lean against the wall beside the glass so Zander and Basuto had a clear view of her. The fact it was out of spitting range was a huge bonus.

"They're outsourcing interrogations now? Seems strange one of my *victims* is here to take my statement."

Stuart shook his head. "I'm not here about you terrorizing Kaylee. Though, we'll be talking about that. Rest assured."

She flashed a grin of white teeth in her haggard expression. "Can't wait."

"You said your dad is Russian."

"*Da.*"

"Nice. Really sells it." He said, "Too bad just any 'ol person can learn any language on an app. Doesn't mean your heritage is any different, regardless of how well you sell it."

He was more interested in the fact she'd told him her dad taught her how to kill. How to *hide.* That was the information he needed right now. Namely, where Silas would have taken Kaylee to wait out the deal. A place no one would be able to find her.

"Yeah." Trina shrugged one shoulder. "He's probably just one of those founders. Not a foreign intelligence agent hiding here for years. Because the fact none of y'all noticed would be pretty shameful, right?"

"Not if he's good." Stuart *would* be irritated he hadn't noticed something about the old man, but it wasn't like he'd have guessed, "Russian sleeper agent." If that was what Silas really was. He said, "I wasn't looking for him. In case you haven't noticed, I've got kind of a lot on my plate right now."

"Poor you. Least you're not in jail."

"They offer you a deal yet—some kind of break in sentencing in exchange for cooperation?"

"Why? You gonna do that?"

"I have no authorization to do so." He figured Basuto was freaking out behind the glass. "I'm not a cop or a prosecutor. I'm just a guy who needs information, and you're a woman with nothing to lose who needs to look good in front of the judge."

"Maybe I'll go for the insanity defense. I could pull off crazy."

Stuart winced just thinking about it. "Not a good long-term plan. Unlike telling me what I want to know. That could get you clout with the judge, right?"

"Cause you're the upstanding citizen who's going to put in a good word for me?" She huffed. "You're as bad as him. Pretending to be someone you're not, trying to fool everyone. Guess what? He does it better."

"And he taught you everything he knows?"

"Doubtful," she scoffed. "No one could learn all that. The way he fooled them all in Vietnam, got in with that squad as one of them. A Last Chance boy. Came back here and helped them set up the town. No one even knew who he was."

"So why is he still here? And why does he want the flash drive."

Trina sniffed. "Who cares? That was like…decades ago? It's a new millennium. No one cares about the Cold War or Russian agents. Everyone's like, dead and stuff." She shrugged. "Is it even a thing anymore? I don't know." She shot him a look, as though she doubted his intelligence.

"You'd be surprised what I know."

"Then why are you asking me questions, Mr. Know-It-All."

"Because you have the chance to be helpful," he said. "And the chance to repair some of the damage you did to Kaylee. Maybe even find a way to get her to forgive you for destroying her sense of safety."

Trina shook her head.

"You don't want to know why I'm asking?"

She said nothing.

"What does he want the flash drive for? Why is he so desperate to get it?"

She studied him. "What did he do?"

"Tell me why he'd need the flash drive. You said he's been here since the beginning of Last Chance. One of the founders, right?"

She nodded.

"That means he hasn't worked in covert intelligence that whole time, or his absence would have been noted." There was nothing in town he could have been reporting back on. Vietnam, Stuart believed. But now the Russian sleeper agent was nothing but an old man. "What does he want?"

"Retirement."

"He doesn't have enough money from the bank? I figured he was loaded."

"He wants to *retire*." Trina leaned forward across the table. "To not be stuck here in this small-town dump, wasting his life away with stupid *work* no one cares about."

"He wants to go home." Stuart said, "And he's taking you with him?"

She shrugged. "As great as *Russia* sounds, I'd rather take the money and move to LA. Or New York. Somewhere better than here."

"Cross your fingers. You could get a federal sentence that lands you in a California prison."

She blinked, lighting up a fraction. As though that sounded preferable to living as a free woman in Last Chance.

Stuart did *not* understand women. He figured he never would.

He put the pieces together. "He's out of favor, and the flash drive will buy him a way back into Russia so he can live out his days in the motherland."

"*Da.*"

Stuart switched to Russian, saying, "Where would he stash Kaylee while he made the deal with me to trade her for the flash drive?"

She swallowed, her throat bobbing. Now she was going to feel bad that a good woman was in danger?

"We both know she doesn't deserve this. You dragged her in anyway, and it was sloppy work. Now you're here. You think Dad is going to come for you when he buys his freedom? You've been scraped off. A loose end he no longer has to worry about."

"Like it's going to work?" She rolled her eyes, using English again to say, "Stupid old man with his stupid plan. Everyone he worked with is dead by now. There's no one left."

Stuart moved to lean his hip on the table, switching back to English as well. "Where would he keep Kaylee?"

"What an idiot, right? He drags me into this, tells me we can make millions and get out from under this mountain of debt. Maybe I'm the idiot for believing him. This was probably his plan all along."

"Trina."

"What?"

"Focus. I don't have much time."

She said, "What do I care what he's doing? I've been scraped off. Remember?"

"Where would he keep Kaylee?"

She huffed.

Stuart grabbed the back of her head, turned it, and slammed her cheek on the table, holding her head there so she couldn't move. He leaned close. "Where. Would. He. Keep. Kaylee, Trina? Tell me now or this situation you're in will start to look like Christmas morning in comparison to what will happen next."

One way or another, he was going to get an answer. She didn't want to look as though she'd given anything up? That was fine with him. But he was going to rescue Kaylee.

Finally, she whispered to him.

"Let her go." Basuto pulled him away from Trina. He shoved Stuart toward the door, where he, in turn, slammed into Zander. "Get out of here. You're done."

"Fine." Stuart strode to the door, pulling out his phone so he could look up the address Trina had just given him.

Twenty-eight

The door swung open. Silas strode in, a jacket on. Under his arm, she spotted a handgun in a holster.

Kaylee flinched at the sight of it. Why, now? She didn't know. Trina had pointed one at her. The cops she worked with wore them on their hips. Somehow, on Silas, it seemed so menacing.

"Looks like your boy came through."

"W-what?" She blinked, trying to remember what he was talking about. "Stuart?"

He cut the cord that secured her to the sink pipe and grasped her bicep in a punishing grip, his fingers like a vice. "Let's go. Leland is going to trade you for the flash drive. Everyone gets what they want, and you go home."

She'd seen him reading that book about successful people at his desk. Was that what this was, a way for everyone to win? Silas was on a path to get exactly what he wanted under the guise of pleasing everyone else so that he could get away with it. And then, before anyone would be able to put two and two together and figure out what had happened, he would be long gone.

That was the worst thing she could think of.

"Everyone wins except Stuart." He would have nothing. Not even the ability to make his own choices for the rest of his life. "Don't do this. The others who are here, men who kidnap and torture, will kill people over this. Innocent people. That can't be what you want. You'll never escape suspicion after terrorist attacks occur in town."

"Obviously Stuart would rather have you than the information on that flash drive, so we're making a deal." He studied her, looking her up and then down. "I can see why. Not that it surprises me."

Her stomach revolted. This whole thing surprised Kaylee plenty, not the least the fact Silas was leering at her. Stuart was really going to make the trade with him? That made no sense. He shouldn't be exchanging her for the flash drive. Not when that meant he lost his shot at a safe, free future.

He was giving up everything, and she wasn't even worth it. This was awful. Stuart wouldn't take long to realize what a mistake he'd made. Her life in exchange for his?

Maybe he only wanted to repay the friendship Brad had shown him. A way to return the favor her brother had done him. No, she didn't want him to save her that way either.

Ugh. Her thoughts and emotions were all mixed up. She was making no sense. She understood why he felt it was his responsibility to do such a thing, and she could appreciate it, but still didn't want him to give up the very thing he'd come here to find.

Kaylee knew what she had to do.

Silas turned to haul her to the door, intent on the trade. Not if she could help it, he wasn't. No way.

She had been scared for too long.

Kaylee lifted her foot and slammed it into the back of his knee. She reached into his jacket for his gun, but he brought his arm down too soon. Their forearms struck. She cried out as the bone reverberated in her arm.

The gun fell to the floor. She dove for it, desperate to grasp it in her hands.

So she could kill him?

Kaylee didn't know if she could do it.

Silas slammed his elbow into the back of her shoulder. Kaylee cried out and fell to her hands and knees, her fingers twisted awkwardly under her palms.

He reached beside her and picked up the gun. "No more games. We're going."

She wasn't going to do him any favors. She stayed right where she was. Kaylee wanted to drag this out as much as possible with the hope that Stuart would have more time to realize the truth and change his mind. He had to be doubting whether she was worth gambling with his future. *Please, Lord. Don't let him do this.*

She knew how much the truth being revealed meant to him. How much he deserved to find peace and healing. Kaylee was content with her quiet life. Her safe and peaceful existence had been perfectly fine for years. The last few months, since the package arrived, had been an anomaly. A detour in her life's story that would be put to rights soon enough. Then everything would go back to normal, or some new kind of normal that had to be better than what she'd had before.

But if Stuart gave up the flash drive to Silas Nigelson and whatever his crazy self wanted to do with it, things would all be over. Not better. Ever. Much worse than anything she could imagine. The fallout for them would be catastrophic. No peace. No safety. Stuart and Brad would have to live their lives on the run, and she would always be a weakness for them. A vulnerability for their enemies to exploit.

"I said, we're going." Silas squeezed the tendon in her upper arm. "So quit messing around and move. This is your ticket out of here. *Both* of our tickets."

She winced as Silas hauled her to her feet. Her fingers hurt. Her entire body ached, bruised, and ready to collapse. But she managed to stay standing. She wanted to go to sleep in her nice comfy bed—not leaning against a wall where she couldn't relax.

And the last hour hadn't exactly been relaxing, expecting to be murdered like her parents at any second.

He dragged her to the hall now and then down a long corridor that looked like an abandoned office building that had been left to the elements. The window at the end had been smashed out and cool night air breezed in to ruffle her hair against her face. He continued to haul her toward the stairs and down through a lobby area, to a pair of glass doors. He used an app on his phone to unlock and then relock the doors, securing the building behind him.

A rundown office building, the business having gone bankrupt. Repossessed by the bank.

"Why are you doing this? Do people's lives mean nothing to you but an asset to be traded for whatever you want?"

He chuckled. "Nobility. How naïve." Silas beeped the button on his car keys, and the trunk popped open. "Get in."

"No. And nobility isn't being naïve. It's the best of who people are, and what they can do. Why would that not be *exactly* what I want to be known for?"

After all, she'd been scared for so long. Why not take a chance now and be something even better? Go after the right thing. The best thing. Despite whatever was happening, she could work for the good of others. To save those who didn't even know they needed saving.

"You think being stubborn is going to faze me?" The corner of his mouth curled up. "I've dealt with much more tenacious companions than you."

"Companions?" What a strange way to phrase it. That wasn't what she represented here. "You kidnapped me."

"To help me solve a problem."

That sounded far too ominous. She couldn't help but think of the young woman whose file she had been reading for days now. A woman she had identified with. Now, more than ever, she understood what it felt like to be at the mercy of an abductor.

Kaylee's mind completed the process of putting the pieces together. "Everything Trina did, it was for you."

He barely acknowledged her comment.

"How many other girls have you tied up in that building?"

"Do not ask questions you don't really want answers to."

That was fair. Still, if this was the last chance anyone had to ask him about it, then Kaylee would get to the bottom of what had happened. "The girl who went missing right after I moved here, the one who was never found. Did she solve a problem for you as well? Trina had her necklace. She was wearing it. Because of you?"

Surely that was a stretch. However, the timing could be off. Trina might have been away, still at college, when the woman went missing. Kaylee hadn't met Trina until later. That meant if anyone in their family had met her, it was likely this man.

The skin around his eyes crinkled in the yellow of the street lights that cast the rest of him in shadow. "I haven't thought of her in years. There have been so many. Why quibble over one?"

Grief rolled over her like a wave. "You killed the girl, and then Trina kept the memento. That, or you gave it to her. Is that what happened?"

"I require a particular kind of entertainment." He shoved her toward the open trunk. "West keeps me supplied now, but years ago I had to find my own. Don't worry. I never leave a mess." He took a half step, moving closer to her. "It's a shame we're on a timeline." Silas reached up and patted her cheek. "Shame."

Yet more of himself that he'd hidden from her. Turned out she knew nothing about him or Trina. He had successfully lied about all of it. A man she had respected. Admired, even. Not only was he a crooked bank manager who utilized repossessed buildings for his own use, but he was a foreign agent.

She backed up. Her legs hit the car, and she froze. There was no way she wanted to be shut up in the trunk. But staying out here with Silas Nigelson and his entertainment ideas? No. That wasn't going to be any better.

He shoved her. Kaylee stumbled backward, hit the edge of the trunk with her shoulder blades. He shoved at her again, and she fell in. Silas reached down with a dark object and hit her with the same stun gun he'd used on Dean.

It crackled.

That was all Kaylee needed to scramble away from it. She didn't want it touching her when she was already in enough pain.

He slammed the lid shut.

She heard a door open and then close. Then the engine turned on. It rumbled under her cheek as she lay in the back of the car.

When it opened, she would see Stuart. She'd be able to ask him why he was throwing away his freedom. Or he wouldn't come, and she could rest knowing he had made the right decision.

She just didn't want to be left with disgusting Silas.

The car stopped.

Two minutes later, the silence was broken by a gunshot. Her whole body flinched and pain throbbed in her face.

The trunk flung open. Two men stood over her and neither was familiar. Words died in her throat. They dragged her out and her legs gave way. Neither man helped her up from the ground, so she just slumped onto the asphalt, trying to hold herself up.

When she finally got her bearings about her, she said, "What's going on?" and looked around to see where she was. The library was across the street. In the yellow light of the parking lot street lights, she could see the freestanding return bin. Bigger than a wheeled trash can and twice as wide. It was the drive-thru spot to drop in finished books.

"Got it?" One man spoke, but she didn't think he was talking to her.

She glanced at them. Uniforms and huge guns. They wore ball caps and vests—maybe bulletproof ones. Professionals who knew exactly what they were doing.

And they'd killed Silas.

"Yep. Let's go."

They both shifted. Kaylee was hauled to her feet, realizing, as she straightened her legs and forced them to hold her up, that the situation had gone from bad to worse. Silas should have given her to Stuart. These men had interrupted, and Stuart wasn't here. Of course, he shouldn't trade his future for her.

She couldn't let that happen.

They shoved her forward. Hot anger rolled through Kaylee, energizing her muscles. She allowed it to fuel her strength as she waited for precisely the right moment, then jerked away from them and sprinted. No more. She wasn't going to be jerked around anymore.

Gunshots peppered the ground around her.

Kaylee screamed, flinging her bound hands over her head as she ran across the street, out of sight and into the darkness, and crouched behind the return bin.

Twenty-nine

Stuart and Zander approached the front door. Two of Zander's guys—the third was with Dean, watching over Brad—went around back.

"Hold up." Zander lifted his free hand and made a fist.

Stuart said, "Security system?"

He didn't think Silas was here, though maybe he'd left Kaylee and gone somewhere else. The whole police department was on alert, expecting an attempted breach in an effort to steal the flash drive. Even Tate was there. It was all hands on deck right now.

Zander pulled out his phone and made a call. "Ted?" For the next minute he said only, "Yep," and, "Yes," and, "Copy," before hanging up. Zander looked up and addressed the group. "He said thirty seconds."

It wasn't long before a click sounded in the vicinity of the lock. Zander pulled the front door open, and they stepped in.

"Empty," Stuart said. "This whole place has been abandoned."

"Business went defunct. Bank repossessed the property." Zander stuck his head down the hall. "I think I know why."

Stuart had seen places like this the world over, covert buildings set up for sex trafficking operations. Each room was outfitted. The farther down the hall they walked, the worse the situation became. Until Stuart couldn't hold back his reaction.

"Yeah." Zander's gaze darkened. "But she's not here, and we have enough problems. This one is for the lieutenant and that detective."

"Mia and Savannah?"

"This stuff happening in their town? You think they're not going to be all-in, kicking doors down and arresting everyone involved."

Stuart nodded. "Okay, that's true." He headed for the stairs and climbed to the second floor. "Not so much activity up here."

This was the place Trina had told him Silas would bring Kaylee. Did that mean Trina knew about the women? Zander was right that they had enough problems, but that didn't diminish the fact a real-world problem had reached this small town. He was completely on board to get his hands on whoever ran this business and help take him down.

Way down.

Stuart didn't appreciate the court system nearly as much as he probably should. Not when it was much cleaner to take out the target himself—under orders, of course.

"Why do you have a murderous look on your face?"

Stuart shrugged, then continued to walk through the second floor.

"Anything?" The man at the end of the hall strode toward them.

Stuart shook his head. "Thanks for being here."

All his roommates had rallied around. Zander's team, Dean, and Ted. Stuart was overwhelmed by all the assistance they seemed perfectly happy to provide.

"Don't get all emotional on us now." Zander clapped him on the back of the shoulder.

Stuart moved away from them. No matter that they cared, he still didn't want them to see his despair. The team knew his trauma was a reality. They had enough PTSD of their own; they'd never judge him. But frustration still boiled in his stomach.

"Where are you?" Stuart whispered the question to an empty room. His eyes snagged on the sink in the corner and a cord that hung from it. Was this where she'd been kept?

"Stuart!"

He strode back to the hall. Zander had his phone to his ear. "We're moving out."

As they stampeded down the stairs and back out the front door, Zander explained, "Ted got into the security system. It's connected to a phone he thinks belongs to Silas Nigelson."

"He can get us a location?"

"He's working it." Zander climbed into the driver's seat of the car. Stuart got in the front, the other two in the back seat. A second after the engine came to life, the phone connected to the car with Bluetooth. "Can you hear me?"

Ted's voice came through the car speakers. "That's a good copy."

Zander shook his head. "You've been watching too much of that TV show."

Stuart needed them to get on with this. "Where is Nigelson?"

Ted said, "Highway 14, where it crosses Candlewood."

"By the library?"

"Yep. Traffic cameras are being a bear today, so I can't get a visual for you. But that's where the GPS on his phone says he is."

Stuart caught something in his tone and asked, "What is it?"

"I need to turn over the contents of his phone to Sergeant Basuto."

"Sex trafficking case?"

Ted was quiet for a second, "It's...he'll want to see all this." The younger man sounded like he wanted to be sick.

"One thing at a time," Zander said. "We get Silas, we get Kaylee. This team in town is in custody. The chief is getting better. Brad is alive. Life keeps going."

"Yeah, case in point," one of the guys in the backseat said. "The next thing pops up and has us all scrambling."

"True." Zander had his lead foot pressed to the floor. In response, the engine screamed as they hurtled around corners all the way to the library.

Stuart didn't care they'd probably die in this vehicle. At least, after they got to Silas Nigelson in one piece. After that, if Stuart slipped and the man ended up with a serious head injury, who was going to argue? Some people—those who targeted innocents just for profit—had it coming. And all of the men in this car were the kind who dished out that kind of comeuppance.

No one would debate that.

"There. Do you see?" Stuart sat up straighter in his seat, pointing to the dark shape in the road up ahead.

The car was stopped in the middle of the street. This time of night, no one had found it yet. They veered to the side of the road, and Stuart hopped out before Zander could even come to a complete stop.

Stuart made a beeline for the car. The trunk was open. No one else in sight.

"Over here."

Zander left the driver's door open and came over.

Stuart had his phone camera flashlight pointed at the ground. "I guess we found Silas."

He heard Ted blow out a breath through the car speaker. "I'll tell the Sergeant."

"We can't wait for them." Stuart couldn't afford that delay. "We're already behind these guys. If they took out Silas, then they also have Kaylee. So where are they? We need to find them."

The other guys had spread out.

Zander said, "If they have her, then they'll contact you."

Stuart circled the area like the others were doing. He glanced over to see where they might've gone, his eyes stopping on the library. If Kaylee had somehow managed to flee, that was where she would go—toward a familiar place.

One of the guys was still in view. The other had moved to where Stuart couldn't see him anymore.

He looked for impressions in the grass—any indication she might have run from the trunk. Where would she hide? Who'd killed Silas? Definitely not Kaylee. That meant someone else had done it, and that person probably then took her away from here.

Which meant this search was pointless.

He should be setting up a trace on his cell phone, waiting for a call. Or protecting the flash drive in person instead of leaving that to the cops.

What am I even doing? She was gone. Stuart hadn't been able to protect her. Now he had no idea who took her, or where she was. He'd failed. His problems had put her in danger, and would likely be the cause of her life ending.

And cost innocent people in Last Chance their lives, too.

Bombs. Helicopters. Who knew what they would do next?

The only thing he could be certain of was that he would give it all up to save Kaylee. Even the flash drive was up for discussion. He'd try to copy it before he turned it over to these men. But the fact was, it wasn't more important than Kaylee's life, or the chance at a safe and peaceful future. He owed Brad, and he owed her.

Stuart was so frustrated, he spun and kicked the stupid return bin. He kicked it for Kaylee. For his stupidity at letting her down. Even for people too lazy to get out of their cars and walk to the drop box by the door.

The impact reverberated up his leg, and the clang of his shoe against metal was loud.

A whimper from inside cut through the quiet after the horrible clanging subsided.

Stuart had already had his gun out and held it in front of him as he rounded the return bin and pulled the back open. Nothing.

He crouched and said, "Kaylee?"

"Stuart!" She launched from the inside and into his arms, nearly sending him back to a sitting position on the asphalt. He recovered his balance and stood, hauling her up and against him.

"It's really you." Her breath came in gasps. "I thought you were one those guys."

Her hands were bound. He pulled his pocket knife and cut her free, then traced the abrasion on her forehead. "There's blood on your face, but it doesn't look like you're bleeding now."

Kaylee wound her arms around him and snuggled close.

She didn't seem seriously injured, just shaken. And she was still standing? He doubted he'd be as together in the same situation, given all the stuff he had in his head. It made him wonder if Brad would be mentally steady when he woke up. Dean could help.

He dismissed the thoughts and focused on her. "They were here?"

She nodded, her face pressed against his shirt. "Ow. My face." She took a breath. "Silas was going to trade me to you for the flash drive, but they killed him. I tried to run, and they chased me." She glanced in the direction of Silas's deceased body and winced. "He wasn't a nice man."

He didn't want to talk about the dead guy. What he wanted to know was where the gunmen had gone.

"I know." Stuart gave her a squeeze, then put some space between them to try and clear his head of the distracting thoughts of having her body up against his. Not the time or the place. "I'm really glad I found you."

He wanted it to be more than that. A more memorable reunion, given everything they'd both been through. Even as far as maybe a kiss between them. And it was clear from the wide-eyed, mouth-open wonder on her face that she might feel the same way—even with the broken nose and all the dried blood on her face and neck that needed to be cleaned up.

Despite how she seemed to feel, there wasn't time for it. Not when this was far from over.

Stuart didn't want to lose the flash drive. But he would hand it over if it saved her.

"Thank you." She took a step toward him, lifted onto the balls of her feet, and kissed his cheek.

Everything in him stilled. He wanted to go for a long walk through the mountains around the town and maybe touch his cheek for a while. Draw the moment out while he was alone and just experience the memory of it, over and over. The feel of her warmth. Her softness.

"We should go, right?"

He nodded, trying to pull his thoughts back to reality. Stuart took her hand and turned back to the car. Zander stood guard. Stuart glanced around, looking for his teammates. "Where'd they go?"

Zander was completely still, his body at attention, and yet he didn't move. Still deep in thought, he murmured, "Following a hunch."

Stuart didn't like the sound of that. Or his friend's body language. "What's going on?"

He wanted to put Kaylee behind him. But what would he be defending her from?

Zander folded his arms and looked at Kaylee and Stuart, accusation in his eyes. "Which one of you sold us all out? That's the real question we should be asking. Because right now, we're surrounded by the very men my guys spotted planting explosives around the hospital. So I want to know what angle one of you played in order to skate out from under this."

Kaylee gaped. "You think we sold you out? What are you talking about?"

Stuart squeezed her arm. "He's talking about the fact we're surrounded."

He heard the movement then.

Seconds later, two gunmen approached from Stuart's flanks. Both had their weapons pointed at Kaylee.

Zander shot him a pointed look.

"I didn't do this." But it was too late to plead his innocence. Zander would never believe him.

Thirty

It was a trap. Kaylee glanced at Stuart, then at Zander, and finally at the two men in turn. Moving that much made her head throb. She wanted to go back to the hugging part of the reunion they'd just had. The fact he was the one who'd saved her.

He hadn't traded her for the flash drive. He'd rescued her instead.

Stuart reached across his body, creating a barrier with his arm before nudging her behind him. He had a gun. So did Zander. And yet, somehow, the two men approaching seemed much more formidable. Maybe it was the body armor. Or the looks on their faces.

"Edmond." Stuart glanced from the man on their right to the one on the left. "Martin."

"You know them?" Edmond and Martin were coming from opposite directions. Even the way they walked was menacing.

"Co-workers." Stuart said, "Brad trained both of them."

Zander lifted one eyebrow. "Not you?"

"I don't do teams."

"Could've fooled me."

Zander's comment confused her. Kaylee didn't know if it was supposed to be a compliment or a dig at something. None of this made any sense. She was so far out of her element, and she needed an ice pack.

"Give it up, Leland."

Stuart angled slightly toward the one he'd called Edmond. "Give up what? You're going to have to be more specific than that. It's been a long day."

Kaylee figured his comment was the understatement of the year.

Zander shifted very slightly. Out the corner of her eye she saw him reach back and crack the car door handle, disengaging the mechanism without actually opening the door. The interior light didn't even come on. That would've caused way too much attention in the dark of night.

Stuart braced. She felt it in his body despite the fact they weren't touching.

Immediately, she spotted the second the guy to her left noted Zander's movement. Kaylee stuck her hand on her hip. "What are you lookin' at?" She tried to sound as confident as someone she had only ever been in her dreams—one of those fierce ladies who seemed so put together and stylish. Kaylee pretended she was one of them. "What do you even want, anyway?"

If Zander was trying to do something, then she would support that even if meant their attention was on her.

They were trained. But that didn't rule her out as being useful.

"I've been tied up all day. I'm hungry." She was determined to continue her performance. "Can we wrap this up and get on with our lives?"

She saw the edge of a smile on Zander's face, though he said nothing and didn't draw attention to himself again.

Stuart said, "She's right. What do you want?"

"They want the flash drive." Kaylee figured he knew that. He must be purposely withholding what he knew to try and get them to share too much. Huh. She should probably back off and let him take the lead. Stuart was far more skilled than her, and if anyone was going to get them out of this situation, then it was likely him.

She pressed her lips together.

This did need to be over soon. Her emotions were so all over the place, she didn't know how to feel. She was exhausted. And hungry.

Edmond said, "Your friend here is free to go."

"No can do." Zander shook his head. "Not till I get my guys back."

"Oh. Those were your guys? So sorry."

Zander's whole body shifted. It was like he'd suddenly morphed into a guy ready an apex predator, though impressively relaxed. "What did you say?"

Kaylee glanced around. Where were the guys? Dead, or subdued as she'd been, or—? And weren't they professionals? How good were Edmond and Martin if they'd taken down guys of such high caliber? A shudder rolled through her. She could pretend to be a stylish, confident woman—with blood all down her front—but she was so far out of her league, it didn't even begin to sound like a joke.

Edmond chuckled. "Get me the flash drive, and you can have your guys back."

"No more bargains." Stuart's body stiffened. "This ends now." Stuart grabbed her other hand and held it. Why would he do that when he might need his hand free? She tried to wiggle her fingers from his.

"Give me the flash drive."

"And if I don't?"

Edmond lifted his gun and pointed it at her. "She dies first."

Stuart whipped her behind him, out of view of Edmond. She stumbled, aware the other guy, Martin, from where he was positioned to her left and in full view of her, could still kill her.

This was bad.

They were like the four points of a diamond, and the first to cross into the middle would get shot.

Stuart said, "The flash drive isn't here. We came here to find Kaylee, that's all."

Edmond was hidden from view, but he didn't sound pleased when he said, "We can all go get it. I'm sure the rest of my guys want to leave their mark on this town."

"I'm not leading you to it if you hurt anyone. I'll order *my* guy to destroy the flash drive before that happens."

She wondered if Stuart was talking about Ted, and whether or not he would follow through with that threat. Could be he had made a bunch of copies of the information found on the flash drive. If she'd been able to access it without the code word Stuart told her, she'd have done exactly that. Hidden a bunch of versions all over town. Sent one to a newspaper, one to the FBI, one to the White House. Everyone would've known who set up Brad and Stuart.

Take away the leverage.

Give these guys no reason to bother her—and no reason to leave her alive. *Okay, maybe not.* If she got out of this alive, she was going to find some books about survival. This face-off-with-each-other, guns-pointed-at-each-other, no one-wanting-to-make-the-first-move thing, was driving her crazy.

She was so nervous.

Her whole body shivered, and she didn't know if it was the night air or her nose or if it was because she just wanted someone to *do something* already. Brad would've shot someone by now. Effective, but not what she wanted to see. Hearing Silas get hit from the trunk had been bad enough. "I wouldn't do that if I were you." Edmond shifted, not nerves as such. Probably adrenaline.

She was certainly feeling it too. Now that she knew these trained men had the same issue with nerves, it made her feel better.

But it didn't get them out of this.

Zander's full focus was on Stuart. She wasn't sure that was wise until she saw a tiny nod of his chin. Barely a movement at all. She wouldn't have thought it meant anything…until he whipped his gun out and shot Martin.

And then Edmond also dropped to the ground, Stuart's gun reflexes sharp and in sync with Zander's. At the same moment, with both men down and her brain struggling to catch up with what had just happened, his free hand grasped hers tightly and flung her toward Zander. "Go."

She slammed into Zander, who shifted her against the car. He covered her with his body while she pulled the door all the way open.

"In. In." Zander crowded her against the car.

A gunshot went off. Stuart cried out. Zander fired a shot. She turned to see what had happened, but Zander shoved the top of her head down. "Go."

Boots pounded concrete in their direction.

Kaylee scrambled over the seat to the passenger side. Zander dove in, started the engine, and hit the gas. "Let's go, Leland!"

She peered out the side window. After a painfully long two seconds, the door swung open and Stuart hauled his body onto the backseat.

"Report in." Zander's yelled command made her flinch. He glanced over but said nothing. Just hit the gas and peeled out, turning the car in a wide arc. "Report in."

Someone running across the parking lot caught her attention. "Look out!"

Zander didn't slow, though. It was Martin, now back on his feet and lifting his hands, his gun pointed directly at them. "Get down!"

Automatic gunfire sprayed the front end of the car. Kaylee screamed. She ducked her head, covering it with her arms as the car swayed. She hit the door and her face brushed her knee. Pain sparked like fireworks had been let off right in front of her.

The car skidded and then a loud *thunk* sounded. They bumped over something—or someone.

But the tires never caught. They had no traction.

She looked up to find Zander desperately fighting with the steering wheel. He had blood on his shoulder. The windshield was shattered. She could barely see out.

"Hold on!"

Kaylee grasped the door handle. The car swerved, and the tires on the right side lifted off the ground, rolling them so far that the driver's side hit the pavement. Metal scraped across the ground. Zander flung about in his seat like a rag doll in the dryer.

Kaylee realized she was screaming and closed her mouth. She had to cough, and her nose thudded with pain to the rhythm of her heartbeat.

Seconds ticked by as the engine made that sound, smoking as it cooled. And then she heard more than one man roar. The car tipped and then slammed back down onto the ground, righted onto all fours by a group. They'd picked the whole thing up?

Edmond stood beside her door with blood on his arm, his gun pointed at her. He shifted his stance, only putting weight on one leg.

"Get out."

Kaylee shoved the door open. She twisted and set her feet on the floor and chanced a look at Stuart. He lay in the backseat, blood on his T-shirt by his left side. Eyes closed. Was he dead, or unconscious? "Stuart."

A huge hand with a punishing grip squeezed her arm, and she was hauled out of the car.

Kaylee stumbled but didn't go down. "People need to *stop doing that.*" She was sick of being everyone else's bargaining chip.

"Give me what I want, and I'm gone." Edmond held his gun loose in front of his body, like he had all the time in the world. Not at all like he'd just been in a gunfight.

She was never going to get away from him. Zander and Stuart were both out of commission. It would be up to her to finish this, and she had no clue what she was doing. All she had was her wits and her brain.

"Let's make a deal."

Edmond grinned. "Brad said you were somethin' special."

She lifted her chin. "You want the flash drive? I want you gone."

"That's not the mission."

If he was supposed to kill her, or Stuart, she figured he'd have already done it himself and then found the flash drive after the fact. While everyone was still reeling.

"What is?"

"You and Stuart come in. The bosses see both of you, and I get paid for that," Edmond said. "And I'll bring the flash drive as well when I deliver the two of you. Double payment."

"Why do they want us?" Why did he not need to bring in Brad, as well?

"Reconditioning."

Whatever it was, it sounded awful. "That's not going to happen."

"No? Brad seemed to think you could do it." Edmond tipped his head to the side. "You don't?"

"My brother—"

"He sold you out." Edmond shrugged. "His freedom, for you and Stuart and the drive. So get over it."

She stared at him. "He...what?"

Thirty-one

"Are you sure that's even going to work?" Stuart kept the words low, underneath his breath. Pretending to be unconscious in the backseat of the car—when what he really wanted to do was dive out and tackle Edmond—was infuriating.

"Yes." A second after Zander spoke, the cigarette lighter popped out. "Go."

They dove for the left side doors. Stuart prayed it would open instead of being smashed tight in a way the door wouldn't work. He had to kick it.

"What?"

Stuart ignored Edmond's exclamation. Zander already had the hot cigarette lighter in his hand, stretched out underneath the car. He touched it to the spilled gasoline that had puddled, trying to ignite the fumes. Inevitable, after a crash like they'd been in.

What Zander hadn't anticipated? Stuart was lying in the pool of gasoline. "Roll!"

Flames whipped across the surface of the liquid. Both of them rolled away from the car as heat gathered, and the whole car exploded.

The boom was deafening.

Stuart kept his gun close to his chest as the car flipped into the air by the sheer force of the fireball.

As soon as he saw Martin, he brought the weapon up and fired. Martin already had a gunshot wound in his thigh. He was limping now.

Stuart fired two rounds into Martin's bulletproof vest. The second bullet hit where he was not protected. Blood spurted from Martin's neck. He cried out and went down, bullets spraying in an arc from his gun.

Stuart scrambled to his feet. He rounded the car and spotted Edmond and Kaylee running toward a side street.

He chased after them, unwilling to allow Kaylee out of his sight again. That had happened far too many times already. They needed another deep conversation—this one about relationships. Specifically, theirs. After that, they'd both have the chance to rest and recuperate.

But not if Edmond took her away.

The only saving grace? Edmond still needed the flash drive.

And he still needed—

Two hundred pounds of muscle tackled Stuart to the ground. His chin hit the asphalt and he cried out. *Not good.* He rolled, kicked out, and found purchase on a shin. The man on him grunted. Another of Edmond's team, hidden out of sight until now.

He brought the gun around.

The man on him shoved his wrist against the ground. Someone else stood on his hand. Stuart's fingers were now mashed between the sole of the man's boot and the asphalt, the metal of the gun making up the middle of this inconvenient sandwich. He gritted his teeth.

"Stop messing around and just get him up."

They rolled him to his front, taped his hands behind his back, and stood him up.

"Let's go."

Stuart was loaded into the back of a vehicle. Before the car door shut, there were two gunshots. The man by the door dropped.

Another two shots.

The second man fell to the ground.

"Why do I have to keep saving you?" Zander reached in and cut his hands free. "You're supposed to be skilled."

At least he didn't say, *skilled like these guys.* "I might have worked for the same company, but I don't do teams."

"Yeah, I remember." Zander sighed. "Good. Because I'm not hiring."

"They would've taken me to Kaylee."

"Eventually, maybe. After you were both sent to a compound and retrained. Isn't that what he said?"

Stuart shoved Zander against the car. "I don't care what he said. It's not happening to her." He roared the words in Zander's face and just about managed to not let spit fly.

"You're gonna want to let go of me." Zander's words were low. "Friend."

Stuart backed up. "I'm not your friend."

He kicked both dead men out of the way, shut the rear door, and climbed in the front seat. He drove to the police station with his foot pressing the gas to the floor until he saw the needle climb to sixty. On main streets in town. Didn't matter what happened, as long as he got Kaylee back. These people would forgive him. And if they didn't? He wouldn't be here to hear about it.

The police station was dark. Stuart drove around to the rear parking lot, trying to figure out where Edmond had gone, and if he could even get inside.

The back door was open.

He dove out, leaving the driver's door ajar and nearly falling on the asphalt. His side stung. He'd been grazed by a bullet. Not that he'd looked at it, he was just assuming that's what it was. Didn't matter.

He stepped inside, gun first. Fear settled on him like an ice-cold climate. He preferred to work those types of missions when he was prepared for it. The right equipment could make or break an operation. Kind of like how the right companion could make any journey seem less like toil and a whole lot more like an enjoyable time. Life was that way, and Kaylee was the kind of woman he wanted to spend time with.

Not going to happen, though, if you don't find her.

The hall door at the end was open, a rubber door stopper holding the door ajar. All the lights turned off. It was never left like that. There was always someone here working, or at least manning the phones. Why was everyone suddenly gone?

Unless they'd known who was coming.

Zander might have alerted Ted. Though, it had to have been done earlier than when Stuart left to come here. Otherwise, they'd never have had the time.

Basuto had to have ordered everyone cleared out. But why? They should be laying a trap, like this team led by Edmond had done. Or lying in wait, as they'd done. Either way, Edmond would be captured and Kaylee would be safe.

Stuart ducked into Ted's office.

Empty, also. Dark and quiet, like the deadliest surprise party he'd never been invited to.

He found the flash drive in a port on Ted's computer tower. Stuart pulled it out, wincing because he hadn't disconnected it properly, and stuck it in his back pocket.

Where was everyone?

The cops had left the flash drive unprotected? The men who wanted it so badly hadn't retrieved it? Nothing about this made any sense.

Stuart listened at the door and thought he heard faint voices. He followed the sound through to the main office, and then to another hallway—the other wing of the building that housed interview rooms and holding cells.

Kaylee.

He waited nearly two minutes until they came out. Edmond, with Kaylee in front of him to shield his own body from any attack.

The sniper who had shot Conroy.

Trina.

All three had guns.

Stuart's body flinched toward Kaylee. He wanted to grab her and run, but blood wet the side of his shirt now. More than he'd thought possible. Unless it wasn't a graze.

Your brother. Edmonds words about Brad rolled through his head as though he was hearing them all over again. *He sold you out. For freedom.*

Stuart smelled the sweat. The sand and urine. Heat rolled over him in waves, sending sweat streaming down his face. *Do it. Kill me.* They'd sat in that cell talking for days. Weeks, even. Until they'd lost track of time. Lost their minds through all the torture. Innocents paraded through the cell. Beheaded in front of them.

We were sold out.

And now Brad had done the same? No. Stuart couldn't believe it.

Kaylee cried out.

Stuart stood. They were in the hall. He raced after them, realizing that he'd lost valuable time by being stuck in his head and the trauma that still lived there. Maybe only a minute, but it could have cost Kaylee her life. Whether Brad had sold her out, or not, didn't matter when she was in their clutches. He couldn't let them take her. The things they'd put him through were so much like special forces training in the military—but without the boundaries.

Kaylee wasn't going to be an asset for their use. Not in any way, shape, or form. Most of which threatened to send him back into his mind. Sucked down by his trauma, and so many things he'd seen. No, he wouldn't allow it.

She would never survive it if he did.

Stuart raced to the hall and saw their group exit. If he was Basuto, the ambush would happen outside, where they would be surrounded. He'd give them no chance for Edmond to take hostages. Or barricade himself inside.

Edmond shoved Kaylee into Ted's office. "Get the flash drive."

Trina shifted. She looked at the sniper who'd shot Conroy. The whole group was a motley crew of people who didn't trust each other. They'd probably start shooting each other at the first sign of dissension.

Stuart stayed out of sight.

"I found it," Kaylee called out. She stepped back into the hall and held it out. Just before Edmond could grab it, she pulled her hand back. "You don't need me. You can turn this over to your boss and tell them I'm dead. That Stuart is dead."

"Doesn't work that way."

"But it can," she pleaded. "You don't have to take me with you."

"If I don't, someone will come back to check that you're dead. My career will be over. The next operation my team goes on will be a suicide mission. After that, you think you'll be left alone? They'll never stop coming for you. For Stuart. No one but me knows the deal Brad made, so he'll be dead too." Edmond paused. "Is that what you want?"

He snatched the flash drive from her hand and shoved it into his pocket, then moved her to the door. "Go."

Stuart had no idea if the flash drive he had was the right one or if the one she'd given Edmond was. Maybe both. Had Ted made multiple copies? Was Kaylee only stringing him along, hoping she had the right thing, and making it so Edmond took her and they left town?

Surely, he'd try and take Stuart with him. He'd find out those men of his failed and come again.

Never stop coming.

Stuart fought the pull of his mind. That long tunnel led to madness. He focused on their figures in front of him. Reality. Truth. Real time events, not memories he could barely trust.

Trina glanced at the sniper. "I go out next. You're the last one."

Stuart figured that was a bad choice, unless she'd prefer to be shot in the back by a man who didn't know her and probably considered her dead weight.

The sniper shrugged. "Whatever."

All of them had weapons, Trina and the sniper had handguns, and Edmond his semi-automatic. Kaylee moved out. Then Edmond and Trina. When the last man took a step, Stuart let out a low whistle.

The man spun, gun raised.

Stuart shot him in the chest.

Trina screamed. Or Kaylee. Or both of them. A commotion erupted outside. "Police! Put your weapon down! Put it down! Drop your gun!"

The answering gunfire was deafening. A steady *rat-tat* of bullets spent from multiple magazines. Not just Edmond and Trina. This was a bigger group. The cops had opened fire? Or someone else?

Stuart raced to the door. He peered out. A bullet sang past his face, and he ducked back inside. It was chaos out there.

He crouched and looked again. Another round smacked the door frame where he'd been standing. Stuart looked for Kaylee in the sea of people.

Cops in full gear.

Zander and his men.

Edmond's guys. Team members Stuart hadn't even seen yet. They were like ants. Or rabbits that just kept multiplying.

There.

Stuart raced toward her. Basuto did the same, and they nearly collided as they chased after Edmond and Kaylee.

Edmond spun, gun up and already firing. Kaylee shoved him. The shot went wide and Basuto cried out, stumbled, then went down.

Kaylee screamed.

Edmond fired again. This time it was Stuart who stumbled. Beyond them, another helicopter—or the same one—landed on a grassy clearing.

Pain shot through his torso. Stuart's legs gave out, and he fell to the ground.

Kaylee screamed.

Everything went black.

Thirty-two

Edmond grabbed her around the waist, his arm banding across her stomach. He dragged her back to the waiting helicopter while the gunfight continued around them. Cops versus bad guys versus Zander and his team guys.

Tears streamed down, leaving muddy tracks on her face. Kaylee wanted to scream again, but he was compressing her diaphragm and cutting off her air.

Stuart didn't get up. Sergeant Basuto rolled on the ground, moaning.

All she heard was her breath and a rush of air in her ears. Not any more gunshots, even though they kept going off.

Tate lifted and fired a shot at Trina that had her yelping and stumbling. No one helped her back up, though she managed to get back on her feet and keep up with them.

Kaylee's world darkened. She tried to get air.

He jerked her against him, adjusting her grip. She sucked in a lungful and screamed. She went limp. If she could be dead weight in his hold, then surely he would drop her. But there was just too much fight in her. So Kaylee screamed, kicked, and fought against his hold. Determined to make as much noise as possible. Cause him as much hassle as possible. Get him to drop her.

Leave her here.

But his grip around her waist only tightened. And then she was tossed in the helicopter. Kaylee's hip slammed onto the floor of the aircraft, and her foot jammed against the open door as others climbed in. She cried out as her ankle was bent unnaturally.

"Shut up!" Trina slapped her across the face.

Kaylee's injured head flashed with a pain that made everything swim. She felt the helicopter lift off the ground and screamed again.

"Someone shut her up."

She focused on Trina's face. Why did her friend sound like she had any authority here? They'd found Trina in the holding cells. The sniper who shot Conroy—the one Trina had killed—had said she made a deal. How would that hold up, now that the guy was dead?

A ping hit the chopper, and it lost a few feet in altitude. Warning alarms screeched. Kaylee held her breath, along with everyone else. Would they be shot down?

But the pilots got it back under control. The screaming alarms shut off, and they kept climbing up as the engines roared, taking Kaylee farther and farther away from her home. Her friends. The family she had made.

Just days ago, she'd been riding her bike through town. Doing her brother a favor, keeping that flash drive safe. Now she was in a helicopter. Kidnapped, again.

"Can this thing go any faster?"

Edmond pointed a gun at Trina. "Shut your mouth. Your place here isn't secure, and you have yet to prove your worth."

Trina's hand whipped up. Nope, it was both hands, moving at a pace so fast they looked like just one hand. In a split second, Trina had managed to confiscate Edmond's gun and was now holding it in her hands.

He slammed a knife into her thigh.

Trina screamed.

He took his gun back. "Like I said. Not secure." He sat back in his seat.

"Yet." She gasped, pressing both hands into her leg.

"You killed one of my men. That's going to cost me. So, you'd better provide restitution for that." Edmond pulled a gauze packet out of the First Aid kit one of the other men was using and tossed it at her.

Kaylee sat up. She tore the gauze pad open and gave it to Trina, shooting Edmond a look. "You're all insane. This whole situation is insane."

She couldn't believe what was happening. After everything that had happened already she was in a helicopter? All because her brother sent her that package. These people had been watching her, trying to get their information back. Why take her too? They didn't need her. And why had they left Stuart?

Because they hadn't been able to grab him in the confusion of the gunfight? Did that mean they would return later to get him? Any surprise they'd relied on before would now be gone. Stuart would be expecting them. Looking over his shoulder all the time. Waiting for Edmond to jump out and attack.

Or Stuart would gear up and mount an offensive.

You've read too many crazy stories. She'd suffered some kind of mental breakdown. Maybe years ago. This probably wasn't even real and she was actually in a mental institution, on medication, having a delusion that felt so real she was convinced it was real life. Would she wake up? Kaylee didn't know which she would prefer.

At least if this wasn't her life, then she was in a place where she was protected, under supervised professional care. There were medical professionals, psychologists, and doctors who cared. Their work was more than a job, it was a mission. People like Dean who believed in what they did. Kaylee wanted to see one of those. They would be able to help her break free of this crazy scenario where gunmen kidnapped her, Trina betrayed her to become one of them, and she was riding in a helicopter. Because there was no way this was really happening. Right?

"I'm exactly who they made me to be. If that means I'm crazy?" Edmond shrugged.

They had to shout to hear each other in the helicopter, but it was satisfying to yell. Kaylee said, "I'm on a rollercoaster I never signed up for, and I want to *get off*."

He flashed his teeth and she was pretty sure he was laughing at her, but she couldn't hear it.

"Where are we going?"

Trina was the one who answered. Through gritted teeth, she said, "To their base, or whatever. For training."

Wait—what did she just say—training? What did that even mean? She didn't want anything to do with this place, even though her *former* friend seemed to be jumping at the chance to sign on.

Who even were these people?

Kaylee moved closer to her former friend. "You really want to be one of them?"

She'd thought Stuart was some kind of CIA agent, but they seemed more like off-book people with no fingerprints and no names. The kind who did anything just for money.

Like her brother.

Or Stuart.

No. She knew the kind of men they were, and it was in no way *this*.

And Trina? Never mind who her father had been. A bank manager who was a criminal hiding in plain sight, someone who used others for his entertainment and destroyed lives in some relentless search for satisfaction. That kind of thing was as powerful as a drug. The high of controlling someone who had no choice but to do what he said.

Kaylee's whole body shuddered. She could see that now. He'd bred that need in Trina, taught her to take charge and go for control in any situation. She recalled even the way Trina had to be the one to decide which restaurant they would eat at *every time* the two of them went out. And Kaylee hadn't even noticed. Or maybe she just hadn't cared enough to object when Trina's personality was the more dominant one. Kaylee just wanted to spend time with her friend instead of arguing about where they would go.

"Uh…*yeah,* I want to join." Trina shook her head, like that should've been obvious. "I've been training for this my whole life. An opportunity like this? I'm not going to pass up the best thing that's ever happened to me."

"You're insane. All of this is insane." She tried to lean back, but there was nowhere to go that wasn't occupied by a sweaty, grimy body smelling like gunpowder. "I'm in a nightmare, and I can't wake up."

Trina laughed. Out the window, mountains passed. Edmond had taken her and Trina and the flash drive she'd given him, and now they were just leaving? To where?

"This is a nightmare." Yes, she was repeating herself. "I'm crazy," she muttered. "I may as well start acting like it."

Maybe they would decide she wasn't worth it, and they'd leave her here. Somewhere. Anywhere. Drop her off and abandon her.

Why do they want me anyway? She could make no sense of it in her brain.

She watched him pull out the flash drive then, turning it over and over in his hand. *Please let there be nothing on it worth anything.* That would be satisfying.

She prayed for Stuart while tears rolled down her face. Her nose was stuffed up, which made her face hurt even worse. Kaylee wanted to collapse to the floor of the helicopter and dissolve into a puddle of emotion.

This whole thing had been the worst experience of her life. If being locked up in a facility for people who needed psychological treatment sounded more pleasant than her present circumstances, then that was saying something. Trapped. No control. Kaylee desperately missed the everyday freedoms she now knew she'd taken for granted. Riding her bike, the wind in her hair. Reading a book in the sunshine.

These weren't going to happen again anytime soon.

Maybe even never again.

The helicopter began to descend, landing on the driveway—a private runway, perhaps—of what looked like a huge ranch house. An airplane was at the end, closest to the house. When they neared it, Kaylee realized the engines were already running. The heat wafted toward the buildings and a small red crop duster that was parked to the side, leaving scorch marks on everything.

Her hair ruffled across her face as she glanced back, looking at Trina. Still unable to process that this person sitting across from her was a completely different person than she had thought she was. Trina looked nervous but, in a twisted way, also excited. Her dad was dead. Did she even know that? She appeared to be satisfied, as if she was holding everything she had ever wanted and bargained for in her hands.

Kaylee wanted to be sick.

Aside from that, her only goals were to stay alive and get away from these people. But at what cost? Would they shoot her? Did she have the courage to find a way to kill herself before they could load her on that plane? Would Stuart jump out from behind cover half a second after her last breath? That would be devastating to be robbed of a proper goodbye.

Kaylee didn't think she should risk it when she was sure that Stuart would come through and try to rescue her.

Unless he was dead.

She let out a sob. Edmond shoved her forward. "Why are you doing this? I'm nothing to you, or the people you work for." She gasped for breath. "What do they want with me when you left Brad back in the hospital? And why not Stuart? Why am I the one you're taking?"

Surely there was a reason. There just had to be, or none of this made any sense—and that would be a waste of time and resources. No one with any intelligence ran a business like that.

"Just get on the plane."

"No. Tell me why you're taking me when you can't be sure that drive doesn't contain a leak." She wanted to wipe her cheeks, but that would be a bad idea. The pain in her head was hard to deal with. "Stuart and Brad are still out there. You've hardly done your due diligence, and I'll tell everyone you work for that you left loose ends."

"Stuart is dead." He shoved her toward the airplane steps. "There can be any number of copies of this flash drive out there, but now that we have one, we can scrub the others from existence as soon as they show up on any network." Shove. "Anywhere." Shove.

She stumbled, spun around, and screamed, "Stop pushing me!"

"I knew your mother's fire was in there somewhere."

She choked on her gasp.

"Stuart needed to believe this was all about him. If he's not dead already, he's destroyed knowing you're in our hands now. He'll never find you. And he can never stop what's about to happen." He led her up the steps and onto the plane. "This is the best result the boss could've hoped for and I have plenty to show for it. That will cover my losses. The main thing is that the mess your family made is now set right."

"My family?" She whispered the words.

"Y'all were always trouble for us. But that's done now." He clapped his hands together and brushed them off. "Problem solved."

Thirty-three

Stuart took the piece of surgical tape from Zander and pressed it on the bandage to hold the edges down. "Thanks." He hissed the word out between clenched teeth.

"You nearly died."

And yet, Zander didn't have a scratch on him.

"Talk to me."

The big man folded his arms. "Alex is in the hospital."

He blinked. "Who?"

"Sergeant Basuto." Zander continued, "Mia left Conroy's bedside to take charge at the police station. Detective Wilcox is at the murder scene working Silas Nigelson's death, and his life—at least what we can ascertain from the evidence found inside the building."

Stuart winced. "Not a job I'd want. There's probably a whole lot of DNA evidence all over that place."

"Yeah." Zander sighed. "Anyway, Ted is with Wilcox, processing everything, running down all the details. Making sure the prostitution operation either died with him or they can ID those involved. But he's certain now that Silas Nigelson was in that photo they have of the soldiers. The one from Vietnam, you know?"

Stuart nodded, since he'd heard about it from Dean and Ellie.

"So he was one of the founders. And also a Russian sleeper agent from the sixties."

"If he's been here that long and no one knew, then he's good. I don't think anyone even suspected, right?"

"I guess." Zander blew out a breath. "And he knew who West is, could've probably ID'd him. Now he's dead, and so is that lead."

Stuart hopped off the hospital bed. "Where is she?"

Zander said nothing.

Stuart had seen her last right before he'd hit the ground and lost consciousness. Kaylee had been taken by Edmond and his men, guys with as much training as he or Zander had. Maybe more, if the fact they'd lost their fight with Edmond meant anything at all. Now Edmond had Kaylee and a copy of the flash drive. And Stuart and Brad had been left behind.

"Tell me."

Zander said, "We don't know. But we're looking."

Stuart shoved his feet into his shoes and shot a glance over his shoulder.

"We're working on it. What we know so far is that she was put on a plane and it took off. We are currently tracking them."

"Why are they taking her in?"

"And not you?"

"Look, regardless of what you think, I'm not trying to figure out why they don't think I'm special," he said. "That's not what this is. I just want to know why she's so important to them if they got the flash drive, the very thing they came here for."

"Did they?"

Stuart shrugged, even though that made the deep gunshot wound in his side tug on his stitches. "A copy of it."

"And what would Kaylee bring to that equation."

Stuart tried to think. The pain meds were working well enough except for the lingering ache. He didn't want to puzzle this out. He wanted to get out there, start knocking down doors, and start shooting everyone he recognized as being part of their group—including Trina. She hadn't been kidnapped. She'd signed on voluntarily.

Kaylee was pretty much the only innocent victim in all of this. Her involvement was supposed to have been done already. Long before anyone showed up with a gun—and a helicopter—looking for the package Brad had sent.

Brad.

"Let's go."

Zander opened the door. "Where?"

Stuart nearly walked right into the men in the hall, two of the three guys on Zander's team. "A whole protection detail of professionals? I'm touched."

One snorted. The other said, "Where to?"

Even though he'd asked Zander, Stuart was the one who said, "I'm going to talk to Brad. I need to know what I've been missing this whole time."

They followed him, a trio. Three points making up the tip of a blade behind him. Despite their extraordinary power and skills, they hadn't saved Kaylee any more than Stuart had. That alone stopped his spiraling thoughts that he hadn't done enough to stop Edmond from taking her.

Stuart stepped onto the elevator and leaned against the wall.

"We're going to get her back."

He closed his eyes to avoid the scrutiny in Zander's gaze. "Not soon enough."

One of the other guys asked, "What will they do to her in the meantime?"

"The plane will go to a holding facility. She'll be kept there a few days, less if they know we're in pursuit. After that there are several options. They have two facilities in Europe, one in Canada, and another in Thailand. Depends on where she's taken."

"Does it matter?"

Stuart glanced at the younger man. Sinewy, built like a warrior.

"I mean, wherever she is, we go get her, right?" He shrugged. "She ain't gonna be on Mars."

"True."

Zander said, "This organization. Who are they?"

"Privatized war."

"So, mercenaries," one of the other guys said.

Stuart shrugged. The elevator slid up to the second floor. "They pretend they're legit. Sanctioned. But in the end, it's just dirty work governments don't want to rubber stamp, so they farm it out."

"You were military?"

Stuart shook his head. "Never. They pulled me out of a life I didn't like, bumming around Poland and stealing from people who didn't care. Running from the ones who did. My first mission, they tossed me in a French prison. Told me to kill a guy in the showers because the spray washes away the evidence."

"And the rest is history, as they say?"

"Let me guess," Stuart said. "You're the poet of the team?"

"Well, I guess that would depend on whether or not you're a poet, and you're gunning for my job. Wouldn't it?"

"Not even close."

All of them shifted. Stuart didn't know if it was because he might want a job, or because they were all super uptight about people not wanting to join them. Either way, he didn't have time to figure out what the answer was.

The elevator doors opened, and they repeated their walking in formation, all the way to where the fourth man on their team, and Dean, stood in the hall.

"He awake?"

Dean spun around. "You're gonna question him?"

"I need to know what Brad knows."

"And if I tell you he's in no condition to talk?"

Stuart moved past him and yanked down on the door handle. He strode in Brad's room, where the machines beeped their steady rhythm while the light of early morning streamed in the windows. That gunfight had been in the middle of the night. Still, how long had he been unconscious? Long enough they'd hauled him here to the hospital. He'd woken up with stitches and warm, soothing medicine in him. It had been so many years since he had taken any kind of pain relieving narcotics, the effect was disorienting.

But he wasn't going to let that stop him from getting answers from Brad.

Finding Kaylee.

Putting all this to rights.

"Tell me what you know."

The men crowded in the room until the testosterone level had a nurse at the door asking Zander if everything was okay. One of his guys smiled a frat boy grin at her, and the two walked back out.

Dean moved close to Stuart's side. "Dude. He's not well."

"Brad." Stuart waited until his friend gave him his full attention. Even though Brad's eyes were glassy, he knew his friend could hear him. Understand what he would say. Be able to give him answers.

Please. There was no one else to plead with. Stuart had come to the end of all his knowledge and all his strength. He had nothing left. *Don't let anything happen to her before I can get to her. Help me make it quickly.*

He leaned against his friend's bedside, hoping compassion would rule this day. But given how they'd been trained, maybe that was a futile hope. "We're tracking the plane, but I need answers. You know they took Kaylee?"

Brad nodded, not giving away any emotion on his face. Were the medicines he was on withholding his emotions from coming to the surface? "If they have her, then it's done." He turned away.

Stuart moved closer. "You sent her the package. This is your doing."

"We were betrayed. I wanted out before that happened. Now that it has? I don't want one more single thing to do with them. It's over."

"You just walk away? When they have your sister?"

A muscle ticked in Brad's jaw. "You're going after her, right?"

"That's the plan."

"With or without my help. You'll get her back."

Stuart appreciated his friend's trust in him. But he wasn't convinced it was a good thing when it meant Brad was essentially quitting and leaving Kaylee to them. "If I walked away too, would you fight for her?"

"Doesn't matter. I know you, and I know that look on her face. She talked about you. Thought I couldn't hear her." Brad swallowed. "You'll get her. Because she loves you."

"Tell me why they took her and the flash drive, but left you and me."

Brad's lips pressed in a thin line.

A heavy feeling rested on Stuart's shoulders. "What did you do?"

Dean shifted beside him. He understood. Did that mean he wouldn't be so inclined to hold Stuart back now? Dean cared about Kaylee. The whole town did. If Stuart put out a call for skilled help getting her back, who would come?

Likely more people than he'd have guessed.

But Stuart was the one in love with her.

A tremor of pure hope rolled through him. Used to denying that feeling his whole life, he immediately dismissed it. Or started to. Stuart stopped himself. Thinking differently about himself, and about his future, was going to take practice.

Can I have everything I want?

It looked impossible. But he knew a God who could accomplish what Stuart could hardly dream.

"I figured it out. Why my parents were killed, why I was conscripted." Brad sucked in a breath that shuddered through him. "They wanted out too, and it cost them their lives."

"Both your parents were in?"

"They tried to hide Kaylee. They knew she'd be looked at as an asset. I tried to make a name for myself so that they'd leave her alone because then maybe they wouldn't need another. Meanwhile, my parents lived under the radar. Kept her safe. When they decided they wanted out, they were both shot in front of her. The asset assigned to it was supposed to kill Kaylee, too. But he left her alive. He couldn't kill a woman."

Brad gasped and then continued, "I was tasked to kill him. I told her when it was done so she would run, but she never did. She stayed in Last Chance. So I spent the next few years doing what I'd done before. Being so valuable to them that they didn't need her." He shook his head. "But when I'd finally had it and wanted out, I knew it would take something big for them to let me go."

"Like a trade." Stuart folded his arms to keep from reaching over and strangling this man who was supposed to have been his friend. Kaylee's brother. "Only, you and I were set up."

"I'd already sent her the information, just in case. When they grabbed me outside the compound, I was at the end of myself. I couldn't go back there. I had to get out. So I told them they could have the information...and her. She has all the skills. She just needs training."

"So you sold her out."

"I did this job for long enough. It's her turn now."

Stuart wanted to be sick. "Your parents never wanted this for her."

"But they had no problem with me doing it."

"Is that true, or did they find out too late?"

Brad pressed his lips together.

"So, this is all about legacy? One you corrupted because you didn't have the guts to finish it yourself. Now you're leaving your sister to suffer alone, with no idea how to handle this."

Dean shoved him back from the bed. The machines beeped, loud and shrill. "He's out."

"It doesn't matter." Stuart strode toward the door. "I don't need him anyway."

Thirty-four

Kaylee lay on the cot. The room was a cell. Bare wood walls, caulk between each panel. She knew the roof was metal because she'd heard the rainfall a few nights ago.

A tiny slit of a window no bigger than an envelope was high on the wall so she was able to track the rise and subsequent fall of the sun.

Four days.

Every time she started to fall asleep, heavy metal music blasted from two speakers above the door. So loud she could still hear it at full blast, even when she had her hands over her ears.

Her eyes burned, hot and gritty. Her mouth tasted like an overripe banana. She hadn't had anything to eat, and the only liquid she'd ingested was a discolored brown substance, given to her in a tiny bottle. It had tasted like muddy river water.

If Stuart can do it, so can I.

Thinking of him was as painful as it was helpful. Picturing his face in her mind, and the feel of his arms around her. His lips against her forehead. *I love you.* They'd had a hundred conversations in her head. Things they had never said. Things she would never get to tell him. All that was gone now.

He was dead.

Her life was over.

She wasn't sure, yet, what they wanted from her, but she'd rather get that over with than continue this torturous waiting. Though, wearing her down past this point—to the point she would scream for it to end—would probably be where they would finally intervene.

Kaylee refused. She stared, bleary-eyed at the caulking on the wall and the knots in the wood and let her mind go blank. The music was too loud for her to think.

What felt like hours later, it finally shut off.

She blew out a breath. Hunger had become a weakness. Thirst was a distant memory. When the door flung open for the first time in what seemed like days, she didn't even blink. She was lying on the bed with her legs bent over the side, her feet nearly flat on the floor.

"You look like crap." Edmond hauled her to a seated position and shoved her back against the wall.

Kaylee wasn't sure she wouldn't fall back down to the bed again, the way her lower body was partially still turned.

Edmond snapped his fingers in front of her face. "Are you even listening to me?"

She blinked up at him.

"Great. I guess that's the best we're gonna get." He tapped the screen of a huge phone in his hand, then turned it. "Smile for the camera."

The flash erupted in her face.

Kaylee's cheek smashed into the bed.

He tapped and swiped. "And…it's sent."

Seconds later the phone started to ring.

"Of course he's calling now," Edmond muttered. "Yes, sir." He had the phone to his ear. "She's not exactly ready. I understand."

He tapped the screen and turned it.

The man on screen had gray hair but a handsome enough face. Tanned skin. "I can see the resemblance."

"Yes, sir. She definitely looks like her mother."

"Can you hear me, Kaylee?"

She didn't move. Maybe she blinked. Kaylee didn't care if that was true or not, or whether or not they wanted her to speak…she didn't have the energy to even finish that thought. *Stuart.* She wanted to go to his funeral. To see him one last time, to touch his face, and to grieve. Even more so because of the memory of their sweet moments. She wanted to experience the loss of what could have been.

What her life would never be.

A family like her parents had. Marriage. Children. *God, You've abandoned me.* She wanted to feel His presence. The warmth of His love. But none of that existed here. It was freezing, and she couldn't remember one single Bible verse, even though she'd tried to bring to mind all the ones she'd memorized. Even just one.

Any of them would do. She just wanted to hear the words.

"What is she talking about?"

"I have no idea, sir," Edmond said.

"Get her up."

Edmond laid the phone beside her nose and then hauled her to sitting again, this time leaning against the corner of the room at the foot of the bed. She rested her temple against the wall while he got on the phone again and stuck it in her face.

"Can you hear me, Kaylee?"

"Yes." Nothing audible emerged from her mouth. She swallowed and coughed, then swallowed again. None of it helped, but she was able to croak out, "Yes," finally.

"Good." The old man on the screen smiled in a perfunctory display of appreciation. "I'd hoped to be there, but this new position prevents me. So Edmond has taken my place. He will be performing the re-education on my behalf."

She flinched.

He continued, completely ignoring her reaction. Or he just didn't see it. "When you're done, there will be a high position in store for you. It was supposed to have gone to your mother, but she decided otherwise. Now that responsibility falls to you. The privilege of being by my side. Someone I can trust with my innermost secrets and, of course, my desires."

Her brain couldn't process the words, but the look in his eyes was clear enough. He'd wanted her mother. Now his plan was to settle for her.

Eight years ago, when her mom and dad had been shot in front of her, gunned down, she'd been barely out of high school. Her mom hadn't wanted this. But he expected her to want it?

"*Kaylee.*" His voice cut through her thoughts. "As I was saying, of course you will be rewarded. If you do well there will be money enough to build the life you've always dreamed of. Travel. Riches. Parties. You can even do some charity work—after we have the wedding of the season so everyone worthy of our company can attend our event."

Beyond the phone, Edmond stared at her. She didn't dwell too long on the look in his eyes.

"Of course, all this is after you've been made suitable. And after that mess on your face heals. Edmond?"

"Yes, sir?"

"You may have to consult with a plastic surgeon. Just to make sure there's no permanent disfigurement."

"Yes, sir. I'll get started with everything right away."

"Excellent. You see, Kaylee? Loyalty is always rewarded."

"What about Brad?" She didn't ask about Stuart. She couldn't even bear to say his name aloud. The feeling she had for him would be there, and then they would know the truth. Edmond would have yet more power over her. He would get in her head and break her down.

More than he already had.

"Your brother has made his own arrangements. Now you're here. It's time to make the best of it, and that starts with Edmond.

Cooperate, Kaylee. There's no use fighting it. You might as well make your time the most…pleasant."

She didn't believe a single word of what he was saying. Maybe he thought it was true, or he wanted to believe what he was doing was acceptable. *Whatever helps you sleep at night.*

"Soon enough we'll be together."

Of course, by that he meant *together*. She saw as much in his eyes. Kaylee swallowed again, enough to say, "You think I won't murder you the second you turn your back."

"Your mother would have." He actually chuckled.

Even Edmond flashed his teeth in a kind of a smile.

"She certainly would have. She was a formidable woman, to say the least. I'm hoping you bring some of that same fire." He touched his tie. "Though, I'm hoping you'll refrain from spilling my blood. Especially when I can give you the world. So many women would jump at the chance to gain the opportunity you're getting."

"So pick one of them." She had no energy for fear. All Kaylee had was the cold, and her broken mind.

Was this what Stuart felt? The way these people had treated him. Missions he'd been sent on. Things he'd been forced to do, and those things forced upon him for "training" purposes. She didn't even want to know how awful it was.

Or how awful it would become for her.

Edmond seemed eager. That didn't fill her with joy, but she doubted anything would right now. *God, don't leave me.*

The old man on the screen chuckled. "Your mother coddled you. She failed to communicate precisely what you were bred to become. That won't happen with our children."

Edmond said, "Your training will be extensive. The idea of killing the man who is responsible for your survival won't even enter your mind. You can rest assured of that."

"I know I will." The old man laughed again, and she thought she heard a tiny murmur of nerves. "But for now, I have much work to do, and so do the two of you. Until next time, my dear. I look forward to seeing what you become."

Edmond tapped the screen and pocketed the phone.

"He's insane." She sounded desperate but it couldn't be helped, and she didn't even care to try and change it. "You don't have to do this."

"And yet I've never had a failure. All the times I've done this, I've never come up short. So don't worry. In a few months, you'll be living that ritzy life in Washington D.C., and I'll be nothing but a memory." He leaned toward her, a mockery of a bow. "Maybe a fond one. Depends on how you respond."

"Probably I'll puke on your shoes, but that's just a guess."

Edmond strode toward the door.

"You're all insane. This whole thing is. People like you shouldn't exist. Manipulating the world according to how you want it to be, thinking others are expendable pawn pieces for you to move around wherever you want."

"Is there a point in there somewhere?"

"It's not right."

He shrugged. "Your friend Trina didn't object. She jumped at the chance to...work with me."

"You're insane." Maybe it was redundant to repeat herself, but limited capacity for thoughts left her with not much to work with.

"That's what breeds success, I'm afraid. Genius with a dash of crazy. Only the strong and the powerful survive, and we all have our part to play in that world." He grinned. "Just lay still and try to pretend you like it." He waggled his brows. "Later, though."

He slammed the door shut, leaving her mercifully, blessedly alone. *To be continued.* Kaylee wanted to vomit, but there was nothing in her stomach. She wanted to scream and cry but was so dehydrated she didn't think her body was capable of producing even an ounce of moisture.

This had been the plan all along. Her brother had fulfilled his usefulness. It was her turn now, and Stuart was dead. She had plenty of friends; cops and people who knew federal agents. But they would never find her.

Kaylee would have to live this life. Until a day came, sometime in the future, when she could make a break for it.

Escape.

It didn't matter how long it took. A month from now. A year, or ten years. Eventually she would find a way to get away from whoever that older man was.

For now, she would conserve her energy. Find a place in her mind where she could detach from whatever happened to her while keeping some of her sanity intact—even as they did everything they could to make her into someone else.

But Kaylee would always know who she was.

A Last Chance citizen. A church member and child of God. A bookaholic. A woman who had fallen for a broken man who deserved far better than life had ever given him.

You were right, Mom. Breaking free is always worth trying. No matter the cost.

She knew that now, despite the fear that would inevitably creep back in. Even though it had destroyed them, it had been worth it to be happy. Even for a short time.

No matter the cost.

Thirty-five

"I've got movement on two."

"Copy that," Stuart said. He turned from his surveillance of the ridge overlooking the compound where Kaylee was being held, and instead trained his attention to the crowd of people gathered around him.

"I'm headed to the van." Mia, the police lieutenant engaged to Conroy, lifted a hand and waved.

"I'll go with you," Officer Donaldson followed.

None of them were in uniform. They'd tracked Kaylee to a remote facility in Utah that was smaller than any of the ones Stuart had even known about. The scope of the organization he'd once worked for astounded him. And yet, why was he so surprised?

Tate pulled up in a car with Savannah and another man. They strode over. "Sorry we're late. This is Phil."

About as tall as Tate, Phil wore cargo pants, boots, and a T-shirt. He'd strapped on a bulletproof vest over his shirt and donned a ball cap. The only reason Stuart didn't kick him out was the ease with which he moved. This guy knew what he was doing.

Still, Stuart didn't like the idea of working with an unknown who didn't have a badge. "I thought you were bringing the FBI as backup."

"Eric is working on the official side of this takedown."

"But he didn't send anyone to help?"

"Like I said." Tate motioned to his companion. "This is Phil."

Even Savannah eyed Phil like she didn't quite understand how he fit with everything going on here.

The local sheriff, two state police officers, and a dog with the K9 unit were here with them providing support. They were as interested as Stuart in what was going on at the bottom of this hill, but only Stuart understood the full scope of it. He would take them down, all the way to the man at the top—who currently occupied the seat of Director of the CIA.

Whoever Zander employed to provide intelligence had uncovered a link between the Director and Kaylee's mother, along with an email that outlined precisely what the Director wanted with Kaylee. Stuart had smashed a laptop and punched a hole through drywall when he'd learned about that.

"Easy." Zander touched his shoulder.

"She's down there," Stuart said. "So let's get to this."

Zander had a map of the facility, a blueprint. He unrolled it on the hood of the closest car and everyone gathered around. No one questioned why he was taking the lead.

As he outlined positions, the plan, and how this would go down, Stuart pretended he wasn't dying to get in there.

"Okay, let's go." Zander slapped Stuart's back. "You're with me."

It was good he'd said that, considering Stuart hadn't heard a word of the briefing. They approached from the south, with Zander reiterating to him what was going to happen. Another team would hit the front gate, big and loud. A diversion that should draw most of the personnel inside out to engage them. Group three came from the rear, while four came from the far side. Four points of a compass, each led by a man of Zander's team.

Each group had cops, local and from Last Chance, and any civilians—like Stuart—were spread out among them with instructions to do as they were told.

Stuart shot him a side glance.

Zander shrugged. "I figured it was worth a try, at least. Kind of like how I told them all to try and not get killed."

"What's the size of the opposing force?"

"We have no idea."

Stuart frowned. They approached the east fence at a crawl, spread out in the long grass, and used downed trees and rocks as cover to keep from being spotted by anyone on surveillance from inside.

Zander looked at his watch. "Three. Two. One."

An explosion split through the sky, rolling up a fireball as though thrown into the air. Trying to reach as high as possible, it turned over and over before falling back down. Smoke darkened the stars.

"Go."

Two men cut through the fence, and they slipped inside.

Zander went first, and Stuart wasn't far behind him. The structure contained multiple buildings, kind of like a hospital campus but much smaller. It could probably house less than a hundred people. Work-out rooms, communal living. Re-education classrooms. Treatment rooms, dorm rooms, prison cells. There was also an entire medical facility—though not extensive, it could provide some surgical services and dental procedures.

Zander placed a small charge of plastic explosives around the handle and breached the side door. As the smoke cleared, Stuart recognized the hallway. The smell. The layout. The feel of it seeped into his bones as memories rushed back, and he staggered back against the wall.

It was like falling into a whirlpool of the past.

Pain sparked across his face. "Wrong answer."

He was tied down, dressed only in his underwear. Blood trickled from the corner of his mouth.

The hand swept toward him again, determined to slap him another time.

"Stuart." Zander shook his shoulders and then glanced behind him. "You guys continue. We'll catch up." His friend crouched and Stuart, looking around, realized he'd slumped to the floor.

Sweat dampened his shirt.

"You wanna go get her, or you wanna fall apart?"

He could barely speak. "Get her."

"Good." Zander bobbed his head down and to the right to lock eyes with him. Stuart didn't look away this time. "That means this thing you've got going on in your head doesn't factor right now. Later you can have whatever mental breakdown you want. *After* you find Kaylee and get her to safety. Copy?"

Stuart nodded. "Copy."

Zander held out a hand. They clasped wrists, and he hauled Stuart up.

Gunshots rang out down the hall. Zander took cover on the opposite side. Stuart opened a door and used it for cover. He waited, then took his shot.

The firing stopped.

They preceded down the hall, guns ready. At the end, Stuart peered around the corner. "Control room is down there."

Already a gunfight was in progress; several men he recognized as part of their group battled plainclothes men he didn't recognize. A state police officer subdued a man, shoved him against the wall, and cuffed him. "Clear."

Two more men emerged from the room, and they gathered all together in the hallway. The state police officer said, "They barricaded themselves in there." He pointed to a door at the end of the hall.

"This place is a maze." Zander sighed. "Blow the door?"

Stuart nodded.

Zander set charges, and the second the door blew open, they barreled inside. Bullets flew around him. Stuart heard one buzz past his ear, entirely too close for comfort. He found a man, half alive.

Mostly covered in blood. Stuart kicked a gun from the man's hand and crouched beside him, while the others took out the rest of the occupants of the room.

"Where is Kaylee?"

The man's gaze flickered around but never settled on Stuart. He gasped for breath.

Stuart knelt on the man's fingers. "Tell me where she is."

"It's too late. The self-destruct protocol…already…" The light in his eyes flickered and then went out.

Stuart sat back on his heels.

"What did he say?" Zander moved close.

"Self-destruct. I was worried about that." He moved to look at the closest computer screen. "Everything on the hard drives will copy to a cloud-based server and then delete itself."

"Charges?"

"Probably. They'll get out, but the buildings will be reduced to nothing but rubble."

"Then we'd better pick up our pace."

Stuart headed for the door. "They'll start from the lowest floors, kill any assets they can't take with them when they flee, and the destruction will go up and out." Like the ripples in a pond; toss a rock in and watch them dissipate. Only this would involve a whole lot more fire and blood.

"We're good." Zander was right behind him, moving at the same speed. "We knew this would happen."

He didn't need to convince Stuart, considering he was the one who'd told them all this information. And it had been corroborated by Mia's interrogation of Brad. Which was all fine, but it didn't tell him where they were holding Kaylee. He was going to have to search room by room.

Stuart found a stairwell and descended to the lowest floor he could access.

Beyond the door were shouts. Fighting. Stuart kicked it open and went gun first. A man raced past him, bloody but determined. He didn't even see Stuart right there as he raced for the door, whimpering and muttering to himself.

"Hold your fire," Zander yelled.

The man screamed, sprinting for the stairwell.

"I'll go left." Zander moved around Stuart.

He already knew where he was going to go. "Right."

Four cells—two to the left and two to the right. At the end were communal bathrooms. Behind him now, at the end and to the left, was a huge training room. Stuart's body shuddered as adrenaline continued to pump through him. Sweat rolled down his temples.

The door at the end opened, and Edmond strolled out.

Stuart fired.

The bullet caught Edmond in the shoulder. He dropped his gun but recovered fast. Too fast. He barreled toward Stuart, and they clashed in the middle of the hall.

Stuart's gun clattered to the ground.

He slammed Edmond against the wall, punched him twice in the stomach, and then when he bent forward, elbowed the back of Stuart's shoulder. Edmond didn't go down. He grabbed Stuart around the waist and tackled him.

Stuart's head bounced off the opposite wall. He grunted and hit out at the man who hadn't let go. He kicked Edmond's legs and was finally forced to slam a fist against the gunshot wound Edmond didn't seem to even feel.

Edmond's legs gave out. He collapsed to the floor, and Stuart kicked him until his head lolled, unconscious.

Stuart bent forward with his hands on his thighs and sucked in a handful of big breaths.

Movement caught his attention. He snatched up his gun in time to see Trina disappear into a room. He followed her, but the door locked before he could get to it.

Inside, a woman screamed.

"Kaylee!" She was here. He'd found her.

Stuart tried the lock. He kicked the door. Kaylee screamed again, and he heard a thud.

A man's deep laughter had him spinning back around. The sound hit him in a place he didn't like, a deep well where he'd stuffed his true feelings for Kaylee.

Edmond was awake again, his menacing gaze now trained on Stuart while his reach inched across the floor toward the gun he'd dropped. Stuart kicked the weapon farther away, down the hall. Still, Edmond tried to inch closer. Stuart couldn't even begin to imagine the medication they must have Edmond on that gave him this much adrenaline—enough he didn't seem to feel the wounds he'd gotten from Stuart, not to mention the fact he had already regained consciousness.

Stuart strode over. He put his heel on Edmond's wound and held his gun steadily pointed at his face. "Keys to that room. Now."

Edmond grinned a mouthful of teeth stained with blood. He coughed and more blood bubbled up. "Too late."

A deep boom shook the building, followed by a rumble. Dust rained down from the ceiling.

Edmond's body shook and laughter emerged from his mouth.

"I can shoot you, or I can haul you out of here," Stuart said. "Now give me the keys."

The laughter grew louder.

Inside the room, he heard a scream. *Kaylee.* If he couldn't do this, he didn't deserve her. He would fail to protect her, and she would die here. Stuart stuck the gun in the back of his waistband and patted Edmond down. He found keys in Edmond's front pocket. Just as Edmond rolled close enough to Stuart's leg to open his mouth and take a bite, he backed up.

Stuart kicked him again, then turned to the locked door.

An explosion tore apart the training room, splintering the door. Flames rushed down the hall. Stuart dove for Edmond's body and rolled the man onto him, using his body to shield him from the rush of scorching air.

Thirty-six

The room shuddered around them. Kaylee lifted her hand and wiped the blood from her mouth with her thumb.

Trina stood across the room, a knife in one hand. She'd hit Kaylee across the face with the hilt of it. "This needs to be done right."

Kaylee just stared at her. The head cold that had been her constant companion since she had left Last Chance crystalized, lighting pain all through her muscles. She took a step back. Trina stood between her and the door, which was locked anyway. She still wanted to shove her former friend back and try the handle anyway.

"What do you want?" Kaylee refused to cower. Never mind that she had no training and no clue, Kaylee wasn't going to back down. Not when this woman, supposedly her friend, had so clearly betrayed her.

Trina wore workout clothes, her hair pulled back in a ponytail except for fly-aways around her face. A bruise darkened her cheekbone. "This doesn't need to take long and probably shouldn't."

The room shuddered around them again and dust drifted down. Maybe this whole place would collapse and Kaylee wouldn't have to deal with the overwhelming terror she didn't even seem to be able to feel anymore.

"Come here. I'll make it quick and painless...mostly. When they come for us, I'll tell them you killed yourself."

"Why?" They would probably die soon anyway. What was the purpose of Trina killing her before then? She shook her head, genuinely not understanding why Trina needed to do this. What was the point? Satisfaction, or something far more sinister? An agenda of some kind.

Seemed like everyone had one, and Kaylee floundered in the middle. Tossed around in a boat on the sea while others decided where she should go and what she should be doing.

Trina's eyes narrowed. She held that knife out, steady like the entire place wasn't coming down around them. "I'm going to kill you myself. Then the director will know I'm the clear choice for his wife. Not you."

"Marry him. What do I care?"

"It'll take more than your disapproval to get him to change his mind. You need to be dead."

"So, stop talking about it, and kill me." She shrugged. "What do I care?" She said it with more emphasis this time.

Kaylee just wanted all this to be over already. What was the point in dragging it out?

She rushed for the door. If Trina thought she was going to escape, maybe she would just stick that blade in her heart and get it done with.

Kaylee wanted to feel the betrayal. To feel the sting of the knife and know it was all done. She didn't want to be here anymore.

She wanted... *Don't think about him.* She had to pay attention to what was happening around her. Otherwise she would never get out of here alive.

Her fingertips touched the door. It wasn't a handle, more like a lever, and it locked automatically when it closed.

Pain cut like a whip of fire across her stomach, a brand, of sorts, that ran from right beside her belly button to her ribs underneath her arm.

Kaylee hissed.

The door could only be unlocked from the other side. Unless the next explosion blew the door open, the only way they were getting out was if someone in the hall had a key. Trina had trapped herself in here with Kaylee.

Unless she had a way to get out.

The crazed look on her friend's face—those wide, glassy eyes—and her quick, panting breaths led Kaylee to believe she wasn't all that mentally stable.

As Kaylee clutched her side and tried not to think about the wet under her fingers or the cut in the material of her shirt, she backed up to the wall beside the metal toilet. She needed to get out of here but that was next to impossible since God had abandoned her so thoroughly. She'd tried to live a quiet, peaceful life, but that had imploded. People with their agendas, who thought they had power over everyone, decided differently.

Those men, especially that one suited, older man and his ideas about how her life should play out.

People like Trina.

Even her brother, who had sold her out for his own freedom. Or Stuart, dying before he could keep his word that he would take care of her.

A sob worked its way up her throat. Kaylee refused to embrace the emotion. It was better to hold onto this coldness she'd discovered. The pure ice of being all alone with no hope. No future. No way to be anything other than a helpless victim of other people's ideas and plans.

"Nice try." Trina launched at her with the bloody knife outstretched.

Kaylee screamed. A protest to getting cut again. Too late she realized Trina had only flinched at her.

Trina tipped her head back and laughed.

The door thumped. Probably debris from an explosion. "We're going to die in here."

"*You* will." Trina grinned.

The latch clicked, and the door flung open. A man filled the doorway, but before she could see who it was, Trina grabbed Kaylee and spun her to the front as a shield. Trina's arm banded around her waist and pressed deeply onto the cut she'd made on Kaylee's waist.

She cried out.

The knife pressed against her neck, Trina spoke right beside her ear, "One step closer, and she bleeds out."

This woman sounded nothing like the friend she'd known. A completely different person than the one Kaylee had spent time with. Felt for. Bought gifts for. Cried and laughed with.

"Let me go."

Trina laughed again. "Now this is interesting."

The man lifted a gun and crossed the threshold. *Stuart.* "Hi, Kaylee."

Trina let out a cry of frustration. "You should worry a whole lot more about me right now. Otherwise she's dead, and all the trouble you've caused is for nothing."

"Let her go." His voice washed over her like a cooling balm. Like her memory of her father's voice, or the way it felt to be held by the man she was growing to love.

"Stuart." She whispered his name. Everything in her tensed to move toward him, to rush over and fling herself into his arms. He was the safe place she wanted to be. But no, not a place—not even Last Chance—just Stuart, and what he had become to her.

She stared at him while a whimper worked its way to her throat. *See me. I'm right here.* Every fiber of her being yearned for him, called out to him, and ached to be by his side. In his embrace.

He didn't look at her. All his attention was on Trina, the lines of his body giving away nothing. Not even tension. His face was blank. So emotionless. She wanted to weep. *Father.*

Stuart had come for her. He wasn't dead. *You never abandoned me, did You?*

She didn't want to correlate the two with one another, or maybe 'shouldn't' was the better word. But in her mind, they were synonymous. Stuart was God's blessing in her life. He was love, acceptance, and peace.

Trina gripped her tighter, causing another stab of stinging pain to catch her breath. Trina said, "You think I can't slit her throat before you even get a shot off? If I don't, she and I are both dead, so I have nothing to lose. The only one who loses is *you*."

He didn't back down or lower the gun. A muscle ticked in his jaw. That was the only indication of his stress level. Aside from that one thing, he looked like a tower. A pillar of strength, everything she wanted to be instead of this blank, frozen being who felt nothing and could do nothing.

All Kaylee had was cold and pain.

"The whole compound is coming down on top of us. Let her go, and we all get out of here."

Trina's body flinched.

Kaylee jumped on the reaction that suddenly flooded her heart; the desire to run. To flee death and escape. "We can go, Trina. Let's just go."

"I'm going to be his wife." She sounded desperate now and not so sure of herself.

"Great. You go, and I'll pretend to be dead." For good measure, Kaylee added, "He'll never know."

The knife dug into her skin. Kaylee sniffed in a breath, her whole body tensing. She was so fatigued, it was like one full body cramp. She wanted to cry out, but there was no breath in her to do so. Her legs started to give out. Until Trina was the only thing holding her up.

"You die. It's the only way."

Kaylee fought the collapse. She started to slide, the knife cutting along the skin on the underside of her chin, and she gasped at the fresh wash of pain. And yet, wasn't this far better than the alternative? If she was going to die, it would be on her terms.

Stuart looked at her then, and she saw an infinitesimally small nod of his chin. Kaylee knew what she had to do.

She looked up, stretching her chin up as far as she could and, in an instant, let her legs give out. It wasn't hard. The gun exploded. In one move she was on the ground, clutching her chin in her hand. Stuart's gun smoked.

Kaylee started to turn.

He reached for her. "Don't look." Stuart pulled her up to stand again, holding up her weight. "Come on. Let's go. Don't look at her, Kay. Just come with me."

Kay. "My dad called me that." She moved her hand away from her chin. It was covered in wet, slimy blood. Her head swam.

"Easy."

The hallway shifted. An explosion tore through the hallway. Stuart half carried her to the stairs where he set her down. She landed on her hands and knees and scrambled up.

She sensed him right behind her and gasped out a sob, tears rolling down her face.

At the top of the stairs, he gathered her up again, and they ran down the hall. Kaylee grasped his arm around her and tried to burrow her face in his shoulder even as they ran. Her side stung. So did her chin. Along with everything else.

Her foot went out from under her, and she nearly dropped. He didn't let her fall. "Come on. Quickly now."

"I'm trying."

"You're doing great, babe. The best."

All Kaylee could do was whimper. She wanted to sleep for a month, but that would bring nightmares. She would wake up still in that room. Edmond would come in... *Don't think about that.*

"Come on!" Zander stood at the end of the hall, holding the door open. "You need to run!"

Beyond him, a helicopter had its rotors already spinning so fast they blurred. Either that, or her eyes just couldn't track the rotation.

"Come on." Stuart's grip on her was tight.

Another explosion threw everything into chaos. Her ears cut off, the boom so loud she could feel it reverberate in her chest.

They cleared the door and were now running outside. Kaylee's ears registered the helicopter, just as Zander climbed in. He reached a hand out, and she took it. Stuart got in right behind her just as she turned to see the building, the one they had been in only a moment ago, collapse into the ground.

An explosion swallowed the structure, tugging it down like a sinkhole. The concussive force rushed at them, swaying the helicopter as it lifted off.

Kaylee gasped. Stuart tugged her onto a seat and clipped a seatbelt around her waist. He pulled back the sliced edges of her shirt. She couldn't help but pant for a stress-free, full breath of air.

"Sorry." His face was close. His eyes soft, and kind.

Kaylee touched his cheeks with bloody fingers. "I guess I can forgive you."

His lips twitched. Kaylee decided she didn't care who was watching.

She smiled as much as she could and pressed her lips to his.

Thirty-seven

One week later

"Do you think she'll ever forgive me?"

Stuart leaned forward in the chair beside Brad's hospital bed. "Honestly, yeah. She probably will."

Now that he had Kaylee back, things were seriously looking up. They weren't perfect yet, and maybe "perfect" wasn't a realistic expectation. But he had a shot at a happy future. A family of his own.

"And you?" Brad said.

"I'm gonna have to work on that." Stuart figured it would take time, but he might get there. When he knew for sure there had been no repercussions in Kaylee's life due to her brother's actions.

"That's all I ask."

Stuart nodded, then leaned back in the chair and blew out a long breath.

"Witness statements?"

He nodded. "We've been at it for a week now, all day conferences at the police department with the FBI and US Attorney. The chief is there, too, looking very pale and not at all like he should even be *thinking* about being back to work yet. It's been pretty hush-hush, and I still can't talk about it."

"They bring him down, we're all free."

And yet, Brad had worked to gain freedom only for himself *and* at the expense of his sister. Stuart wasn't anywhere near being ready to offer forgiveness. Brad had done a bad thing. Unthinkable, even. Who hung a family member out to dry like that?

But the lives they'd lived led to blurred lines. Considering the duress Brad had been under, and all they'd gone through that had left even Stuart barely sane, he'd taken the only out he thought was available to him. It was a failure of character or moral fiber. Not something the cops in town could prosecute, even if they weren't working with the feds to bring down the CIA director right now.

Last Chance could wind up making a name for itself. Getting on the map, and not for good reason. Most in town preferred the more anonymous life they all lived. No one wanted national attention.

Least of all Stuart, when Kaylee was technically still in danger—and would be until the CIA director was in federal custody. His network was broken down. The organization disbanded.

The last thing he wanted was for someone with a grudge to crawl out of the woodwork with Kaylee in their sights. But the FBI had promised them protection by way, specifically, of Special Agent Eric Cullings, who had turned out to be Tate's brother-in-law. He'd given their word she would be guarded until she was out of danger.

Stuart was exhausted, wrung out from talking his way through his entire life since the company had first made their approach. Everything he'd seen. All that he'd done, and the name of the person who'd had given him those orders in the first place. Not one thing had been left out, which meant the federal authorities knew the truth of every single thing he'd perpetrated. The good, the bad, and the ugly. Even so, Eric didn't look at him with disdain. Not even once. Instead, he looked at Stuart as though he was a valuable asset. A man whose hand he shook firmly in a greeting.

Someone worthy of respect.

To a man who hadn't thought of himself in those terms...not just in a long time, but *ever* in his life before, Stuart would have trouble putting into words how it made him feel.

But he was working on it.

Thank You. God had shown up—in a big way. His many blessings were making themselves evident. The truth was out now. With it had come freedom, peace, and joy. A woman he loved. One he desperately needed some quiet time with, not surrounded by recording equipment and people with notepads talking about depositions and hearings.

Brad had drifted to sleep, so Stuart stepped into the hall where Dean was on protective detail to make sure the director didn't retaliate and come after any of them.

"What did he have to say for himself?"

Stuart lifted a brow. "He's sorry."

"So you're just going to forgive him?"

"Would Ellie?" Stuart needed his friend to realize the good people they loved were choosing to forgive.

Dean blew out a breath. "Is that the point?"

Stuart grinned. "I'll be sure and let your girlfriend know she still has some work to do."

"She loves me just the way I am. Kind of like how Kaylee feels about your sorry self." Dean wiped his brow in mock relief. "Good for us."

"Yeah." Stuart took a step back. "Good for us."

He took a side door out of the hospital. One most people didn't know about, let alone use. It led to the rear of the building. He double-timed it into the trees. Instinct was like a second skin. But those highly-trained senses didn't alert him to anyone watching him through a scope. He didn't feel the itch between his shoulder blades that would indicate crosshairs aimed over his heart.

Stuart jogged anyway, using the exercise to dispel all the nervous energy pent up in him. Living in one place this long was unfamiliar. As was having people in his life he cared about—and who cared about him in return.

Two miles of running got him to the isolated cabin where they'd stashed Kaylee until they got word the CIA director was no longer a threat. It was supposedly owned by a former resident of the town, Victoria Bramlyn. Talking about her was the only time he'd ever seen Zander look nervous. Not even in the heat of a gunfight or buildings exploding around him had Stuart seen that look on his friend's face.

He whistled.

Zander, who'd turned from his post just off the front step, was watching Stuart approach out of the trees.

"All quiet?"

The big man nodded. "I'll make another round. We got ribs in, and we're gonna fire up the barbeque if you can persuade that woman of yours to make cornbread."

"I'll see what I can do." Stuart had requested all the fixings for a salad and knew they had baking supplies as well. Kaylee was welcome to help, but he felt like cooking tonight.

Walking in the front door felt more like coming home than any other time in his life. Stuart stopped just inside the door and pressed his palm to the wall.

"Hey. You're here." Curled up in the corner of the couch, Kaylee set her book on the coffee table. She started to stand.

He shook his head, moving toward her. "You don't need to get up."

She held out her hand, a smile teasing her lips. He saw none of the disassociation he'd seen when he had brought her out of that cell in the compound. She'd suffered. He had rescued her. Was she good now? Or would the trauma resurface in the future?

She hadn't had a nightmare since then. Neither had he.

Stuart pressed his lips to that smile and sank onto the cushions next to her, gathering her against him with an arm around her shoulders.

"Did you tell him?"

Stuart reached over and touched the ring on her left hand. "He was more interested in whether or not you were going to forgive him than hearing about your dress and what kind of flowers we had."

Kaylee sighed but didn't comment. She leaned her head on his shoulder. "You don't think it was too soon?"

He turned his hand and looked at her ring, then his. The one she'd slid on his finger six days ago in a ceremony held at six in the morning with four armed men and a pastor present. "Do you think it was?"

"No."

"Probably we're both just delusional, and it was way too soon. Likely this will turn into a nightmare, and we'll end up screaming at each other and throwing stuff around this cabin because we're sick of being in such close proximity for weeks and weeks until the trial is done." He shook his head for emphasis, "But there was no way I was going to go home at the end of the day while someone else protected you. It's easier to keep two people safe when they're living in the same house."

"Is that the reason?"

"Dean reamed me good when I told him I wasn't leaving. He told me how staying was supposed to be for good folks who are in love. Those who are sick of being apart for the sake of being noble." He shrugged. "So, I said, 'okay. I'm in!'"

She shifted, lifting her head from his shoulder to look at him. "Okay?"

"Am I gonna go anywhere else?"

Her eyes narrowed. "When we get all worked up about stuff and start throwing things…are you going to throw my book?"

"Of course not."

"None of my things?" She motioned to the vases perched on the bookcase, "What about any of this Victoria person's things?"

"No."

"So when you get upset, you'll just throw your stuff." She lifted one eyebrow. "And then clean up after."

"This is a very bizarre conversation. I'm not sure what's happening." But considering he got to hold her close whenever he wanted, including in the dark when the memories threatened, he was going to just go with it.

"I'm just laying down some ground rules."

"Great," Stuart said. "I've got one. You don't ever leave, and neither do I."

"Because it's more convenient than picking up and going somewhere else?"

"It isn't. But that's not why." He touched her face. "Stay. Always."

Her gaze softened. "Okay."

Stuart laughed. "I feel like maybe we skipped the whole dating thing."

"And the whole engagement thing. Pastor Daniels didn't seem worried; not if we take the class and 'do the work.'"

"I wouldn't miss it."

She snuggled against him again. "So long as you don't touch my book, we'll be good."

Stuart chuckled. Then he stopped when he realized his laughter was shaking her.

She sighed and whispered, "Love you."

He held her close while she drifted off to sleep, and he wondered how his life had come to this. "Love you too, Kaylee."

Whatever it took, Stuart was going to make sure this lasted. He was going to do the work. Because, for the first time in his life, he knew where he was supposed to be and what he was supposed to be doing.

This would be the most important mission of his life.

Thirty-eight

Eric walked down the hall, flanked by two Secret Service agents. Bringing up the rear was two US Marshals and two agents from Homeland Security. Everyone wanted a piece of the pie on this one.

At the back of the group, the US Attorney walked beside the Secretary of State.

He didn't knock. Eric lifted a hand to the sputtering assistant and let himself in the office of the CIA director.

The old man looked up. "I'll call you back." He set the phone in its cradle on the desk. "This looks ominous."

Dismissing them with a poor attempt at humor was a mistake.

Eric set the arrest warrant on the desk. "It would be best if this happens with the minimum of fuss."

The old man scoffed.

"Whether you like it or not," Eric said. "Adrian Pierce West, you're under arrest."

Up next
Book 5: Expired Game

This book will be released late
September 2020.

Did you enjoy this book?

Please consider leaving a review on your favorite book retailer! You could also share about the book on Facebook! Your review will help other book buyers decide what to read next.

Visit **www.authorlisaphillips.com** where you can sign up for my NEWSLETTER and get a free copy of Sanctuary Buried!

About the author

A British ex-pat who grew up an hour outside of London, Lisa attended Calvary Chapel Bible College where she met her husband. He's from California, but nobody's perfect. It wasn't until her Bible College graduation that she figured out she was a writer (someone told her). Since then she's discovered a penchant for high-stakes stories of mayhem and disaster where you can find made-for-each-other love that always ends in happily ever after.

Lisa can be found in Idaho wearing either flip-flops or cowgirl boots, depending on the season. She leads worship with her husband at their local church. Together they have two children and an all-black Airedale known as The Dark Lord Elevator.

Lisa is the author of the bestselling Sanctuary (WITSEC town series), the Double Down series, and more than a dozen Love Inspired Suspense novels. Her 2019 series of Northwest Counter-Terrorism agents was a big hit.

Find out more at www.authorlisaphillips.com where you can:

SIGN UP FOR MY NEWSLETTER

FIND A COMPLETE LIST OF BOOKS

SEE WHAT'S COMING NEXT

Lisa Phillips also writes Christian thriller supernatural novels under the name JL Terra
You can find these at www.jlterra.com

Made in the USA
Middletown, DE
01 June 2021

40811655R00158